BRIANA COLE

in

their

shadows

www.kensingtonbooks.com

DAFINA BOOKS are published by

Kensington Publishing Corp.
119 West 40th Street
New York, NY 10018

All Kensington titles, imprints, and distributed lines are available at special quantity discounts for bulk purchases for sales promotion, premiums, fund-raising, and educational or institutional use.

Special book excerpts or customized printings can also be created to fit specific needs. For details, write or phone the office of the Kensington Sales Manager: Kensington Publishing Corp., 119 West 40th Street, New York, NY 10018. Attn. Sales Department. Phone: 1-800-221-2647.

The Dafina logo is a trademark of Kensington Publishing Corp.

ISBN: 978-1-4967-3876-9
First Trade Paperback Printing: November 2023

ISBN: 978-1-4967-3878-3 (e-book)
First Electronic Edition: November 2023

10 9 8 7 6 5 4 3 2 1

Printed in the United States of America

in

their

shadows

To my baby sister, Paige Christina. I dedicate this book to you like I dedicate my life and creative ventures. As always, you are my inspiration and my motivation. I hope I'm making you as proud as you made me.

#Forever28

"The past is never dead. It's not even past."

—William Faulkner

Prologue

April struggled to restrain her rising panic as she approached the hotel desk. Usually there was a rush of adrenaline. But not tonight. Not this time. That had been superseded with a fear so chilling it left her breathless and trembling. *Would it work? Would they recognize something was off?* But she kept those thoughts to herself. As far as everyone else was concerned, she was just another guest, weaving through the maze of elite patrons peppering the hotel lobby. Blending in was the easy part. Not getting caught—well, that was the challenge.

Muffled laughter and music wafted to greet her, evidence of a party in full swing in the ballroom. The merriment was almost mocking and April quickened her pace. She had to get away. She had to think. She knew if she acted on impulse, she would make another mistake. And she couldn't afford any more of those.

April scissored her legs across the floor with a panicked urgency. A laptop bag was slung over her shoulder and knocked against her hip, throwing off her stride. She wheeled a Montblanc suitcase along, with a grip so tight it felt like the handle would crack the bones in her hand.

She was nearly nauseous. It was his musky vanilla scent that clung to the trench coat she wore. She hadn't wanted to take his, but it was the only one she could find in her haste. Anything to hide the blood coagulating in the fleece of her sweatshirt.

The hotel attendant—Wendy, by the gold name tag pinned to her breast pocket—looked up with a warm smile. "May I help you?"

April forced a smile of her own, hoping her face relayed the casualness she didn't feel. "Checking in," she greeted.

Wendy nodded and began pecking away on her keyboard. "Of course. Name?"

April's voice quivered over the name, and she licked her lips. *Breathe, just breathe*, she coaxed herself.

"ID, please."

April tensed as she pulled the stolen driver's license from the front pocket of her computer case and slid it across the marble countertop. She held her breath.

Wendy's eyes flickered to the laminated card. One moment. Then two. Each second was more excruciating than the last. April felt like she was going to combust.

Finally, the attendant nodded her approval and resumed typing on the computer. Desperate to remove the evidence, April all but snatched the license from the counter and shoved it into her coat pocket.

"Only one night with us?"

"Yes." And because she felt like she needed more to corroborate her story, April added, "Just passing through to take care of some business and enjoy the Atlanta nightlife."

"I completely understand." Wendy pressed a button and the printer at her backside hummed to life, generating a receipt. "It's so crazy here during this time of year. If I didn't have to work, I would spend tonight by myself in a remote cabin with some wine. I hate crowds. Big crowds," she amended, with a chuckle. "And Atlanta sure has plenty of those. This your first time here?"

"Yes." The lies were coming easier now.

"Well, when you get all settled, you should join us in the ballroom to ring in the new year."

April nodded politely, though that was the furthest thing from her mind. She reached for the key cards. The gesture prompted her sleeve to rise just a little to expose a piece of her arm. The sight of dried blood checkered on her skin had her immediately snatching back, praying Wendy hadn't seen.

Thankfully, the sweet hotel attendant was preoccupied, her head dipped low as she circled the room number on April's receipt with an elaborate flourish. "Room four-two-two-eight," she was saying. "Anything else I can do for you?"

"Can you please make sure I'm not disturbed?"

"Absolutely. Enjoy your stay and good luck with your business."

April's face was ashen as she hurried to the bank of elevators. Of course, Wendy had no idea exactly what *business* she was up to. But the comment's double meaning was eerily appropriate.

The cavernous presidential suite was elaborate, adorned with high-end finishings and offering a panoramic view of the skyline. City lights pulsated in the distance and for the briefest of moments, April was lulled by the pensive hum of downtown nightlife. She was sure if she looked hard enough, she would see her condo nestled on the outskirts of the city. Far away enough for privacy, but not far enough to escape.

Which was why, instead of basking in the luxurious accommodations or indulging in the complimentary wine and charcuterie board with its arrangement of fruits and cheeses, April immediately peeled out of her clothes and rushed to the bathroom.

Water sprayed from the rain shower in scalding splotches, rinsing her skin until there was a dirty, crimson puddle collected at her feet. She couldn't risk the blood staining the white hand towels, so instead, April used her hands to lather the soap, inducing the smell of lavender to fuse with the metallic stench in her pores.

Desperate, she scrubbed and scrubbed until her body was inflamed from the friction.

Maybe one day she would become immune to the guilt. A piece of her was comforted by that hope and she clutched it like a lifeline. But that day wasn't today. Today, with the steam pluming around her and the ominous burst of fireworks echoing in the background, April sank to the floor, wrapped her arms around her knees, and let loose a defeated sob.

Ten minutes. That's all the time she allowed herself to be emotional. When she was done, April took a breath, wiped her face, and got to work.

PART I: DENIAL

The refusal to accept the facts of the loss, either consciously or unconsciously.

Chapter One

April awoke, disoriented; briefly unsure which one of her husbands lay beside her. Her vision cleared enough so she could make out the red digits illuminated from the clock on the nightstand: 1:43 AM. Her peripheral vision caught the floor-to-ceiling windows adorning one whole wall of the industrial high-rise. The Atlanta skyline glittered through the glass, sweeping and majestic in all its early-morning splendor. She was in a penthouse suite. That meant . . .

April glanced at the figure sleeping beside her. Sure enough, Carter was in his catatonic position, left side, mouth open, and a nasally snore that seemed magnified in the silence. *Her husband Carter, not her husband Ramsey.*

April relaxed against the leather headboard as the last bit of haze cleared from her head. She hadn't meant to fall asleep, but Carter had wanted them to enjoy themselves the previous night. *"Since you can't be here for New Year's Day, then we'll celebrate tonight."* And they had. Wine, slow music, dancing in their living room. Intimate and therapeutic. For a moment, it was as if it had been real. But this time of year, just like it had been for the past eight years, was triggering. No matter how much she tried to assuage the lingering trauma.

April eased from the comfort of the satin sheets and padded across the hardwood floor. The room's sudden chill peppered goosebumps on her forearms. Carter insisted on keeping the air conditioner on sixty-eight degrees, no matter the weather or the season. It was a habit she wouldn't miss when she got back to her other husband. The two men were similar in more ways than one, but it was those kinds of differences she could appreciate.

April rested her forehead on the window, letting the coolness of the glass soothe her hangover headache. Too much to drink. That wasn't like her. She was usually sober and in control. She had to be. Thankfully, last night was over. Carter was asleep and she was alone. This was one of those rare moments that she could be herself, her *real* self, and not the women that she pretended to be. She savored it. Even if it was only temporary. Finally, almost regrettably, April tore her gaze from the view, all emotion suppressed. No, now she was . . . numb, moving on an autopilot that had been perfected like second nature.

Carter had converted the second bedroom into a minimalistic office. As an architect, he was so meticulous she could recite everything in this room by memory. A glass drafting table buried under a cluster of blueprints dominated the room. Vague outlines of pictures hanging on the walls; proof of his brilliance in the designs of the commercial properties captured in each frame. The only light was from his laptop, which cast a chilling glow on the neatly organized files stacked on his desk. His next projects. She had been half-listening and feigning excitement the previous night as he raved about his new bids.

April slid into the executive chair and, as she had done numerous times before, typed her birthday (more like the fake birthday that Carter knew) into the password box. The Microsoft desktop appeared on the screen, cluttered with entirely too many spreadsheets, folders, and programs. Three clicks and she was on their joint banking website, keying in the same log-in information she had used too many times in the past.

She knew never to transfer too much money. Only what she needed for now. Carter wasn't one to notice fifty dollars here, or a hundred dollars there. But he sure as hell wasn't stupid.

Seven minutes. That was all it took for her to steal from her husband. She was used to the routine, had calculated every best- (and worst-) case scenario down to the excuses she would use if she were ever caught. Even still, as prepared as she always was, it didn't make the task any less difficult. *Or troubling.*

"It's pretty easy to have more than one life; you just have to know how to balance them. Like shifts, you clock-in one while you clock-out from another." Even though the years had bred a dissonance between April and her mother, she still couldn't shake the words playing in her head as she waited patiently in the dark. Like some kind of sick and twisted lullaby. Erika sure as hell hadn't given her much in the way of an idyllic childhood. But the little tidbits of knowledge that *did* manage to seep through during her moments of sobriety—well, those gems had proven priceless. Like now.

As always, April tried to keep her eyes focused on the screen and ignore the photo Carter kept right beside the keyboard. Their wedding picture. She had seen it too many times to count and still, the image managed to unravel the threads of her guilty conscience. The frozen memory made her look so deceptively happy. Carter had managed to smear a bit of icing on the tip of her nose, and she had opened her mouth to laugh at the gesture. And the photographer had caught just that. Her laughing with a mouthful of red velvet cake clumped on her tongue and Carter watching her in adoration.

Never mind her embarrassment, the illusion in the picture looked entirely too . . . natural. Too comfortable. She hated it. He loved it. Which is why he hid it in his office, tucked away from the myriad of photos decorating the rest of their apartment.

A sudden light shined through the pocket of her robe. Her cell phone. Silenced, but the screen signaled the incoming call. She knew who it was without even looking at it. Deciding he could wait, April took her time finishing her transactions. She then cleared the browsing histories and recycle bin, making sure every trace of her deception had been carefully and neatly erased. By the time she readjusted the chair and swept from the room, there was only a phantom of her presence.

It was done and according to her balance, she was a few dollars closer to her goal. Her feelings weren't as intense anymore, which was progress. The first few times, April's eyes would sting with the threat of tears at what she did. At what she had *become*. Looking back on it now, it was almost humorous because she couldn't explain her distress if she tried. And how could she even justify being a con woman with feelings, anyway? *What's wrong? Nothing and everything.* Thankfully, she was past that part. Or so she liked to tell herself. It was easier not to feel at all than to feel too much.

April checked the bedroom to confirm Carter was still sleeping before settling on the couch, tucking her legs underneath her. She swiped her screen to toggle to the missed call.

The late hour was never a deterrent for Ramsey. She used to wonder if he slept at all. Another one of the subtle differences between her husbands. Carter lived by his *early-to-bed-early-to-rise* ideology, energized and ready to get his day started at the crack of dawn. Ramsey, on the other hand, was like a vampire, often spending the nights painting in his art studio because he insisted those were the most creative hours. She could already picture him hovering at his easel, flecks of paint caked on his fingers, guiding his brush across a half-finished canvas in methodical strokes. Creating picture poetry, he called it. For someone like April, who had never cared about painting, she now found herself fascinated by his talent. Even to the point where she chanced picking up a paintbrush herself, mimicking his movements. Of course, her artwork never turned out as beautiful as his, but she was proud just the same. Interesting how she was discovering more about herself by pretending to be someone else.

Ramsey answered on the first ring as if he'd been waiting. "What are you doing up so late, Mrs. Duncan?"

Without realizing it, April's lips curved at the sound of his voice. "I should be asking you the same thing, but I already know you're in the studio making something great."

His chuckle glided through the receiver. "My wife knows me so well."

"Of course, I do."

"How is Virginia?"

Once again, her eyes lingered over the scenic Atlanta view through the window. Of course, she wasn't in Virginia, but Ramsey couldn't know that.

"Great," she lied with practiced ease. And then just as genuinely, "Wish you were here." That much was true. She would be lying to herself if she said she didn't have feelings for both of her husbands. Was it love? Not necessarily. She wasn't even sure what love was. But they did make her feel special in their own ways. And they provided her with an escape from reality. It was . . . reassuring. Which was close enough.

"I miss you too, babe," Ramsey said. "Maybe if you can get away from work for a few days, we can take a little vacation this summer. Maybe a cruise or something. I think we both need it."

April didn't bother responding. If she voiced what was on her mind, she would have to admit that she didn't plan on being around during the summer.

Ramsey didn't seem to notice her hesitation and instead asked, "What time will you be back tomorrow?"

April looked toward the front door, where her packed suitcases already sat waiting. The flight attendant uniform that she kept for appearances' sake had been steamed and hung near the closet, thanks to Carter. She mentally checked off her routine once she got back to her place. As laborious as it was, Mrs. Carter Evans had to switch to Mrs. Ramsey Duncan. Like rotating shifts.

"Not sure." Her answer was intentionally vague. "It'll probably be after six. I have some things to handle before I leave the airport."

"Okay, well, I have a surprise for you."

April tensed. She hated surprises with a passion. And even though Ramsey knew her attitude about his little unexpected tokens of love, he seemed to enjoy the challenge. Perhaps he thought if he impressed her enough with his affectionate spontaneity, she would learn to love it.

"I promise, it's a good surprise," Ramsey rushed on, clearly reading her mind.

Highly doubtful, but she would keep her thoughts about that to herself. "Okay, we'll see."

"By the way, I put your packages up."

"Great, thank you. How many were there?"

"I don't know. It was a stack of boxes on the porch. Though I'm not sure what else you could possibly be ordering."

"Just a few things for the house." That was partially true. Somewhere among those new boots and designer sweaters, she was sure she had purchased some new bedding and throw pillows for the living room. It usually softened Ramsey's disapproval of her spending habits. He'd once exaggerated her shopping with the word *addiction*, and April had immediately dispelled the absurdity. She liked to look nice because it made her feel beautiful and valuable. Was that so bad?

"Well, it looks like you confused the delivery driver," Ramsey said absently. "I think I saw someone else's package mixed in with yours. Poor *April* is going to be upset when she doesn't get what she ordered."

April's chest tightened. It felt like someone had snatched her breath from her lungs, leaving her strangled with confusion and enough fear to send a rippling tremor up her spine.

"W—what did you say?" She didn't even realize she was whispering until she heard her voice, now suddenly foreign to her ears.

Ramsey chuckled. "What's wrong?"

"What's the name on the package?"

"April *somebody*. Not sure. Want me to check? Do you know her?"

Her mouth soured as he repeated what she had clearly heard the first time. "No," she murmured, weakly. "Just . . . maybe leave it with the rest. I'll check it out when I get back." Before he had a chance to respond, she hurried on. "I'm feeling tired, so I'm going to get some sleep."

"Erin, you okay, sweetie?" Ramsey's voice was heightened with concern.

She couldn't even stomach the strength to reply. Because she wasn't okay. Not at all. She was nauseous to her core as the beginning tendrils of tension careened from temple to temple. *April, April . . .* the name singed clear through to her bones. Like an aggressive poison. It was a name she hadn't heard in lifetimes. Because that's not who she was. Not to anyone. Not anymore.

She didn't even remember what lie she told to placate Ramsey and end the call so abruptly. But suddenly, she was alone with her thoughts, her worries, and yes, her terror.

Like a sinister collage, her aliases flooded her vision. She was Ramsey's wife, Erin. She was also Carter's wife, Michelle. And she had been a tapestry of women, professions, and identities in between. But only to those from her past, a past that her manipulation had forced her to bury years ago, she was April. And expected or not, a mysterious shipment to her house was the least of the baggage she would need to unpack.

Chapter Two

"Who were you talking to last night?"

April kept her back to Carter so he couldn't see the twinge of panic that flickered over her face. She willed her movements to remain calm as she finished filling the Keurig. "What are you talking about, sweetie?"

"Did you watch TV?"

She paused. "Maybe for a second. To be honest, I was so tired I really don't remember." April turned around this time, now completely composed and feigning ignorance with a downward turn of her lips. "Why? Did you hear something?" She studied him as his eyebrow creased in concentration.

It was obvious the wheels were turning in his head as he attempted to replay the previous night's events; muddling through the aftereffects of inebriation to scrap together some semblance of coherency. He gave up with a half-hearted shrug. "I thought so. I was out of it too, so I could've been dreaming."

"Well, thank you for a great night," she deflected with a warm smile. "Obviously we both needed it."

Carter's face softened with adoration. "We did. I just wish you didn't have to work on New Year's Eve."

"You know flights are crazy during the holiday season." The excuse was especially true, though the airport congestion wasn't affecting her plans in the least.

April disguised her dread with a yawn as she turned back to the counter. She hadn't been able to sleep ever since hanging up with Ramsey. Her mind was equally exhausted, leafing through a Rolodex of people she had encountered, conversations she'd had, and anything else that could help make an association with the nameless, faceless person who had sent the mystery package. Whoever it was had done their due diligence to discover she was living under the identity of Erin Duncan. So, the fact remained. As careful as she'd been, as much as she'd covered her tracks, there was someone out there who knew the truth. Which meant he or she knew more about her than she did them and well, that was enough to have a swell of anxiety settling like a brick in her chest.

April lifted a mug to her lips and took a generous swig of coffee, the scalding liquid searing her throat like a cathartic release. But it was not enough to settle her nerves. It just didn't make sense. There was no way someone from her past could know who, or where, she was now. It had been years since there was even a trace of *April*.

A mistake. That had to be the most logical answer. She had done a little shopping online before she left Ramsey last week. The packages had arrived. Of course, something had gotten mixed up during the shipping process. It happened all the time. Warehouses shipped to wrong addresses, or drivers accidently transposed numbers when really, the package was for the next house or the next street over. What were the odds that the package in her real name was actually intended for her when that identity had disappeared years ago? Pretty much nonexistent, April mused with a little more reassurance. It wasn't like the name was uncommon. That had to be the sensical explanation. *Right?*

Carter must've sensed the slight discomfort hanging thick in the air. He was behind April in three strides, his gentle hands kneading the tender spot between her shoulder blades and the base of her neck. His fingers moved with artistic precision, using his fingertips to apply just enough pressure to have her skin pulsing in response. "Babe, you sure everything is okay?" he asked.

No, not really. "Yes. Just work." Instinctively, her muscles tensed when his lips replaced his fingers on her neck, his hands trailing down to caress her shoulders, then arms. His breath had grown heavy with arousal, and she could only swallow her repulsion. "Carter—"

"If you weren't working so much, then we would be able to start our family." As if to emphasize his point, Carter's arms circled her waist to rest, almost wistfully, on her flat stomach.

April grimaced as the words scratched her throat. "We will."

"When?"

She pursed her lips, the familiar conversation instantly dampening her mood. Of course, he wanted children. Didn't they all? It was only a matter of time before Ramsey would mirror those same sentiments, but thankfully, he had other things to keep him distracted for now.

But not Carter. He was on an accelerated path to creating the perfect family, the perfect *image*. As if he had something to prove to himself and everyone in his circle. If April were another woman, another wife, maybe. If she actually wanted that life with him, perhaps. So many variables that made his desire and hers irreconcilable.

But she had to put her desire out of her head. She had to remember she was currently playing the role of Michelle Evans, and *Michelle* wanted what Carter wanted. Instead, she got back into character and reasoned, "I told you I just wanted us to be married for a while first. We have plenty of time to have kids." And she planned to be long gone before then.

The brisk knock on the door was both startling and a welcome reprieve. Instinctively, April snatched back, coffee sloshing over the lip of the cup to sting her hand. "Dammit!" She winced at the burn, immediately dumping the mug and the remaining contents, into the sink.

"Let me see it." Carter was in his protective mode as he reached for her hand to assess the damage.

April shook her head, sidestepping his embrace. "It's fine. Can you just see who's at the door?" The gesture was blatantly dismissive. She knew it. He knew it. But he said nothing. April's sigh was one of relief when she heard him move to answer the door.

She couldn't help but feel bad about the circumstances. Was it his fault that she didn't want kids? Or had no sexual desire? It was just another by-product of her less than idyllic past. Asexuality aside, intimacy was just not a high priority. April had been self-sufficient since the age of twelve, so she achieved gratification by other means. It was all she knew. It was all she had.

A triad of voices wafted into the kitchen, lifted in apparent merriment. Carter's brother, Ian, and sister, Valerie. Flustered, April busied herself with wetting a paper towel and applying the cold compress to her singed skin. It shouldn't have been a surprise that the Evans siblings decided an impromptu visit was in order. Much to April's frustration, their close relationship compelled them to often stop by for one reason or another. She would never admit she was envious, not even to herself.

"Hey, little sis." Ian was first in the kitchen, already swinging open the refrigerator and pulling out a fresh carton of orange juice. Noticing April nursing her wound, he frowned. "What happened to you?"

"Coffee spill," she confessed with a strained grin. As if to prove the statement, she peeled back the paper towel and held up her hand, exposing the area below her thumb, now tinged red.

Valerie was, not so obviously, cutting her eyes in April's direction. Then she looked at her brother, a distinct proprietary scowl marring her face. It was evident she had some kind of slick comment marinating on her tongue. Good for her for deciding to keep her thoughts to herself. April didn't mind Ian. But as far as the middle Evans sibling, she didn't care for her. Valerie had made it clear the feeling was mutual. Somewhere between her first date with Carter and their wedding, the women settled on tolerance; a silent understanding to stay out of each other's way. It was just easier to keep the peace.

Ian nodded with a sympathetic frown before glancing toward his brother. He stepped closer, lowering his voice. "Can I talk to you for a minute? Alone?"

Paranoia had April hesitating at the question. She had never had a problem with Ian. It was his sister that she couldn't stand. Then why in the world did he need to speak with her? She didn't even realize she had been clenching her teeth until she felt a dull ache throbbing at her jaw. Maybe Carter would intervene to keep her from having to entertain the conversation.

"Sweetie, Ian needs to speak with me for minute," she voiced lightly. "I'm just going to step out in the hall." To her surprise, Carter didn't seem too curious or fazed by the request, merely nodding his nonchalance.

Ian led the way to the front door and April shuffled behind while her mind toppled over legit responses to the accusations that were surely coming. Plausible deniability would work in this case.

"I wanted to ask you something," he started as soon as they were alone in the hallway. If he was suspicious, he wasn't showing it.

April narrowed her eyes. "What is it?"

"You know I'm planning Carter a surprise birthday party, right?"

It felt like the pressure valve had been released and April allowed herself to relax, grateful her stammering heartbeat was beginning to subside. Thank God he didn't know anything. Since he was watching and waiting for a reply, April nodded absently, though she had absolutely no recollection of him mentioning anything about a party idea.

"Well, it's nothing too big," Ian went on. "Because you know Carter is so low-key. But I thought it would be nice since he just got that big contract for the city, and we can celebrate both."

"When are you trying to do it?"

"Two weeks. And before you say anything—" he added. "I would just need you to help me make some calls for a caterer and maybe a DJ. I already booked a venue."

April took a steeled breath but kept her voice optimistic as best she could. "Sure, I'll make a few calls." That was the least she could do. Because really it was a coin toss whether she would actually attend. Sure, it looked distasteful and downright tacky for Carter's wife to be absent from his party. But since when did she care about people's perception? Especially Ian.

"Okay, I'll call you and we'll get some details finalized." He glanced behind him toward the closed door and when he turned back, there was something else in his gaze. Hunger? Desire?

April shifted and cleared her throat. "Thanks for keeping me in the loop about the party, but I better get going. I have a flight."

She had become too good at reading other people. Either that or Ian was making a point not to hide the lust flickering over his face. So much so that she was already anticipating the kiss, even before he leaned down to inch his face closer. His tongue snaked out to lick his lips and April recoiled. In that brief second, she knew she had a choice. Well, if she were her mother, Erika would say there really was no choice to be made. *"Give a man what he wants, April, and that will allow you to use him for what you need later."* Of course, Erika would encourage her to do what any respectable wife with a strategy would do and let her brother-in-law kiss her. And maybe before, April would have. Sometimes, she was so drowned in her deception that she didn't know where the truth ended and the lies began. But not this time. Not when she was still haunted by the visceral memories of an assault years ago.

"What the hell are you doing, Ian?" Her hands were shoving against Ian's chest before she even realized she was reacting. It felt like she was pushing against a rock.

Ian's eyes rounded. Did he really have the nerve to be shocked?

"I'm married to your brother," she reminded him with a pointed glare, taking care to strengthen her voice so he wouldn't hear the trembling. "Don't ever do anything like that again."

"Yeah, but I know you—" he cut himself off and shook his head, raking his fingers through his beard.

April wasn't sure if his apparent disbelief was at his own actions, or hers. But his words, then subsequent silence, sent an uneasiness rippling through her spine.

"You know I what?"

"Forget it."

He started to turn for the front door and April grabbed his arm, snatching him back around to face her. "No, go ahead and say it."

Ian's eyes leveled at the silent dare. "Do you really love my brother, Michelle?"

"Of course, I do."

"Then, I'm sorry." He sure as hell didn't sound sorry. "And I think this little misunderstanding needs to stay between us."

Was that a threat? He watched her as if he expected her to respond. She didn't. No, she couldn't. Not when her tongue felt numb. He retreated back inside the apartment, leaving her alone. His behavior, albeit bold, hadn't been completely unexpected. Sure, he had given her one too many lingering looks before or found weak excuses to get close. But she had ignored him. The last thing she needed was a complication with Carter because his brother didn't know how to respect boundaries. But Ian had never initiated any type of exchange, sexual or otherwise. Until now.

April's body felt weak and she leaned against the wall, wiping clammy hands on the side of her pants. She wasn't sure what prompted Ian's brazen behavior, but the underlying warning in his words was more than clear. Now the question was, what was she going to do about it?

Chapter Three

April Garrett's Journal

I just got back from the mayor's annual charity ball fundraiser and something interesting happened. I don't even like to go to these things anymore, but Erika does. She says it's an opportunity to mix and mingle with the upper echelon and indulge in their free liquor and gourmet food. She's been telling me that for years. But I've been to enough of these prestigious functions to know she uses them as a ruse to scout for the next target. Looking at who she can scam and whose circle she can infiltrate to get what she wants.

At first, I didn't realize that's what she was doing. I just thought it was a great opportunity for us to bond and have some fun at somebody else's expense. She used to almost make it like a game. "Let's see if we can get in and out without getting caught." Though now I know better, I have to admit there is still a certain thrill to the endeavor. For one night, I get to be someone else. Someone I want to be. Wiping the slate clean and writing my own narrative instead of the ugly truth. There is a certain power that comes with that. It's liberating. It's . . . therapeutic. That's why I agreed to accompany her tonight. I didn't expect to meet anybody, that's for sure.

I've been many women but tonight, I was Michelle Price, a woman who Erika confirmed was on the guest list but wouldn't be in attendance. We'd gone shopping. I don't know whose credit card we were using, but I purchased a black sequin gown that both the driver, and even the valet, complimented once we arrived. As soon as we were escorted into the banquet hall, Erika disappeared into the crowd, presumably to "work the room." She said she had her eye on some judge with a fetish for Black women. About an hour later, I was having another drink at the bar when she'd made her way back to me, this time with her arm looped around a man. He was average, in every sense of the word. Average height, average build, average chestnut brown complexion. And he wore glasses. No way would any woman classify him as traditionally sexy. In fact, he could easily blend in with a sea of other quirky-type professionals. But judging by the noticeable age difference between him and Erika, and the fact that she was steering him in my direction, that meant (a) he had money and (b) he was now my target.

"Michelle, you have to meet Carter," Erika gushed with exaggerated enthusiasm. "Carter, this is my friend. She's into drawing and stuff like you." And that was how it started. Carter's face was flushed, clearly from embarrassment. I sized him up. He was a shy introvert. The thing is, those are the ones you have to be careful with.

After having made introductions, Erika gave some half-assed excuse in order to leave us to ourselves. Carter and I exchanged some idle conversation about the ridiculously overpriced food. It was his weak attempt at flirting. But it was cute. Then, he asked me about myself and I was able to spin a little story about Michelle, the flight attendant raised in a loving two-parent household instead of the projects by a drug user and con artist single mother; Michelle, who has an affinity for jazz music, sushi, and the color pink, all the things I feel like I would've been able to appreciate if I had been given the opportunity as a child. That's when Carter had been pulled away and Erika had riddled me with possibilities. A prominent architect. Why not entertain a little luxurious lifestyle for a while? I deserved it, right? Therefore I did what I had done before. What I had been taught to do with prospects. I faded into the background and did my research.

I watched Carter for the rest of the night, mingling with high-level executives and councilmen. I noted what he ate, what he drank, who he laughed with, who he knew and who knew him. I kept my ears peeled for conversation about him, how the crowd responded when he'd given his small speech, and what items he'd found interesting or bid on during the silent auction. I had scrolled his online presence, his website, his social media, press releases, and news articles. Erika and I compared our findings. Honestly, I didn't know who was more vested. Her or me.

By the time the fundraiser was over, I knew Mr. Carter Evans of Chicago, Illinois, surprisingly well. All the way down to the third-place award he'd won in a ninth-grade English essay contest (that one was thanks to his very vocal high school ex-girlfriend who enjoyed walking down memory lane). When he finally approached me again and offered to walk me and Erika to our car, I agreed.

I can see something serious with Carter. I think that's what is risky. He's sweet. Generous. And he likes me—well . . . the woman I presented to him. It's obvious he's looking for a wife. I'm not the marrying type; it's an inconvenience. But Michelle is. And honestly, it feels good to be cherished even if it is a lie. Even if I know it won't last.

Chapter Four

She lied.

After his siblings left that morning, April rushed Carter out the door, claiming she needed to make an 11:30 AM flight. Though she had a perfectly good and brand-new car (thanks to him), he still insisted on driving so they could spend as much time together as possible. She would be gone for a few weeks, but thankfully, Carter was very understanding of her unpredictable schedule. He had to be in order to date someone he thought was a flight attendant. Truth was, she had no plans of leaving Georgia at all.

Carter was unusually quiet as he wheeled onto the turnpike. Part of her was curious what Valerie had been talking to him about while she was in the hallway with Ian. The other part of her, the part that she was more focused on, was enjoying the silence—as stifled as it was—because it was allowing her to get her thoughts together about seeing Ramsey.

She hadn't talked to him any more since the previous night which, in and of itself, wasn't at all worrisome. He didn't too much disturb her when she was away, since he thought she was working. But pulling out her cell and seeing the lack of notifications on the screen, April had to admit, was a little unsettling. She just hoped—no, *prayed*—that his curiosity hadn't gotten the best of him, and he'd opened the mystery package. Trying to explain whatever it was brought this crippling angst that only heightened as the airport peeked into view.

Judging by the clock on the dashboard, Ramsey would be working down at the restaurant for another hour, so he probably wouldn't respond to a text. But she sent one anyway, quickly keying in a message to let him know she would see him soon, with some heart emojis.

April put her phone away and turned to study Carter's profile. His lips were turned downward into what looked to be a scowl, a clear indicator that something was indeed wrong. Feeling compelled to ease the awkward tension, she reached across the console to gently squeeze his arm.

"You going to miss me?" she teased. She expected Carter's face to relax into an amused grin as it often did when she played cute.

Instead, he moved his arm from her touch and pretended to fiddle with the air conditioner. "When will you be back?" he asked instead, keeping his eyes on the road.

April frowned at his attitude. "A couple weeks or so, why? What's wrong with you?"

"I think when you get back, we just need to discuss some things."

A plane took off overhead, its thunderous ascent nearly drowning out the dialogue. April remembered their conversation from earlier and had to keep from rolling her eyes in agitation. "Is this about having kids again?"

"Not just that." Carter blew an exasperated breath as he steered the car to the curb under a DEPARTURE sign. He finally turned to look at his wife. "I feel like there's . . . I don't know, something going on with us."

April kept her expression neutral. One thing for sure and two for certain, she knew the importance of a poker face. "Something like what?"

"I don't know. Like there is this divide between us. And I can't figure out why. Maybe it's this"—he gestured vaguely to the plane departures and airport activity—"getting to me. I knew you were a flight attendant when I met you, but I think your job could be getting in the way of our marriage. I feel like we don't spend enough time together."

Carter's leather seat was suddenly hot and sticky, and April shifted uncomfortably under his stare. "What are you wanting me to do, Carter? Stop working?"

"No, I just—"

"Because you know I damn sure wouldn't tell you to do that. Would you honestly quit being an architect, your lifelong dream, for me?"

Just as she knew they would, the words silenced him, and he lowered guilty eyes to his lap. "Maybe we just need to get on a better routine," he offered, gently. "I don't know. Something. I just love you, Michelle, and I hate being away from my wife. That's all."

Her heart stung with his admission. She swallowed, unable to coax herself to meet his gaze. It was easier not to. Seeing the sincerity was too painful. Not bothering with a response, she opened the door and stepped out, grateful for the comfort of the noisy congestion.

By the time Carter joined her at the trunk, handing over her garment bag and suitcase, April had softened her demeanor and even risked a kiss to soothe the tension. His lips relaxed against hers. "We'll talk about it when I get back," she promised with a warm smile.

He nodded, seemingly appeased for the most part, but she could tell something heavy was still on his mind. She made a mental note to dig a little deeper when she had more time. The last thing she needed was any negative influence unraveling all of her hard work. April hugged Carter one last time and hurried off through the automatic doors of the airport.

A cool gust of wind hit her as soon as she entered the lobby. Canned announcements echoed from the speakers, infused with the inaudible chatter of families and their travel discussions. She didn't break stride as she rounded the registration kiosks and made her way to the restroom.

An unsettling prickle rippled along her back and neck and April paused, resisting the urge to spin around. Crazy, she knew. She was in a crowded airport with a number of people who certainly wouldn't be able to identify her. However, that last part brought more apprehension than comfort.

April stopped at the restroom door and risked glancing toward the window, which boasted a good view of the pickup and drop-off roadways in front of the terminals. To her surprise, Carter was still standing at the curb where she left him. But even through the fogged glass, it was clear that he wasn't looking at her. Something or some*one* had caught his attention across the airport lobby, and he was watching with an intensity that made April nervous. She turned in the direction he was looking, but of course, all she saw was a blur of travelers bustling by. No one even appeared to be returning his gaze. Just as quickly, Carter pulled out his phone and began making a call as he climbed back into his car. *What was that about?*

Again, April chastised herself for being so paranoid as she pushed into the restroom. Did she have any right to be suspicious? Of course not. But was she? Absolutely. It had undoubtedly become second nature.

April bypassed the few women at the sinks and made a beeline for the handicapped stall. If Carter, or anyone for that matter, ever went through her suitcase, it would look very generic. A few outfits, a pair of heels and sneakers, and a small Face Shit bag that contained makeup and travel-size toiletries.

Now, tucked away in her own private dressing room, she pushed those items to the side for the small, barely noticeable zipper pocket lining the bottom of the bag. Inside, a neatly folded sweatsuit, dingy from wear and one too many washes, was stuffed along with a baseball cap and a braid wig.

April didn't even bother changing clothes, since she would be making a pit stop anyway. She dressed quickly, pulling the sweatpants and sweatshirt over her leggings and T-shirt. She eased off the glamorous beachy wave wig that Carter loved with its flowing tresses and packed it neatly in the secret compartment, along with her flight attendant uniform. Braid wig first, baseball cap on top, then she shoved her feet in the sneakers, and she was ready to go.

Emerging from the stall, she had to grin at the drastic change in the mirror. No one would suspect she was the same woman who'd entered only moments before. Well, no one who should've been looking that closely anyway.

Satisfied, April reentered the lobby and instead of heading toward the gate departures and security checkpoint, she doubled back and took the escalator down to the parking garage, deck two. Her navy blue Genesis was parked right where she left it and she quickly loaded her trunk and slid into the crisp, beige seats. It was a stark contrast to the Tesla she drove when she was with Carter, but the difference in luxuries was yet another necessity for the lives she juggled.

April didn't fully relax until she eased on the expressway to downtown Atlanta. As anxious as she was to get to the home she shared with Ramsey, it would still be a few hours. Besides, she needed to fully prepare. The sweatsuit and braid disguise were just to get her discreetly out of the airport (never could be too careful) but Erin Duncan had a different look altogether.

April had a condo in the heart of town, a safe haven of sorts, where she could relax, regroup, and replenish. But like always, she detoured around a longer route, navigating her car into a

neighborhood saturated with more negative memories than positive ones.

The area used to look pristine, but now it just reeked of distress with overgrown weeds and shrubbery flanking narrow
streets. Surprisingly, some of the mini-mansions were just as de-
bilitated with their peeling paints and sagging rooftops. Of
course, it didn't look like this when she had moved into the home.
No one would look at the neighborhood and think this used to be
the location for the upper echelon. But then again, she had been
confined indoors with a task to focus on—Warren, so it wasn't
like she could appreciate its grandeur—or lack thereof. April
shuddered at the thought. After all this time, his name still gripped
her with fear. Even more so when she pulled up to the actual
structure with wooden planks boarding the doors and windows;
completely abandoned. Just like she had done to it.

Erika would probably kill her if she knew April was there; that
she went out of her way to drive by any time she was in town. But
she wouldn't get it. Wouldn't understand why the building's
trauma, haunted with all its skeletons and sordid memories, was
so magnetic. How it brought back a pain that was, in a warped
and karmic sort of way, morbidly poetic. Plus, and this was something she would only admit to herself, it was comforting to know
those secrets were still buried in that backyard, now glazed over
with cement and seasons of neglect. It was always easier to forget
the blood on your hands when you knew no one could see it.

There was another stop she wanted to make, but April knew
she didn't have time. So instead, she headed toward her condo,
anxious to unwind and peel off the layers of her deceit.

The shrill ringing of her cell phone pierced the air as soon as
she pulled into the gated community. The number flashed across
her screen and she groaned in response. Not Ramsey, or even
Carter like she expected. Those two she could handle. This one
required another level of strength altogether.

"Are you tracking me or something?" The question was every bit as irritable as April intended.

Erika smacked her teeth with equally mutual disdain. April could picture her taking a drag of her cigarette, probably her third one for the day, with an avalanche of liquor flowing through her bloodstream. Her mother was nothing, if not predictable. "Well, aren't you a ray of sunshine this morning."

"It's been a long morning. But anyway. Where are you and what are you doing?"

"Oh, you know me. Here. There. Everywhere." Erika laughed off her ambiguity. "I wanted to tell you I'm visiting Atlanta for a few weeks, and I would love to see you if you had some downtime."

"Why is that?"

"Because you're my only daughter and contrary to your wild beliefs, I actually love you."

April swallowed the slick comment on her tongue. As toxic as their relationship was—and it was as toxic as it got—Erika had done a good job in establishing a codependency. And she knew exactly what buttons to press to make April feel guilty about it.

Balancing her phone with one hand, April stepped from the SUV, lifting her hand to wave at a neighbor who passed by with an arm full of groceries.

"Hey Brenda," the neighbor greeted April with a warm smile.

"April, did you hear me?" Now it was Erika's voice again humming in her ear. "I asked is there anything new that's been going on."

April debated relaying the package mix-up. But then, wouldn't that be too premature? As threatened as she felt, she didn't even know if there was anything to be threatened about. "Nope. Just the usual," she said.

"How is Carter?"

"He's good."

"Okay, well, I see you're being short like you don't want to be bothered again." Erika blew an impatient breath. "Let me know when you're free. We can do lunch and maybe a spa day or something."

"Sounds good," April responded dryly.

"Be sure to call me, for real. I can't wait to hear about your latest ventures." And with that, she hung up. No "goodbye," no "I love you" and no waiting for affection that they both knew would never come.

That last thought had a wave of repulsion coursing through April's body as she took the stairs to the second floor. As pathetic as it was, their history was the only thread that salvaged their strained relationship. But that too, like everything else, was beginning to deteriorate. Pretty soon, there would be nothing left between them. Such a shame that April was looking forward to that.

April's condo was a charming blend of warm hues and characterful accessories that enhanced the space's art deco aesthetic; exactly how she liked it. Splashes of purple adorned every swatch of furniture, from the deep-set throw pillows on the L-shaped couch, to the lampshades, to the accent rug swallowing the rich hardwood floor. A stone-paneled peninsula fireplace served as the makeshift partition between the living room and the dining area, enriching its age-old glamour. It was an inviting retreat, uniquely hers. Well, in *Brenda's* name, but still, it was hers just the same.

April kicked off her shoes as soon as she entered and left her bags in the foyer. She continued shedding her clothes as she walked, the garments making a bread crumb trail to the master bedroom. Soaking in a bubble bath was the first order of business. As always, she paused briefly at the nightstand. The picture was still there, as expected, its corner anchored under the digital clock. Even from a vantage point in the doorway, she could still make out the silhouette of the baby's tiny frame in the sonogram, its head and body like a floating peanut encased in the concentrated shades of black and gray. April allowed the familiar twinges of sorrow to consume her. The pain was a welcome reminder that she would never forget. *One breath, two breaths, three.* Only when she was sure she wouldn't crumble under the weight of her memories, April moved on into the adjoining bathroom. She would have to worry about herself later. For now, she needed to get back into character.

Chapter Five

By the time she hit I-85, putting miles between her and her first husband and the life she'd built with him, April was a completely new woman. Both figurately and physically. She had even taken a little extra time to indulge herself in a bubble bath and a glass of wine. Then, she had set to work on her makeup. It was truly amazing how a palette could completely reshape the planes of a face. Erika had once told her it was an art form and April had to agree. After years of perfecting her artistry, she prided herself on her transformations. A new look, a new life . . . being who she wanted, when she wanted just came down to a few brushstrokes.

As April drove, she angled the rearview mirror to take a look at herself from behind the dark tint of her sunglasses. While Carter liked her long hair, Ramsey loved the cute pixie cut (she was sure because he, like every other man, had a Halle Berry crush growing up). Now, April took the time to run her fingers through the short wig, making sure her natural hair was still neatly tucked in. And because she knew Ramsey would like it, she had changed into a simple maxi dress that accentuated the contours of the frame her surgeon had given her.

If she was lucky, Ramsey wouldn't be home for another few hours, which would give her the opportunity to settle down, maybe check in with Carter, and take a look at her packages. She relaxed as she turned onto the quaint, suburban street.

Columbus was a far cry from Atlanta and she had to admit, it had taken some getting used to at first. However, when she had settled down with Ramsey, she realized it was a refreshing change of pace from the congested city life. Though it didn't (and probably would never) feel like home, it was home for Ramsey. April didn't mind the cookie-cutter homes and manicured lawns. Or the overbearingly friendly neighbors with their book club meetings and ice cream socials by the pool house.

April wheeled past a pop-up lemonade stand on the corner and lifted her hand to greet the twins (who no one could tell apart) manning the booth. Today it was lemonade. Tomorrow they would probably be ringing doorbells to sell their homemade M&M brownies that were never quite cooked all the way. Ramsey usually bought them all to give away at his restaurant. The man was endearing like that.

It started drizzling as April pulled up to their ranch home nestled in a cul-de-sac. The fixer-upper had been another one of Ramsey's passion projects. She remembered the hodgepodge of brick and crumbling concrete had been riddled with cosmetic issues and in desperate need of repairs. Whatever modern charm the house had was buried beneath years of neglect. But Ramsey, being the visionary that he was, had not only seen the diamond in the rough, but had executed a majority of the renovations himself.

Now sitting in the driveway, April could hardly remember how wrecked it looked before. It was the kind of picturesque home that, as a little girl, she would've imagined for herself with picket fences and swing sets and a puppy frolicking in the grass, and a daughter who looked like her miniature twin with lopsided pigtails and a gap-toothed grin. It would've been easy to dream had she not been tainted with such a crippling reality. But living here with Ramsey allowed her to have a taste of that illusion.

The rain was picking up now, coming down in blinding sheets and pelting her windshield like bullets. April eased into a garage with cluttered shelving units and lawn equipment. She pictured the twins shrieking and scrambling to salvage their drenched lemonade stand. Poor things. April would make a point to give them a little something extra when she saw them again. She had always admired their ambition.

April left her bags in the car, resolving to unpack later. Right now, she needed to get settled before Ramsey—

"Surprise!" The chorus of voices roared with exuberance as soon as April opened the door into the house. Startled, she staggered backwards, sweeping confused eyes over the group of people assembled in the living room and kitchen. It didn't take long to identify her neighbors. But what the hell were they doing? That's when she noticed the decorations. Bouquets of black, purple, and gold balloons hung suspended from the ceiling and crepe streamers had been braided between cabinets and columns. The dining room table was now obscured by a black, disposable tablecloth and an assembly of cone hats, tiaras, horns, noisemakers and light-up necklaces, all branded with celebratory slogans of the upcoming New Year's Day.

Finally, Ramsey stepped through the crowd and pulled her in for a hug, his woodsy, citrus cologne familiar and intoxicating. She dissolved into his embrace.

"Welcome home, babe," he said, his voice lifted in amusement at her shocked expression.

Because everyone's eyes were fixated on her, April plastered a contorted smile on her face. "Thanks, but what's all this?" She gestured to the festivities with a wave of her hand.

"Don't get mad. It wasn't my idea. It was actually Brynn's."

As if summoned, Brynn rushed forward in a blur of perfume and honey-bronzed ringlets framing her flushed face. Brynn Sunderland, HOA president, event planner, new resident greeter, community baker, and neighborhood watch, plus a host of other self-nominated responsibilities no one asked nor objected that she volunteered to do. And apparently, April mused as she was pulled into Brynn's arms, her best friend.

"I'm so sorry, I couldn't help myself," Brynn gushed with a sheepish smile. "When Ram told me you were coming back in town, I figured it would be a great time to celebrate."

Ram? April frowned at the nickname as she slid her eyes to Ramsey. *What's that about?* She bit her tongue and kept her smile firmly in place. "Celebrate what?"

"Your anniversary, silly!"

"Anniversary?" April turned back to her husband. An anniversary was something she would've remembered.

"Not *our* anniversary," Ramsey corrected quickly. "She means since we moved in."

"Of course. It has been three whole months since we welcomed you to the neighborhood so we—" Brynn turned and waved to the neighbors at her back "—just want to thank you both for making Westmoore Oaks your home and are so proud to call you family. And we figured it was a great excuse to have a New Year's Eve party to commemorate the occasion."

On cue, an eruption of claps and cheers reverberated as if she had just presented the couple with an Academy Award. It was an uncomfortable ordeal and April couldn't help but cringe at the theatrics.

"I told you all she would be surprised." Brynn's laugh erupted as if she'd made the funniest joke. She used her elbow to nudge Ramsey's arm. The exchange was playful enough, but April's gaze narrowed, her eyes volleying between the pair. They did that often, inside jokes and sideways looks that stopped short of being misconstrued. She'd surmised it was harmless. Actually, if she could be honest with herself, she didn't feel she was in any kind of position to voice suspicions of infidelity. Plus, it wasn't like they had said or done anything to warrant her distrust. April just knew she'd always been overly suspicious of everything and everyone. She kept her thoughts to herself.

April was distracted, so she didn't realize Ramsey had leaned in to kiss her until she felt his lips rub against hers. "Sorry about this, babe," he whispered earnestly. "But you know how your friend is. I didn't even have time to object before she was parading the neighbors in here to decorate and set up food."

April relaxed. She really couldn't be mad at the man. "You're such a softie."

"That's why you love me."

A weighted pause. Her cheeks were beginning to ache with the smile she kept planted in place. "I take it this is the big surprise you were telling me about?"

"No, I have something else for you."

April groaned. She didn't know how much more she could handle.

Ramsey lifted both of her hands to his lips and gave the back of each one a dramatic kiss. "Just give it an hour," he said. "And I promise we can get them out of here. We can tell them we want to bring in the new year alone, just us."

Grateful, April wrapped her arms around his neck. She could deal with the party for an hour.

An hour turned into two and April tried her best to keep her attitude at bay. She had just gotten home from traveling. The last thing she wanted to be bothered with was a slew of people she didn't even know that well, or really care for, if she could be honest, grinning and chatting and laughing in her face as if they had known each other since elementary school. And Brynn was bouncing her from conversation to conversation as if she were showing her off like a prized poodle. Someone had turned on some music and since it had stopped raining, the party had filtered into the backyard, despite the wet grass and soaked patio furniture. Like they always seemed to do at these types of functions, the women had branched off to gossip among themselves while the men stood drinking and laughing with Ramsey around the grill.

In a matter of minutes, April was caught up on all the community updates since she'd been gone for the week. Apparently, Ms. Snyder's dog had to have surgery, the Braswells' son had dropped out of college (again) and moved back home, and the twins had started ballet. Oh, and the twins' mother was pregnant. A boy this time. April had to massage the beginnings of a headache as she nodded and feigned murmurs of interest. Finally, she excused herself from the various clusters of conversation and wandered off to find somewhere private.

To her surprise, Ramsey's mother, Edith, was seated on the sectional in the living room, her floral-print dress fanned across the gray upholstery. One of her legs was elevated across the tufted ottoman, exposing a knee brace. April took a seat next to her. Sure, she was pleased to see the familiar face, but more so, it was an excuse to disassociate herself from mingling with the rest of the guests.

Edith was the spitting image of her son, with a salt-and-pepper crop of curls that softly framed her sweetheart face. They shared a warm smile and expressive eyes. Edith's now widened with genuine warmth at the sight of her daughter-in-law. And April appreciated her sentiments. She loved Edith like the mother she always wanted. The woman reminded her of a country grandmother, evoking feelings of Christmastime and chocolate chip cookies and money she would sneak in your hand when your parents weren't looking. April didn't know firsthand what any of that felt like, but something like longing nostalgia began to ache in her belly as she leaned down to wrap her arms around the woman's frail shoulders.

"Mama Edith, it's so good to see you."

"Sweetie, where have you been? I missed you."

"Just working. Staying busy."

Edith's lips turned down in a curious frown. "Oh? What do you do?"

"I . . ." April hesitated. "Remember, I'm a flight attendant." She conjured a mask of calm as her neck heated with shame. It was bad enough she had to keep up the façade of her false identity, but flat out lying to this sweet old woman felt blasphemous. Didn't she already know her profession?

The blank expression in Edith's eyes was a clear indicator that something wasn't registering with the statement. Then that too dissolved into a polite nod. "Of course, dear," she said, recovering a smile. "I'm so glad you were able to make it home before the new year. I wasn't sure if you would with the airports being so busy."

Strange. April cleared her throat to dispel the awkwardness and nodded toward Edith's brace. "What happened with your knee, Mama Edith?"

"Just a little fall." She winced in pain as she readjusted her leg. "I tried to tell my son it's not as bad as it looks and that you wouldn't want an old lady in your space, but he insisted it wouldn't be a problem."

April's eyebrows creased in confusion. "What wouldn't be a problem?"

"For me to stay with you both for a few weeks." A pause before the realization settled. "Oh no. Ramsey didn't tell you, did he?"

Of course he hadn't. But judging by Edith's horror-stricken face, she felt bad enough for the imposition. April grinned to disguise her ignorance and quickly dismissed the woman's worry with a gentle pat on her hand. "No, that's not it. He told me." It wasn't a complete lie, considering she knew Ramsey would tell her eventually. "You know it's never a problem to have you here, Mama Edith."

Edith visibly relaxed, even as April suppressed her own worry. It wasn't like Edith was the problem, but she'd been right; April would rather do without a houseguest. It meant another pair of eyes and ears in the vicinity, so she would have to be extra-vigilant. Ramsey may not notice a few lies, but that's not to say his mother wouldn't. And April had enough to worry about without adding to her trepidation.

"Excuse me." Brynn appeared at April's side with those dimples of hers winking in each cheek. "Would you mind if I borrow my friend for a quick moment, Ms. Edith?"

Edith waved them away. "No, not at all. I'm sure you two need to catch up anyway."

April wanted to express to her that wasn't the case; that she would rather stay and keep Edith company because it was nice and peaceful and welcoming. But Brynn was already propelling her through the spirited activity and laughter toward the kitchen. She was clearly enjoying herself and April had to question the woman's motives. Who throws a surprise new-house-versary, New Year's Eve party anyway?

The thing was, aside from Brynn's bubbly and zealous personality, she was pretty harmless. Which was why April tolerated her impromptu visits to check in or keep her company or bring wine and Instant Pot recipes because she "made too much food for one person." Sure, she wasn't used to that type of companionship, but that didn't make Brynn a bad person because April was so guarded. "She's probably just lonely," Ramsey had said once after April had shared her apprehension with the attachment. "You know she lost her husband, doesn't have any kids . . . she just needs a friend." April just had to remember to play her part.

Eventually, Brynn had grown on April. She was fun, entertaining and, despite her obnoxiousness, she was another semblance of normal. Of simple. She was, in all honesty, the closest thing to a friend April had ever had. And that wasn't saying too much. So rather than fight it, she realized it was so much easier to just go along with their friendship. Lord knew it was less exhausting that way.

The galley kitchen carried the overwhelming scent of a campfire. Someone had laid out a spread of finger foods and all the trimmings for a country barbecue feast, complete with an array of desserts a neighbor had either baked or bought. This area was Ramsey's domain since he did most of the cooking, so he'd accentuated with light wood cabinets to add a jolt of warmth to the gray floors and maximize the otherwise narrow room.

Brynn immediately went for the assorted fruit tray, peeling off the plastic lid and popping a grape into her mouth as she leaned back onto the counter. "I'm so glad you're enjoying this," she said, beaming.

Was she? Funny, April didn't remember telling her such. Still, she didn't object. "You really didn't have to go to so much trouble."

"It was no trouble at all. I just knew something like this was what you and Ram needed. You've been working so much." Brynn was plucking the stem from another grape as she spoke. "Besides, what kind of friend would I be if I didn't throw you a surprise party?"

The preferable kind. April swallowed a laugh at her own thoughts.

"I'm glad you're finally home because I did have a favor to ask." A smirk flitted at the corners of her lips, making April even more wary.

"What kind of favor, Brynn?"

"Nothing big. I've been having . . . sort of . . . a *thing* with this guy I met online a few months ago. He seems nice and he wants to meet up. I was wondering if you and Ram would mind doubledating with us. Just so I can make sure he's not crazy," she added quickly with a roll of her eyes. "You never know with people these days."

The accuracy of her phrasing had April grimacing. Brynn

probably wasn't addressing anyone in particular, but she might as well have been since the comment pricked just the same. "We'll see." April's tone was conciliatory. "Let me ask Ramsey before I commit to anything."

"Oh, don't worry, I already did. He wants to vet the guy too. You know, man-to-man. He said as long as you were in town that he was happy to do it." Brynn flashed another one of those bright smiles that was beginning to make April's head hurt. Leave it to Ramsey to be so chivalrous.

Since she was still standing there waiting for an answer, April lifted her shoulder in a half-hearted shrug. Brynn's face lit and she all but squealed as she flung her arms around April's neck. "You are the absolute best. I owe you big-time. Let's set it up for next week."

"Let's set what up for next week?" Ramsey entered through the sliding glass door in a billow of grill smoke. He carted a pan piled with seared burger patties, chicken, and hot dogs that sizzled against the foil.

"Our double date," Brynn said with an appreciative smirk in April's direction. "Prez will be in town and he's dying to meet you two."

"Prez?" April tried to keep from rolling her eyes. "His name is Prez?"

"Well, I thought that was a cute name," Brynn clarified with a blush. "It fits him."

Ramsey slid a gaze in April's direction, his face transparent with his skepticism. "Okay, well, as long as Erin doesn't mind—"

"Perfect! I'll let him know." And with that Brynn was strolling from the kitchen, her heels echoing on the linoleum.

April felt an amused grin tug at the corners of her lips. "That woman is something else," she murmured with a shake of her head.

"That's your friend." Ramsey's customary response to any of Brynn's antics, expected or unexpected. He placed the food on the counter and, resting his hands on her waist, guided her hips toward him. "But enough about her, I missed you."

April's hands were already against his chest, halting whatever movements he was initiating. "Why didn't you tell me about your mom, Ramsey?"

A labored sigh. The mention of Edith wrinkled his face into a troubled frown. "I was going to. I'm sorry."

"You should've told me."

"I didn't think it would be a problem. Is it?" He lifted a brow at her prolonged silence.

"No, of course not." How could she tell him that without sounding completely heartless? "I just . . . wish you had communicated that so we both could agree on it first. I like to know what's going on in my home, even when I'm away."

That roused a grin to spread across Ramsey's face as he pulled April's body closer. "I'll tell you what's been going on," he murmured against her neck. "I've been missing and needing my wife."

His lips found hers, soft and warm like satin, just like she remembered. Her body didn't hum to life like it should've. April couldn't even remember the last time it had. But she put her dispassion out of her mind and succumbed to the motions to reciprocate his affection.

Outside had given him a distinct flavor of woodsmoke and musk. Even now, his shirt was damp with droplets of sweat that glazed his arms in a sticky residue. She squeezed the bunch of muscles bulging from under his rolled sleeves. Unlike Carter, Ramsey was more toned with a body that physical labor had definitely blessed him with.

"Are you thinking what I'm thinking?"

He was backing her against the counter and April felt the slab digging into the small of her back. "Yes," she whispered. Her hands reached up to cup both sides of his face. "You stink."

That prompted a burst of laughter. "I love you too." A final kiss from him, this time a noisy and playful peck before he took a step back.

Making her movements as casual as possible, April stopped him with a gentle grab of his wrist. "Hey, listen. Where did you put my packages?"

"Don't worry. I put them out of the way when everyone came over. No one's going to steal your precious shoes."

She ignored his teasing. "You put them away where?"

Ramsey's eyebrows knitted together. "In the bedroom. You want to open everything now?" As if to prove the absurdity of the idea, his eyes flicked behind her, making a veiled reference to the party's audible merriment that wafted from the backyard. It didn't look like it would be winding down anytime soon, so there was no point in pushing the issue without looking completely silly. *Or suspicious.*

She put on her best smile and wrapped her arm around his waist. As anxious as she was, April would have to contain herself for a little bit longer. Even while she was riddled with a nagging feeling that something dangerous was lurking within reach.

Chapter Six

April Garrett's Journal Entry

I'm getting married again and this is one of the worst days of my life.

First off, it's a beautiful day for a wedding. You wouldn't think anyone had a reason to complain. A small backyard wedding was my idea. Something quaint and casual. But I didn't expect more than ten people to come. Everyone there was one of his family members. I wanted—no, needed—something short and to the point. Just enough to appease him while I go through the motions of becoming his wife. Then I can take what I need from him and disappear. I hate it has to be this way, but I've learned to play the hand I'm dealt. Thing is, I don't feel like me. I feel like I'm on autopilot, staring down at myself. Or a version of myself rather. A business arrangement. That's what I've convinced myself this is.

As I'm sitting here writing, I should be getting ready. But I'm nervous. And it's not a regular, bride-on-her-wedding-day nervous. I've been down the aisle before. No, I'm always on edge with the acting part. It's like, my middle school drama teacher used to quote this speech from Shakespeare: "All the world's a stage, and all the men and women merely players. They have their exits and their entrances; and one man in his time plays many parts." That's like my life, but every day.

I know as soon as the doors swing open, I'll need to get on "stage" and start playing my part. I'll have to ACT happy and smile for the cameras and ACT like this ridiculous wedding gown doesn't itch like hell, and ACT like I actually plan on spending the rest of my life with the man at the end of the aisle instead of just the next few months. I've been acting so long that it's actually starting to feel real.

It's interesting. I never planned on having one husband, much less two at the same time. And I sure as hell didn't plan to start liking them. You see, when I met Ramsey Duncan, my goal was just the opposite. He was sexy, don't get me wrong, but I'm not swayed by a man's physical appearance. I saw past the smooth, chocolate complexion and deep-set dimples that added to his charming demeanor. I saw an opportunity.

Ramsey is your classic small-town Southern boy but he has certainly made a name for himself as the owner and manager of an upscale dining establishment in the heart of Columbus, Red Velvet Bistro. But not only is he an artist in the kitchen, but he also loves to paint and, well, really anything that allows him to use his hands. That's honestly one of the attributes that drew me to him. He is, in the most respectable of

*ways, simple. And after the kind of life I've lived, I didn't re-
alize simplicity was so damn attractive.*

*I met Ramsey during a spontaneous dinner at his restaurant.
I was passing through town and had heard so much about
the delicious salmon, so I figured, what the hell. Might as
well stop in and give it a try before I head back to the hotel. I
had no idea who he was, or even that he owned the place. I
was actually in the lobby, admiring artwork that I didn't
know he painted. It was one of those extra-creative retro
pieces that was so abstract, you had to stare at it for a long
time in order to determine what you were looking at. Like an
optical illusion. But me being an artist myself, it definitely
had my attention.*

*I didn't even realize a man had sidled up to me until he
spoke, asking me if I liked the painting. I told him, sure, if
you're into that sort of stuff. He asked me if I understood it
and I told him that I didn't think you were supposed to since
it's the artist's voice. You just appreciate it for what it is. And
I left him standing right there.*

*Lo and behold, this man followed me to the bar. I'm waiting
to place my order and he's standing there, damn near breathing down my neck but still smelling so good in that cologne
he was wearing. I placed my order and was handing over my
credit card when he asked me what else I could conclude
about the artist from the pictures hanging around the restaurant. He told me he was a painter and was always looking for
ways to improve his own work. I understood how good it
was to hear how something was perceived so I admit, I entertained him a little, telling him how I interpreted the artist as*

passionate and because of his use of bold colors, how he liked to make a statement. Plus, how he was into abstract, so he was complicated and enjoyed a mystery.

It wasn't until the man introduced himself and gave me my meal for free that I realized his prominence in the establishment, as both the owner and artist. And it was also then I decided I wouldn't tell him I was married. It probably looks bad, but I really wasn't trying to be intentionally deceitful.

I don't necessarily love Ramsey any more than I love Carter. I enjoy them both and I am at peace with their protective natures, both physically and financially. I like not having to worry about life's hardships. I like being comfortable. Carter makes me feel like I can conquer anything. And Ramsey takes an interest in the things that matter to me, like my art. That appreciation makes me feel complete. He allows me to see the world through his eyes. And it's quite beautiful.

I know it can be considered selfish. But I never want to let that go. There's too much pain on the other side. It's easier to just comfort myself with the lies.

Chapter Seven

"Five . . . four . . . three . . . two . . . one . . . HAPPY NEW YEAR!"

A melodic symphony of voices rose against the crescendo of fireworks exploding in the night sky. It felt like déjà vu all over again. Except this time, she wasn't hiding in a hotel bathroom shrouded in the stench of blood.

April stood with Ramsey's arm draped protectively around her shoulders. Scattered across their backyard, neighbors were assembled with their heads angled skyward to watch the gorgeous display. Each burst of the pyrotechnics colored the shadows with eerie prisms of light that danced across their faces, illuminating the wonderment. Like zombies. She shuddered at the thought and pulled her jacket tighter against the bite of the cool, night breeze.

"You cold?" Ramsey's breath was warm on her forehead.

"A little." She couldn't even be sure it was the temperature or something else entirely.

A vibration in her pocket had April angling her cell phone to sneak a look at the screen. Only one person would probably be looking for her at this hour. Sure enough, *Work* flashed on display. Which meant Carter. She swiped a discreet thumb on the screen to ignore the call. Just as quickly, an incoming text notification popped up: **Happy New Year, babe. Love you. I know you're probably asleep so call me when you get up.**

"Everything okay?"

April casually shoved the phone back into her pocket. "Yeah, why do you say that?"

Ramsey's expression was masked in the dark, but she could tell by his silhouette and the whites of his eyes that he had pivoted to stare at her. Had he seen the message? "Aw, you're a trouper, babe. I know you're probably tired."

"Yeah, it's been a long day." April didn't have to fake her yawn as she rested her head on Ramsey's shoulder. She was, indeed, physically and mentally exhausted.

Thankfully, he nodded his understanding and began shepherding her toward the patio. "Of course, sweetie. Let me get everyone out of here so I can have you all to myself."

April waited in the living room, peering through the glass as Ramsey began rallying up the neighbors. One by one, they spilled back into the house with pleasantries and farewells as they collected their belongings.

"Erin, we love you."

"Thanks for a wonderful party, Erin."

"Erin, let's do some shopping later this weekend."

She nodded politely as the women took turns exchanging hugs with her and each other, their speech slightly slurred from intoxication. You would think *she'd* organized this little get-together. Was that Brynn's plan all along? To better integrate her into the community by getting her acclimated with the neighbors? Apparently, it had worked like a charm.

After to-go plates had been wrapped with foil and the last person had been ushered out of the front door, April made her way back to the kitchen. She was dreading the cleanup process, but now that everyone was gone, and Edith had already retired to the guest room, it was an excuse to prolong the night until Ramsey had showered and fallen asleep. Then she could pull out those packages and make sure it was a mix-up. It was the most logical explanation, but she wouldn't be able to rest until she found out for sure.

April stopped in the doorway with a frown. She was mistaken. Apparently, she had misjudged the number of attendees.

Brynn tossed a glance over her shoulder as she stood at the counter, scraping food into Tupperware containers. "Hey, girlie," she said, entirely too jovial for the late hour. "Did you have a good time?"

April sighed and trudged into the kitchen, her mind shuffling through polite ways to encourage her friend to leave. She certainly didn't want to be rude, considering Brynn was helping her. But still . . . "Brynn, you don't have to do all of that. I got it."

Brynn didn't break stride, popping open the dishwasher and stacking dirty dishes onto the racks. "Oh please, you know I don't mind. This whole thing was my idea, so it's only fair. I hate everyone left you to clean up this mess by yourself."

April started to object once more but stopped short when Ramsey entered from the backyard with a bag nearly bursting at the seams with garbage.

"Everyone walked over so they should be good getting back home. I'll finish cleaning up outside in the morning." He carried the trash with him into the kitchen and stooped down to tie a knot in the bag. "Brynn, it's late. You should head on home before you end up cleaning the whole house," he joked.

Brynn turned to offer him a smile. That's when April caught it, a little more pronounced this time. It was fleeting, a lingering stare so brief that someone else would've probably missed it. Someone else that hadn't had a lifetime of vigilance, making her more observant than the average person. April for sure caught every second of the exchange. She knew Brynn had this exuberance about her that often skirted the edges of friendliness and flirtatious. But that look, that *smile* she was giving Ramsey . . . there was some meaning behind it. Some meaning she wasn't sure she was supposed to be privy to.

Then just as quickly, Brynn disguised the affection with jest, using her shoulder to give Ramsey a playful nudge away from the sink. Amusement colored her cheeks. "Erin, can you *puh-lease* go entertain your man so he can leave me alone?"

Again, the few stings of jealousy left a rancid taste in April's mouth. And again, she willed herself to purse her lips against the streams of accusations she was sure to let loose. It wasn't like she had room to feel any type of way. Not against Ramsey, who was as faithful as they came, nor Brynn, since she wasn't his type. And sure as hell not with Carter a few hundred miles away, who was probably waiting on a call from *his* wife. But still, April felt compelled to join them, inserting herself between their bodies as if the distance would disperse any budding chemistry.

"Ramsey's right," she said. "You should get on back. It's already dark."

Brynn's gaze flickered to the window as if she were just now realizing the time. "You're probably right. I should've left with everyone else, so I didn't have to walk alone. Do you mind if Ram walks me home? I promise not to keep him long."

She definitely minded. But she shouldn't have. Not when Brynn was her friend. Not when she only lived a few blocks over on the next street. Now when it was a good opportunity for her to look at her packages. Instead of opposing, April nodded. "No, of course not. Better safe than sorry."

"Not that anyone is trying to kidnap me anyway," Brynn teased with a laugh. "That would probably do wonders for my love life, so I know I'm not that lucky." She gave April a quick, friendly hug and followed Ramsey to the front door. "I'll call you tomorrow, girlie. Love ya." And the two stepped out onto the porch.

As soon as the door clicked shut, April hurried to the living room to peek through the blinds. They were cutting across the front yard before they faded into silhouettes against the yellow streetlamps. Then it looked like they stopped walking. Were they talking? Hugging? April squinted into the darkness, unable to make out any kind of clear distinction between the figures. Not from this view anyway. She was tempted to go out and see for herself, or at least change windows for a better angle, but something more pressing eclipsed her concern. Whatever they were, or were not doing, it wouldn't be long before Ramsey returned, so she had to move. Fast.

First, she poked her head into the guest bedroom to check on Ramsey's mother. The door was slightly ajar, letting through a sliver of light from the muted television. Sure enough, Edith was swathed in the sheets, a light snore escaping her parted lips. Her suitcases were stacked under the window and she'd started unpacking, as evidenced by the jewelry and medicine bottles littering the dresser. Ramsey had obviously attempted to make her feel more comfortable by hanging some personal pictures on the wall, as well. Satisfied, April closed the door and made her way back down the hall.

The master bedroom was right off the foyer. Ramsey had spent a great deal of time with this area during the renovation, combining two bedrooms to create what he considered their retreat.

The room looked like something from one of those home-designing shows. She should know. She'd taken the initiative with decorating and had managed to give the room a touch of chic luxury. The decor was accented in a mélange of pastel blues, creams, and grays and spacious enough to comfortably accommodate an upholstered California king bed with a matching chaise, along with two sets of dressers and an armoire. Ramsey's abstract paintings checkered the walls, along with a few candid shots of the couple. He'd taken the liberty to clean up this time, judging by the neatly-made bed and distinct smell of fresh linen that hung in the air.

Something different caught her eye and April turned to look at the space above the headboard. Whereas it had been empty before, now it was dominated by a huge canvas wedding photo. The photographer had captured a candid shot of the couple as they made that joyous trek up the aisle as husband and wife. Goofy grins adorned their faces as Ramsey clutched his wife's waist. April's arm was lifted in the air as she gripped the bouquet and the flash of the camera had brilliantly captured the sparkle of embellishments on the bodice of her wedding gown. That same sparkle reflected in her eyes. She looked different from her wedding with Carter, but equally radiant. Apparently this was his big surprise. It was a stunning photo, but yet another reminder that April could've done without. She snatched her eyes from the image, telling herself not to be irritated with the gesture. Why did he have to be so damn romantic? Why did he have to make it so . . . *hard*?

A handful of packages in various sizes were stacked in a tiered fashion in the corner of the room. Most she recognized by the label, all addressed to Erin Duncan. She shifted those to the side until she got to the very last one. Curious, she observed the neatly taped flap and the carefully tied red ribbon and bow adorning the simple brown packaging. It was compact, roughly the size of a sheet of paper both in length and width, but inflated with the bulge of Bubble Wrap lining the inside. And sure enough, neatly scribbled on a label in handwriting she didn't recognize, was *April*. That's it. No last name. Just April. There was no evidence of a postal service delivery. No return address. Not even a stamp. Whoever it was had personally placed it on her doorstep.

Anxiety pounded her temples like a hammer. April sat back on her heels and lifted the package. It was light, so light it felt empty. She shook it and heard the rattle of something inside. A mistake, she told herself over and over. She desperately wanted to believe it, even as she used her fingernail to puncture a thin hole in the adhesive and rip the flap open. Her blood surged with the escalating apprehension, even as worry itched her trembling fingers.

She took her time, pulling open the package as if she were dissecting an animal. With a clenched breath, she peered inside . . . and froze under the ripple of fear that gathered in her bones.

The white gold of the necklace chain had her shutting her eyes. She didn't need to pull out the piece of jewelry to know what it was. Or where it came from. She easily remembered the simple infinity symbol–shaped design of the charm, its featured overlay of dazzling diamond accents that would catch the light and bounce kaleidoscopic sparkles across her collarbone. It was Warren's favorite. April recoiled as every sordid memory came barreling back in snippets that snatched the air from her lungs and sat like weights on her chest. Even just having the necklace exposed left a residual terror, its metal soiled by her experiences. It was too much. For a brief moment, the stillness was just as haunting as the memory, the anguish just as crippling. Like something was lurking in the corner, only to be unleashed by this stupid package. *How? How? How?*

"Erin?" Ramsey's voice pierced the silence, interrupting April's disquiet. She swallowed, struggling to keep the panic attack at bay. Their eyes locked in the mirror, and she saw him now standing behind her in the doorway with his face furrowed in concern. *Or was it calculating?* One glance at her own reflection told her why. She looked like she'd seen a ghost, which, in a condemning way, was true. Her own.

Ramsey eased closer and peered into the package. Her breath caught in her throat as he reached in and lifted the necklace into view, letting it dangle like a pendulum between his thumb and index finger.

"What's wrong? This isn't the necklace you ordered or something?"

"No, I . . ." she swallowed. "I didn't realize it would come so soon, that's all." *Put it back. Please put it back.*

Ramsey lifted the strand higher to study the infinity-symbol charm. "I like it. Never saw you really wear much jewelry other than earrings though." He fiddled with the clasp and held it out in April's direction. "I can put it on now if you want."

"That's okay." She didn't mean to snatch the necklace from him, but the idea of it around her neck, again, felt as harrowing as a noose. Her movements were brisk as she dumped the jewelry back in the packaging with more force than she intended. "You got Brynn home safe and sound?" she asked.

"Yes, she's good." Ramsey lifted April's chin to bring her face closer. She shrank under his scrutiny. "Babe, you sure you're okay? You've been acting a little weird this evening. And you look like you're getting sick."

She was unraveling, she knew it. April mustered as much strength as she could to stretch her lips into a thin smile that she didn't believe. "I'm just tired," she said, which was 100 percent true. "I told you it's been a long day. Work and then the party. I just need to take a shower and relax. That's all."

His eyes searched hers a moment longer, as if he were trying to gauge the honesty. Because she was afraid of crumbling underneath his stare, April cradled his face and leaned in to kiss him. It worked. His body seemed to melt against hers with the gesture.

"Okay, want me to run you a bath?"

"I'm good. Thanks, babe." And with that, she pulled back and headed to their adjoining bathroom, praying he wouldn't notice that she had to brace against the wall to keep her legs from buckling. Her body was going through the motions, but her mind was lost in the fog of past trauma.

She closed the door and looked down at her hand where she held the package. Abruptly, she shoved it into her vanity drawer with a resounding *slam*. Even through the wood, its presence was just as palpable. And just as ominous.

PART II: ANGER

A strong feeling of displeasure and belligerence aroused by a wrong; wrath. A defense mechanism that helps us feel in control and avoid our helplessness and grief.

Chapter Eight

Before

Something was wrong. April pretended to eat dinner but couldn't help but keep a questioning eye on Erika. At sixteen, she didn't know everything. But judging by the cigarette that bounced between her mother's trembling lips and the pacing that was sure to leave a hole in the dingy carpet, there was definite cause for concern. She kept her head bent low, raking spaghetti noodles across the Styrofoam plate while Erika shuffled on the edges of her peripheral vision.

Her mother's eyes looked sunken in, almost hollow, and the disheveled housecoat was a huge contrast to all the designer clothes adorning her closet. Her new boyfriend had been spoiling them both, keeping their hair and nails done, showering them with gourmet dinners at five-star restaurants April couldn't pronounce. Plus, he kept their refrigerator stocked so she appreciated not having to go to the grocery store and use stolen EBT cards or sift wallets from the other shoppers just to keep them from starving. They were good. Great, actually. For once in all of their years of struggling, scamming, and living dollar to dollar while they scrapped to keep the raggedy Section 8 apartment over their head, April could sleep peacefully. Erika's boyfriend had even promised they could move in with him and she, for one, was looking forward to living in a neighborhood without roaches and shootings and burglaries. So why, then, was her mother looking so damn stressed that she was taking huge drags of that Newport like it was oxygen?

Finally, Erika crossed the room and took a seat at the table in front of April. The hard plastic of the foldout chair groaned under her weight as she shifted to get comfortable. She took another puff of her cigarette and blew a stream of smoke in the air. "We need to talk," she said, her voice rusty with nicotine and alcohol.

April didn't like the sound of that. Usually, it meant she needed her to do something. Forge check stubs or get a Social Security number from a classmate so they could open a credit card, or pee in a cup so she could sell it to some people who didn't want the labs to pick up the drugs in their systems. At this point, there probably wasn't anything that would surprise April. But still, she was nervous as she pushed her plate to the side and rested her palms flat on the table. She didn't speak, but they both knew her silence was permission for her mother to continue.

Erika exhaled; her expression shrouded in the smoke that permeated between them. She ripped her eyes away from her daughter's as if she couldn't bear to look at the shy innocence, or the subsequent result of the ultimatum she was about to enforce. "You know I would do anything for us, right? To make sure we're taken care of. To make sure we have everything we need, want, and deserve."

Something stirred in April's belly. Something slow. And agonizing. "Of course."

Erika released a weathered sigh. "What about you, April? Are you willing to do anything?"

April's lips hardened into a thin line, insulted by the question. Hadn't she always? "What is it, Erika?" she prodded, her voice laced with irritation. Not *Mom*, but Erika. They'd never been close enough for anything else, their relationship diluted to disassociated formalities. Partners in crime. Hadn't that been Erika's label before? April already knew whatever Erika was tap-dancing around was something she needed her *partner* for. Why else would she want to talk? What April didn't understand was why she didn't just spit it out. It couldn't be any worse than the scams they'd already pulled together, right?

"We've always done what we needed to do to survive," Erika said, stabbing her cigarette out in the overflowing ashtray. "It's always been us against the world, because why?"

"Because the world ain't never gave a shit about us," April finished the familiar quote. Her mother had preached this gospel all her life. But it wasn't that she'd heard it enough, she'd lived and breathed it. It had been ingrained into the very core of her existence like the bones, muscle, and tissue that made up her anatomy.

Erika's smirk was one of satisfaction. "Exactly," she said. "And this time is no exception." She paused. April didn't know if she was asking for a response or strength with the delay, but she offered neither. "I need you to do me a favor. A big favor. But it would change our lives forever if you did it. Can you do that for me?"

"What?"

"First, promise me you'll do it." Erika's reiteration was more forceful. "I need to know you understand the magnitude of what we're about to do." As was customary between them, she held out her pinky in April's direction and waited for her daughter to reciprocate. The silent bond was completely unspoken but once they locked pinkies, both knew that the gesture sealed the deal between them as permanently as if they'd taken blood oaths. Everything and everyone outside of them came and went, but they'd always been able to rely on each other. That was all they had.

A sliver of dread had April hesitating only briefly. She reached out to hook her finger around her mother's. "I promise," she said, eyeing their joined fingers. "What do I have to do?"

She almost didn't hear the words as she watched her mother's lips move. Knew she couldn't have heard what she thought she heard. It was as if the lingering cigarette smoke had created some kind of buffer that muffled the noise. April remained expressionless.

"I need you to marry Warren," Erika repeated.

There it was again. The punch of the demand had left her breathless and April recoiled in disgust. Marry her boyfriend. Her *forty-seven-year-old* boyfriend. The thought brought on a wave of nausea that had the aftertaste of her spaghetti pervading her throat. "Why?" was all she could stomach.

Erika rose to her feet. She was headed into the kitchen as she spoke, banging around cabinets and drawers, then the refrigerator for her weapon of choice: vodka. She poured it into the only clean dish she could find: a mug. Like it was coffee. "Trust me, it's not as crazy as it sounds," she was saying. "Apparently, he loves you or some shit. I tried to make him love me. Gave that man everything he asked because I was just happy that he was taking care of us, so we didn't have to resort to scams like we're used to." She knocked back the liquor in two gulps, slamming the cup on the counter so hard it was a wonder it didn't crack. "He said we could move in with him, but he had the nerve to give me an ultimatum," she fumed, her eyes wild with fury, her lips clenched with the potency of her words. "That fat bastard really had the nerve to tell me that he's had his eye on you and that you were the one he wanted to be with. Otherwise, he's leaving and taking everything with him." She shrugged. "I told him the truth. The only way that would work was if he married you."

"Why the hell would you say that?" April didn't bother hiding her own budding anger. Not like it was good news that she was being auctioned off to the highest bidder.

"Because we're going to cash in, that's why." Erika was back in her seat, now leaning across the table so April could smell every molecule of the alcohol staining her breath. "Because after this, we won't have to run any more scams. Ever. Boyfriends are smart, husbands are stupid, April. Remember that. It's risky, but the reward outweighs the risk. I've learned where you have to fight for even a house key as a girlfriend, having that wife title can afford you a key and the house that comes with it. Passcodes, bank accounts, deeds, titles . . . More trust, less questions. Being tied down for a little while is just a temporary inconvenience." Erika was firing up another cigarette, rushing on with renewed enthusiasm as the idea materialized. "We give him what he wants. That way, we can take what *we* want."

Unable to sit with the repulsion any longer, April rose to her feet. Try as she might, she couldn't bring herself to do it. The thought of having to commit herself to that man, to kiss him, have him touch her in ways only she touched herself, was sickening. And for what? "I can't do it," she mumbled, spitting each word with all the disgust she'd tried to quell. "We'll make another way like we always do. We'll take what we have and let him leave because this ain't worth it."

"April—"

"I said no." She didn't even have time to react. Hadn't even realized Erika had risen to her feet and scissored across the room in a matter of strides. But she did feel the slap sting her face with enough force to have her head snapping on its axis. Pained tears threatened to sprout from her lids. Erika had done a lot of things. But hit her? Never.

As if realizing what she'd done, Erika balled her hand into a fist and shoved it in the pocket of her robe. She straightened her back. "I'm not going to argue with you about this," she said, her voice surprisingly calm despite the tension lobbed between them. "You need to think about all the damn sacrifices I've made for you. Trying to keep your ungrateful ass out of jail. Doing what I needed to do to give us opportunities and make a way when there were none. The best decisions aren't always the easiest. Life ain't giving no damn handouts to us so we have to take what we can. And Warren is who we need to work on. You can either get on board or get the hell out there and try to make it on your own." Then, a smile broke her face as she reached out. April flinched, but Erika's hand was gentle as she brushed a strand of hair from her face. "It's just for a little bit. Just enough to get some of his money so we'll be set and never have to do any of this shit again. Trust me, April. You deserve your happily ever after."

Stunned, April could only watch Erika for an extra moment before she managed to find her voice. Slowly, she nodded. "Okay," she said, her tone obligatory. "How are we going to do this?"

Chapter Nine

She was being strangled. Her breathing was raw and jagged as she tried to suck in greedy gulps of air. Her vision wavered with the lack of oxygen, but still, she could make out a shadow looming above, using the necklace to choke the life out of her with inhuman strength. A shadow with no features.

The chain bit into her neck like a razor, so thin she couldn't get her fingers around it to pry it away from embedding in her skin. She flailed her arms out to grab the person's wrists, arms, *anything*; scratching at flesh until she felt blood curdling under her fingernails. The whimper that escaped from her parted lips was desperate. And useless. She was meant to die this time.

"It's over," he said. *His voice.* Even on the precipice of unconsciousness, she could make out the voice corroded with hatred. And triumph. It was Warren. He'd won. She felt his breath hot and heavy in her ear and her scream erupted as she jolted upright in bed.

The sheets were tangled around her legs, her frenzied breaths like an echoing roar in the empty room. Her fingers flew to her neck to claw the necklace from her throat. But there was nothing, her bare flesh a surprising relief. Still, she couldn't help but grip her knees as her chest rattled with panicked breaths. She felt wet and her hand slid to her chest, half expecting to feel blood staining her shirt. No, not blood. But sweat soaked the cotton material, spreading through to dampen her skin. April pulled the shirt over her head and tossed it to the floor. With a labored sigh, she sat back against the cool sheets and struggled to calm down.

A nightmare. She hadn't had one of those in a while. She wanted so much to tell Erika they had returned. No, she really wanted to go see another psychiatrist. But she couldn't risk it. If it was one thing she'd learned, it was the value of remaining hidden.

For a moment, April could only lie in the sweat-drenched sheets and listen to the low drone of the ceiling fan blades slicing the air overhead. She pressed her fingers to her closed eyes, struggling to extinguish the headache that had bloomed. She couldn't remember much from the dream, but she knew it felt real. It was a wonder she didn't wake her husband. The clock read 3:23 in the morning but she already knew going back to sleep was not an option.

April reached across the plush mattress for Ramsey, not at all surprised when her hand brushed the empty pillow. Knowingly, she kicked the covers off and pulled her weakened body from the bed. She cast a fearful look to the closed bathroom door; at what lay on the other side of the plaster, in a cabinet drawer under bonnets and scarves and bobby pins. Tormenting her. It was wistful to think the package had disappeared, but she couldn't bring herself to go in and see.

Ramsey had been up for a while. That much was clear from the nearly finished painting propped on the easel in front of him. April leaned on the doorframe and peered through the pane of the closed French doors.

His studio was organized chaos, with a slew of easels, shelves, art supplies, and canvases—both finished and unfinished—cluttering the workspace. Windows lined three walls facing their backyard, allowing the night sky to create a soothing ambiance. Ramsey's back was to the door where April stood, so she watched him lean backwards on his stool and angle his head to better assess the results of his creation. Then, he rose from his perch and carried his paintbrush and tray to the stainless steel sink.

Now, with a better view of the picture, she could make out the exaggerated contours of a woman's body with no clothes and no face. *Was that her?* She couldn't be sure. An artistic interpretation, he would say, with its slashes of reds and oranges. The man prided himself on being a master with his hands, creating both works of art on the canvas and in the kitchen.

A low buzz had April frowning in response. *A vibration.* Ramsey's phone, by the looks of it. He was still preoccupied at the sink, washing his supplies; perhaps the noise from the water faucet drowning out the notification from his cell. But April heard it loud and clear from her position near the door. Even more prominently with the phone's screen glowing with the incoming call. The phone stopped, then immediately started again. *Buzz, buzz, buzz* that had the device inching toward the edge of the table. *Who the hell could be calling him at this hour? Repeatedly.* Even with his business, April couldn't recall this type of emergency.

Ramsey finished up at the sink, just in time to catch a glimpse of the phone before it finished droning. April kept her eyes peeled as he leaned to pick it up. But he didn't answer. Instead, his thumbs began flying across the screen to compose what she assumed was a text message response. She caught the amused smirk that crossed his face, which only piqued her interest even more.

When he stuffed the phone in his back pocket and resumed tidying his workspace, April made her way back into the bedroom. She would have to find a way to ask him about the suspicious call without looking too obvious. Not that she was without her own secrets, but Ramsey had never given her a reason to distrust him. *Until now.*

April crept into the bathroom, closing and locking the door behind her. This time, without Ramsey watching her, she pulled open the drawer with the package and opened it once more, turning it over to dump the necklace into her hand. The metal felt surprisingly warm against her palm, with its infinity charm glistening in all its brilliant splendor. She closed her eyes, remembering when Warren had surprised her with the gift. He'd stood behind her as he clasped it around her neck, his fingers feeling grimy against her skin. *"All my love, for all eternity,"* he said with a smile. April opened her eyes to dispel the memory and held the necklace close to her face, searching for any evidence. It had to be there. But surprisingly, there wasn't a shred of blood or dirt on the white gold finish. Not even a speck of dust. It looked just as polished and new as when Warren had presented it to her, which couldn't be right. Was this the same one from that night, or a different necklace entirely? And either way, who else but a very twisted (and very dead) Warren would understand its sinister meaning enough to send it to her?

Chapter Ten

"I still can't believe you, Erin." Brynn gave an animated shake of her head.

Across from her, April stabbed at her salad. She was too preoccupied to eat so instead, she was using her fork to scatter the vegetables around the bowl. At Brynn's continued silence, she glanced up to see her staring at her. "What's wrong?"

"No, nothing's wrong. I just can't believe you bought this dress for me." Brynn gestured to the shopping bag in the chair next to her. "I told you I had nowhere to wear it."

April shrugged. "And I told you, it wasn't a big deal. Plus, you looked good in it."

Brynn rested her chin in her hand, crumbs of the club sandwich she'd ordered sprinkled on the plate at her elbow. "You're right, I did, huh?" She laughed. "Well, thanks anyway. You really didn't have to."

April nodded even though she wouldn't divulge the truth. Sure, she had paid with a credit card, but it hadn't been hers. So as far as she was concerned, the expense hadn't been a problem for either of them.

She hadn't planned on shopping today. But Brynn had called wanting to go to the mall to find an outfit for their double date. April considered it a blessing in disguise because she wanted—no, *needed*, to get out of the house and away from that damn necklace. She probably should've thrown it away, but she couldn't bring herself to do that either. Not until she figured out where it came from and who sent it. But leave it to Brynn to intervene with gossip and girl time. April just wished it was enough of a distraction.

Brynn polished off her sandwich and took a generous sip of her Coke. She frowned at April's barely touched food. "What's wrong, girlie? You not hungry?"

"No, not really."

"Is this about Ram?"

April frowned. "What do you mean?"

Brynn glanced around the crowded food court and shifted in the booth to lean closer across the table. "I mean about the restaurant."

April's frown deepened. *What was she talking about?*

"I know he's been a little stressed lately," Brynn revealed with a sympathetic smile. "Money issues, I guess. Red Velvet isn't really doing so well." She paused, taking in April's shocked expression. "Oh my God, you didn't know?"

"He didn't tell me anything about it." *Did he?* April hated the guilt tugging at her heart.

Brynn reached across the table. Her hand was soft and compassionate as it rested on April's. "He probably didn't want to worry you," she offered. "You're so busy with work and stuff."

And stuff was certainly the bulk of it.

Brynn went on with a comforting smile. "I'm sure he's got it all under control."

April nodded, though she still didn't feel any better. Why hadn't he mentioned it? Better yet, why had he mentioned it to *Brynn* and not her? Was she really missing the obvious now? That would certainly account for her anxiety, especially with the mysterious package.

She glanced toward the window. She didn't know who this person was or what he or she looked like. It's as if it were a ghost. A woman strutted by in heels and a skirt extremely too tight. A teenager in earphones and swaddled in a tapestry of tattoos nearly broke his neck to turn and look at her. A man in a business suit with a cell phone fastened to his ear didn't even break stride when he bumped into the brunette with the pregnant belly bulging from a floral dress that kissed her ankles. Any one of them could be the person who sent her the necklace and April wouldn't have known them if they looked her in the face.

One man in particular caught her eye. He was sitting alone at one of the high-top tables wearing a black sweatsuit with an angular face and twist curls peeking from underneath a hoodie. April couldn't tell, but he seemed to be looking in their direction. She tensed, narrowing her eyes. *Was he looking at her? Or Brynn?* She kept her eyes on him as he rose from the table and headed in their direction, only relaxing when he bypassed her chair. She turned in time to catch him greet a group of men and she blew out a breath. She really needed to pull herself together.

"Okay, change of subject," Brynn stated, pulling April's attention back to the table. "Let's not let that sour the mood." She clasped her hands together. "I was thinking I wanted to put in for a flight attendant job."

April's eyebrows drew together. "Where is this coming from?" As far as she knew, Brynn was happy with her management job at some clothing boutique. The woman's outgoing personality made her a natural in the retail industry.

"I just need a change of pace. Something different. You know I don't really get out of Columbus. And your job seems like so much fun. Traveling all the time." She shrugged. "I don't know, I figured it couldn't hurt to look into it, right? Maybe put in a good word for me."

The way her eyes were twinkling made April nervous. Was she really serious about this? "I'll ask around when I get back to work."

"Okay, don't forget about me now. I already told Prez I didn't know how available I would be in the next few months if I could get on with you. Which airline is it again?"

Now April did reach for her drink. Something, *anything* to dislodge the lump in her throat. "Delta," she lied, taking a sip.

Brynn nodded and tapped a finger to her cheek in consideration. "Yeah, I can see myself doing that. Maybe I'll get lucky and meet a pilot."

She *was* serious. And she didn't sound like she was going to let it go. April didn't know which part of the conversation was worrying her more. She took the opportunity to change the subject.

"A pilot, huh?" she tossed back with feigned amusement. "You think *Prez* would mind?"

Brynn chuckled as she began to pile discarded napkins and other trash on her tray. "Prez and I are still in the talking phase. Besides," she added with a gleeful wink. "If I had your kind of job, I could do what the hell I wanted because honestly, who's going to know?"

April felt convicted and since she wasn't really sure how to respond to the accurate assessment, she remained quiet as she followed Brynn to the garbage bins. As she looked up, she caught the man in the black sweatsuit, now standing alone. Watching her. And from this distance, she couldn't tell, but it looked like he smiled before turning to disappear through the exit doors.

Chapter Eleven

"Fire! Help!"

April heard the desperate shriek, which was nearly eclipsed by the sudden piercing of the fire alarm. Her heart leapt into her throat as she pushed out of the shower stall and snatched a nearby towel from the rack. It was Edith's voice. *Oh God, what had happened?* She was soaked, or maybe because she was terrified, but the gust of air felt like frost on her skin. Still, her wet feet slapped the hardwood as she stumbled toward the kitchen.

The flame caught her eye first, crackling up from the pan with roaring sizzles. Edith was standing entirely too close to the stove as she attempted to fan and blow out the blaze. Bursts of heat licked April's face and for a moment she stood in the doorway, paralyzed with shock at the scene.

Edith turned wild, panic-stricken eyes to her daughter-in-law. "Put it out, Erin! Put it out, please! Oh my God, what's happening?" Her cries were nearly drowned out by the deafening shrill of the siren.

April snapped from her daze and hurried to grab the fire extinguisher from under the sink. Panic had her fumbling with the spigot. She was nearly blinded with helpless tears as she struggled to concentrate and not grow fearful as the flame intensified. *Please, please* . . . She didn't even realize she was mumbling until she heard her own voice.

A set of firm hands snatched the extinguisher from her grasp and she was pushed backwards, away from the heat, away from the threat. Ramsey was planted in front of the stove now, dousing the fire until the pan was now caked under a mound of foam. Then just as quickly it had started, the frenzy was over with only the smell of smoke billowing in the air.

Ramsey sat the extinguisher on the counter and looked first to his mom to pull her into a hug. He was visibly unnerved as his gaze met April's over Edith's shoulder. "Is everyone okay?"

April stared as if in a stupor at the black marks now streaked across the backsplash. The fire was gone but she could still see, smell it, taste it. The house could've burned down.

"Erin?"

It was Ramsey's voice pulling her focus once more and she forced herself to tear her eyes from the stove.

"Yes, I'm—we're fine," she squeaked, struggling to calm her racing heart. Still wet from her shower, she was dripping water into a puddle on the linoleum and now, without the heat from the fire, she was shivering. The room had dipped a few degrees.

"What happened?" Ramsey said, looking between the women.

Edith coughed. "I'm sorry," she said, wiping her watery eyes. Whether from the fire or tears or both, April couldn't tell. "I just . . . I wanted some sausage."

"Why didn't you ask Erin to help you, Mama?" He was talking to his mother, but simultaneously throwing a look in Erin's direction. A look that was entirely too accusatory.

April blinked. Did he think this was *her* fault? "I was in the shower," she said. "Besides, I didn't know she needed supervision cooking breakfast."

She watched Edith pull her robe tighter and tie the belt around her waist. The woman suddenly looked small, more like a reprimanded child than a woman in her seventies. April felt bad for even speaking her mind on it. The last thing she wanted to do was make Mama Edith feel bad.

Ramsey sighed. "Mama, can you give us a minute? I'll clean up and get you some breakfast."

Obediently, Edith trudged off down the hall.

The cabinet slammed as Ramsey replaced the fire extinguisher to its place under the sink. "I'm sorry." He was already speaking as soon as they were alone. "I didn't mean to act like you did anything wrong. I just . . . didn't know she was going to try and cook by herself."

April crossed her arms over her chest. "You want to tell me what's going on, Ramsey? Your mother has cooked plenty of times. I don't recall her starting a fire before."

An awkward pause stretched between them. He actually had the nerve to look conflicted and his hesitancy was infuriating. Maybe the conversation with Brynn about the restaurant had some truth to it. What else was he keeping from her?

Finally, Ramsey leaned on the counter and rubbed the back of his neck. He looked exhausted. Much more than usual. "I want my mom to come live with us . . . permanently," he said.

April blinked, her mind already flipping through the many reasons why that was a horrible idea. "All this because of her knee? I thought it was temporary."

"It's not just her knee." Ramsey sighed as if the weight of his next statement was taking all of his strength. "My mom has dementia. It's getting worse. They diagnosed her when she went to the hospital after she fell."

April looked down the hallway, now empty. Her heart ached for the poor old woman. "Ramsey, I'm so sorry." And she was. Edith had been the closest thing to a real mother she'd ever had.

From the moment he first brought April to meet Edith, she had opened her arms, her heart, and her delicious Southern recipes, all of which she had passed down to her only son. She had gushed how happy she was that Ramsey was finally settling down with someone he was happy with. April remembered she was afraid the dinner would be awkward, mainly because of her, but Edith, or Mama Edith as she insisted, had been happy to finally have a woman around to bond with. Especially one that, she thought, was so good for her son.

Ramsey squeezed April's hands, bringing her attention back to him. "I need you to do me a favor, babe," he said, his voice in a hushed whisper. "Please help me look after Mom. I'm going to look into getting her an aide, maybe part-time. But she needs us. I don't want anything else like this to happen."

April started to object; offer some sort of compromise so Mama Edith could obtain the proper care she needed. She wasn't a nurse, by any stretch of the imagination. Nor did she have the time to be saddled to the house looking after anyone. If she could be honest, it would be a hindrance. And when April left to go back to Carter, or better yet left for good, then what? Where would that leave Ramsey and his ailing mother?

But when she searched his eyes, she saw it. Fear. Ramsey was genuinely scared. And even with the smoke gone but the smell hanging strong between them, April could understand why. He didn't have to say it. Edith wasn't safe being left alone. *They* weren't safe if she were left alone. Because what had just happened could have been much, much worse. "Of course, I will."

He nodded his appreciation and glanced back to the stove. "Well, on the bright side, at least you get to do what you do best. Shop. Do you mind ordering another one of those?"

His weak attempt at humor had April's lips curving. "Sure."

"I need to finish cutting the grass before I head to work. Would you mind running out to grab Mama something to eat?"

"Okay."

"By the way, would it be too much trouble for you to stay home and watch Mama today?"

April hesitated. She needed to handle some business. Make a visit to someone she hadn't thought she would be seeing again for a while. "Well, I actually was going to run some errands," she responded.

Ramsey brightened. "Oh, great idea. Why don't you take her with you? It would do her some good to get out of the house and get some fresh air."

April's spirit deflated. Well, so much for handling her business. Even if Edith had dementia, it was too risky because she *may* just remember where they went and who they spoke to. Her plans would have to wait. At least until she could coordinate with Ramsey about watching his mother so she could sneak away for the day without looking suspicious.

"Sure," she said with a smile. "Maybe we'll go to the park or something."

Ramsey pecked her on the forehead. "Thanks, babe. What would I do without you?"

April nodded and started to leave but Ramsey's arms circled her waist, pulling her into a hug. "Hey," he murmured, his voice muffled against her hair. "I'm so glad you're both okay. And thank you for loving me and Mom. This will be good to have her here. I promise."

She didn't bother verbalizing her uneasiness since Ramsey had already made up his mind. She would have to just keep up the charade a little while longer. And she knew she would have to hurry to finish what she started, so she could disappear. And hopefully, he would be able to handle his mother alone.

Chapter Twelve

She had a bad feeling about tonight.

April finished up her makeup in the bathroom mirror, but her eyes were magnetized to that damn necklace tucked in the drawer. She was tempted to pull it out, just to see it once more. She could already feel the flood of painful memories, could smell the brazen stench of liquor and Marlboros. Eight years ago. Had it really been that long? That night had been a catalyst, setting off a chain of events that ultimately led to a fight for survival. And she had been running ever since.

April pulled the spaghetti straps of her dress onto her shoulders, the neckline dipping invitingly low, the bottom brushing a little below her knees in sheer layers. Reflexively, her fingers lingered on the stomach area where she could almost feel the baby's delicate nudges. She shut her eyes against the familiar taste of guilt. Trying not to think about it only heightened the sorrow.

"You look amazing."

April met Ramsey's eyes in the full-length mirror as she finished putting in her earring. He was giving her an appreciative scan from head to toe, and she couldn't stop the blush that warmed her face.. But she had to admit, the dress did look gorgeous on her. She twirled, giving her husband a 360-degree view of the dress from all angles.

"I wish we could stay in so I can take that off you," he teased.

A fleeting glimmer of hope. She didn't want to do Brynn's double date tonight either, but their friend was so excited. That was all she had been talking about, especially after she had found, in her words, the "perfect" outfit during their shopping trip at the mall. And she'd relayed how nervous she was for them to meet the infamous Prez. "We could just skip dinner . . ." April said, almost wistfully.

Ramsey sighed and crossed to the dresser to spray on his cologne. "No, we promised Brynn we would do this for her. Apparently, she's nuts about this guy—"

"No, Brynn is just nuts, period," April teased and had Ramsey laughing in response.

"True too. Let's just go and have a good time. But . . ." he added with a wink. "I wouldn't be upset if we cut the evening short. Especially since Mom will be here with Tabitha and we don't want to be out too late anyway."

April stooped down to step into her heels, praying that she wouldn't have to keep them on too long. Brynn was the type of woman she could only handle in doses. Very, very short doses. At least Ramsey shared her sentiments.

"Hey, why don't you wear that new necklace you bought."

April froze and she was grateful to be out of Ramsey's eyesight. "It broke," she said, dismissively.

Ramsey was now on her side of the bed and, without asking or waiting, he knelt to assist her with her shoes. He worked easily to secure the straps, his fingers comfortable with the familiarity of the task. "Sorry about that. It was a nice necklace," he mused. "Make sure you send it back and get a refund."

April didn't comment.

Finished, Ramsey pulled her to her feet with an approving nod. "Ready?"

No. "Of course."

They found Edith in the living room with her new aide. Tabitha was a sweet, young, premed student, and the daughter of one of the waitresses at Ramsey's restaurant. April was thrilled when they hired her, but she had to admit, Tabitha's demanding school schedule wasn't as flexible as she would have preferred. But so far, the young lady had been amazing and both Edith and Ramsey adored her.

Right now, Mama Edith was seated on the sofa next to Tabitha with her injured leg propped up on a pillow across the ottoman. A TV tray sat between them that they were using as a playing table, clear from the deck of cards that Tabitha was shuffling like a pro dealer. They both glanced up as the couple entered, hand in hand.

"You look beautiful, Mr. and Mrs. Duncan." Tabitha was the first one to speak.

"Thanks, Tabitha." Ramsey gave his mother a kiss on her forehead. "We shouldn't be too long, but please don't hesitate to call if you need anything at all."

"Oh, Ms. Edith and I will be just fine, I'm sure. She's teaching me Bid Whist."

"Of course, we will be fine," Edith piped up with a smile as she patted Tabitha's hand. "My granddaughter always takes good care of me."

April and Ramsey exchanged worried looks. But no one bothered correcting her.

———⊷◦⊶———

April wasn't surprised when Brynn insisted that they meet at Red Velvet Bistro promptly at 7:00. Not only was it Ramsey's restaurant, but the dining establishment was ritzy, one of the few in the downtown Columbus district. It was the perfect place for a date night.

They were early. Ramsey bypassed valet and instead, wheeled his truck into the crowded self-parking lot. His space was reserved, right in the front. April flipped down the sun visor and checked her makeup and wig for what must've been the fifth time during the drive over.

"Babe, you look great, I promise." Ramsey watched her from the driver's seat with amusement coloring his handsome face.

Her smile conveyed more of a grimace than she intended. "I know, I just have to make sure." She eyed the parking lot, noticing how packed it looked. Nothing like a restaurant that was struggling, as Brynn alluded. "Ramsey, is everything okay with the business?" she asked.

Ramsey's face crinkled with a weird expression. "Yeah, why?"

"Brynn mentioned that you were stressed, and she didn't know if it was because of the restaurant not doing so well."

His face smoothed over with ease. "Yeah, dealing with the situation with my mom and of course, work can be stressful. But that's nothing new."

"Oh." She paused. "Then . . . there's nothing I need to be concerned about? Money or otherwise?"

This time, Ramsey leaned over the middle console and pressed his lips to hers. "Nope. Nothing to worry about, babe."

She believed him. She should've known Brynn was just being Brynn and may have overreacted. So why then, was she still so nervous? Her hands felt sweaty and she would've wiped them on her dress if she wasn't afraid the residue would leave a damp streak on the satin material. Normally, she would've been excited for an elegant evening at a nice restaurant. But there was this dull drone in the back of her head, something inaudible, but distracting. It only got louder as they climbed from Ramsey's truck and approached the restaurant. She was just ready to get this over with.

The luxurious atmosphere boasted sleek and sultry decor, with intimate lighting and suede banquettes. A low-level jazz instrumental of R&B classics played in the background, only adding to the ambience. April knew that Red Velvet Bistro had been Ramsey's dream since he was a child, and it was clear he'd put everything into making the place just as beautiful and opulent as he envisioned. He even had his paintings displayed in some of the prominent areas, such as the lobby and restrooms. April remembered their first chance meeting with a reflective smile. Her intentions hadn't been the best, but she could always appreciate how her husband made her feel, even from the beginning.

The hostess, a sprightly young woman named Kimberly, gave them a wide grin as soon as they approached. No, not *them*, April noticed immediately. Ramsey. Of course, being the owner of the establishment would afford him a companionable rapport with the staff. But it still made her slightly uncomfortable. Especially because Kimberly was not bothering to hide the lust oozing from her pores. April tucked that piece of information away for later.

The hostess did a sultry lick of her lips before she spoke. "Good evening, Mr. Duncan. Always a pleasure to see you. And good evening to you as well." Kimberly turned quick eyes to April to mask her initial disregard for Ramsey's wife. "Come to check in on us?"

Ramsey chuckled. "No, not this time."

"Dag, and here I was getting excited."

April lifted an eyebrow.

Ramsey grinned, not seeming to mind the banter. "You're too funny. Actually, we're here with a reservation for Brynn Sunderland."

Kimberly glanced at the tablet as her manicured nails scrolled the screen. "Yes, I see that here. Ms. Sunderland has already arrived. I would be happy to show you to your table."

Just as she started to take a step toward the dining room, Ramsey quickly held up his hand to halt her movements. "Oh, you're fine, Kim. I'm sure I can manage. What table number?"

"Thirty-four."

"Thanks. You have a great evening." Ramsey took April's hand and led her to the expansive dining area. They weaved through the cluster of booths and tables as the patrons' hushed dialogue murmured around them. Ramsey lifted his hand in greeting to a few of the waitstaff as they passed.

Sure enough, Brynn was tucked away in a corner, seated in a round booth way too big for their small party of four. Her hair was swept up in a ponytail and the candlelight from the table flickered over her downcast face. It immediately brightened when she looked up as they approached.

"Hey guys," she said. "I'm so glad you both came." She scooted from the booth and rose to greet them. April regarded how the fitted red bandage dress she wore accented the undertones in her mahogany skin. She hugged Ramsey first, then April before gesturing back to the empty booth. "Well, sit down. Prez isn't here yet."

April caught how she snuck a look at the watch on her wrist. "It's still early," she felt compelled to offer.

"Or he stood me up," Brynn retorted with a snort. Then immediately waved her hand to ward off any compassionate words. "I'm not surprised. It wouldn't be the first time."

April watched her from across the table. Had there really been a date to begin with? She didn't want to think Brynn was lying, and judging by the hurt look wrinkling her face, she definitely didn't seem to be. But she knew, all too well, how to play the victim for sympathy.

A waiter came to take their drink orders and after Ramsey acknowledged him by name and requested a bottle of wine for the table, Brynn eased from the booth and began smoothing the wrinkles of her dress. "I'm going to freshen up," she announced. "Just in case. Erin, can you come with me?"

"Sure."

The restrooms were a luxurious extension of the restaurant, which were designed to recall the abstract spirit that Ramsey loved while celebrating the surrounding charm of his beloved city. Stained concrete floor tile featured stencils of contemporary

African-American motifs with wall tiles adorned in organic shapes that looked fresh out of an interior design catalog. A citrus fragrance welcomed them as soon as they'd pushed into the relaxing spa-like oasis, with its generous space mirrors that scaled the length of the wall behind a row of stone rectangular vessel sinks.

Instead of going into a stall like April expected, Brynn snatched a paper towel from the dispenser and stood at the counter, dabbing at the corner of her eyes. "I'm sorry," she said with an embarrassed laugh. "I'm sitting up here crying like a damn baby, so I know I look crazy."

April frowned. This was certainly something she didn't expect. Not from Brynn. "What's wrong?"

"I just . . ." Brynn released a frustrated breath and gazed up to the ceiling, as if to keep her tears back with gravity. "It's weird, starting over. I haven't really dated much since my husband died, so this is all new to me."

April closed the distance between them. She didn't consider herself much of a friend, but the least she could do was offer some words of solace. "Listen, Brynn. Are you sure you're ready for this? Maybe it's too soon."

"I . . . I didn't think about that." Brynn's bottom lip quivered with the admission. "I don't know. I just want what you and Ramsey have, you know? It's lonely sometimes."

April nodded, pursing her lips to suppress a reply.

Brynn forced a watery smile. "You're so lucky, girl, I swear," she said. "But maybe you're right."

April smiled and forced herself to ignore those tugs of unease whenever Brynn spoke of Ramsey. "I just don't want you to get your hopes up," she admitted. "There's someone out there for you. Maybe Prez, maybe someone else. But you will find love again. Any man would be lucky to have you."

Brynn wrapped her arms around April with a grateful breath. "Girl, thank you so much. I needed that."

The dining room had gotten more crowded in the few minutes they had been in the restroom. April glanced at her cell phone: 7:38. Maybe Brynn was right and her mystery man had stood her up. If there was one at all. But after their conversation, she hoped Brynn felt a little more confident, no matter the outcome for this evening.

Just as they rounded the corner and Ramsey's head popped back into view at the table, April stopped in her tracks, paralyzed with shock. Her eyes ballooned at the sight of the man Ramsey was talking to.

He looked the same. Sure, he'd gained weight and had grown more facial hair. But those eyes, April remembered staring into them plenty of times. Of course, she had been someone else then, but she'd never forget them. Just like she was sure no matter what disguise she wore, he would never forget her. Or what she'd done. But what the hell was he doing here? And how did he find her?

The man's head lifted, his gaze meeting hers. She didn't have the opportunity to try and recover from her astonishment. A hand was on her arm, Brynn's, and she was being pulled toward the table.

"Oh my God, he came," she squealed. "And I was ready to call it a night."

They were at the table in a matter of seconds and April could only stare helplessly as Brynn all but jumped in his arms. She then turned around, looping her arm through his, a proud grin spread on her face. "Ram, Erin, this is Prez. Prez, this is my best friend, Erin, and her husband."

Prez? No, that couldn't be right.

The man extended his hand in her direction, the smallest of smirks on his face. "Nice to meet you, Erin."

April's hand was limp in his. This man standing in front of her was her ex, Jameson. And he certainly didn't know her by her current identity *Erin.* What the hell was going on?

Chapter Thirteen

April felt like her heart was in her stomach. Around the booth, Ramsey, Brynn, and Jameson (or Prez, as Brynn kept calling him affectionately) were engrossed in a spirited discussion of health-care among the Black community. No doubt thanks to Jameson's employment as a cosmetic surgeon. But April knew that before he'd even volunteered that information, considering he'd done an amazing job on her body.

Still, she had to question if he recognized her. He hadn't said anything suspicious, nor had he bothered sparing her more than cordial looks across the table. He seemed completely oblivious, which almost made April question if she was going crazy.

Drinks were passed around, along with bread and appetizers. By the time her meal had arrived, April hadn't been able to stomach anything more than a few glasses of wine.

Of course, he should've remembered her. She'd married him and the next day, had disappeared, intent on taking his money. She hadn't realized he'd somehow been privy to her motives and had blocked all access to his accounts. She'd moved on to her next identity, chalking it up to a lesson learned. She sure as hell didn't expect to see him again. And most certainly not with Brynn.

"So why do women opt to have plastic surgery anyway?" Ramsey was topping off everyone's glass of wine as he spoke. April may have been imagining things, but she could've sworn Jameson's lips turned up into an amused smirk before he lifted his glass. Or maybe that was her paranoia.

"I get that question a lot," he answered, sitting back in the booth. "And surprisingly, it's not just women. It's men too. It's a way to not only improve a person's appearance, but their self-esteem and confidence. And as long as people are fully aware of the risks and benefits, I am happy to help that person feel better about themselves."

"I don't think it's necessary." It was Brynn this time, her voice laced with judgment as she spoke with an upturned nose. "I mean, I commend Prez on his profession because I think that's awesome that he's helping others. But I think everyone should just be happy with their natural bodies."

"But you wear makeup," Jameson pointed out.

"That's not really the same thing."

"I have to agree with Brynn on this one." Ramsey tapped his glass against Brynn's in a mock toast. "Men already have trust issues as it is. Now we have to worry about our woman's body being fake. There's nothing like the real thing. Makeup is used to enhance. Some women just go overboard to change their appearance into something else completely."

April wanted to sink into the cushions.

Jameson took his time answering, as if he were picking his words carefully. "Well, with modern medicine, oftentimes you can't even tell the difference. The bodies and faces look and feel just like the real thing."

Ramsey grunted. "I'm sure I could tell the difference."

"Oh, you'd be surprised."

April felt nauseous. She rose abruptly, nearly knocking her hip against the table in the process. "Excuse me," she said. "I need to use the ladies' room."

Brynn was already nudging Jameson to move out of the booth. "Oh good, I'll come with you, girl—"

"No, no. I don't want to take you from your date." April didn't have to look at Jameson to know his eyes were now drilling into her profile. She kept her eyes trained on Brynn. "I won't be long. Promise." And before anyone had a chance to respond, she hurried off toward the back of the restaurant.

She might as well have been drowning. April took in greedy gulps of air as soon as she was tucked away in the privacy of the ladies' room. She gripped the sides of the sink, bracing on the porcelain so she wouldn't slink to the floor. He knew. He had to. There was no way he didn't. But what did he want? What kind of twisted game was he playing?

Her cell phone vibrated with an incoming text message. April pulled her phone from her purse and her breath quickened at the blocked number. Her thumb trembled as it hovered over the screen. Then, before she could change her mind, April opened the message: **You look gorgeous. I love how you're wearing my favorite color.**

She gasped and quickly deleted the message. Just as fast, she powered down her phone and watched the backlight wink off until she only saw her reflection in the black screen. He was definitely toying with her.

April lifted her head to the mirror. She took in her hollow expression as another thought crossed her mind. Was it Jameson who sent the package? It would make sense. Since he knew enough to be here, he must've tracked her down somehow. After she left him and disappeared, maybe he went digging. It seemed too far-fetched to be true, but too much of a coincidence to ignore.

April took another steadying breath and turned to swing open the door. She had to get out of there. She would make up something, anything to keep from having to torture herself through the rest of dinner. Ramsey would understand. Brynn may not, but she didn't have a choice at this point.

"Hey."

April stiffened.

Jameson approached from the men's restroom, wiping his hands with a paper towel. "Erin, that's your name, right?" His voice was husky as he let her name roll off his tongue. Just like she remembered. He was taunting her. Wasn't he? He had to be.

April shifted uncomfortably under his scrutinizing stare. She didn't know which was worse, a lie or the truth.

Jameson seemed humored by her lack of response, and he stopped about a foot from her. "I think we may have gotten off on the wrong foot," he said, the hint of something April couldn't pinpoint glinting on his face. "Can we start over?" As if to prove his intentions were pure, Jameson extended a hand. "I'm Jameson. I think Brynn would really like us to get along."

"What are you doing?"

Jameson was stunned silent at her accusatory tone.

"Are you the one who sent me that necklace? You trying to threaten me, Jameson?" Adrenaline fueled her to take a daring step closer, closing the gap between them.

Still, his gaze remained unreadable. "I think you got me mixed up with someone," he said.

"Do I?"

Jameson eased backwards with a shake of his head. "Look, I'm going to head back to the table." And with that, he ducked back into the dining hall, leaving April staring after him in confusion.

She expected him to confront her, or at the very least admit he knew what she was talking about. The fact that he did neither was what scared her.

PART III: BARGAINING

A stage in grief in which you may try to negotiate with yourself or with a higher power to try to undo the loss.

Chapter Fourteen

Before

April felt numb as she stood at the bathroom sink. It felt strange. She was a teenager, but the reflection staring back at her was one of a grown woman. Erika had taken great care with her makeup. Her bronzed skin seemed suffocated by the streaks of eye shadow and blush. A subtle pink hue tinted her plush lips that were now turned down in a piercing frown. "We have to make sure you don't look like a child," Erika had said when she was painting the gunk on her face. April had wanted to snort in mock laughter at the irony. That's because she *was* a child. She had to admit, though, eyeing her reflection once more, she felt more exposed. And the makeup definitely brought out her bold features. Some people might actually consider her attractive, though she had never used such an adjective to describe herself.

April wasn't like most girls. No, she hadn't planned out the intricate details of her wedding because she had never considered herself the marrying type. But getting ready in a courthouse bathroom with the smell of tainted sewer water and Clorox in the air was definitely not what she would have pictured for herself.

The tiny knock on the door had April's eyes looking in the mirror past her expression. She didn't even bother responding and her mother, not waiting for one, invited herself into the room. She was dressed in a simple navy blue dress with a delicate lace over-lay that flirted at her thighs. Her fresh weave had blond highlights with swept bangs pinned to the side and bundled spiral curls at the nape of her neck. With her own makeup masking whatever emotions she had managed to conceal, they almost looked like twins.

Erika closed the door behind her but didn't make a move to scoot further into the bathroom. April was grateful. Ever since the big arranged marriage announcement, an increasing resentment had begun to settle in her stomach. And now, eyeing her mother standing there feigning excitement, the feeling threatened to rise and spill out on this simple white wedding gown she wore. April busied herself with fingering the beaded trim at the bodice of the dress. Anything to keep from looking at the woman.

"You would look even prettier if you smiled." Erika's attempt at a joke only stiffened the tension. On a sigh, she finally crossed the room. "I came to finish your hair," she said. "Then . . . well, then you'll be ready."

Would she? April pursed her lips together as Erika began fluffing her weave. Highly doubtful. She would never be ready.

She wasn't used to all of the hair on her head, but the wavy tresses cascading down her back suited her. Erika pinned them up into a stacked ponytail before completing the look with rhinestone hair clips and a veil. The flimsy material made it hard to see. Just her luck, she would trip down the aisle in the six-inch white pumps and bust her face on the floor. But she would risk it before parting her lips to say otherwise.

Erika's reassuring smile was forced as she nodded at her daughter in the mirror.

April choked back the tears. She already felt violated and completely degraded and the man hadn't even touched her yet. He had wanted to relish her innocence on the wedding night, he had said. "It should be you," she blurted out.

Erika sighed and gently nudged April to her feet. "I know," she agreed without hesitation. "But . . . we can't always get the life we want. So instead, we'll settle for the life we deserve."

A light knock on the door broke through her thoughts and April welcomed the distraction.

Erika was the one who spoke up. "Come in," she called.

A well-dressed gentleman in a suit entered the bathroom gently shutting the door behind him. He looked way too professional for a simple day wedding. He was bald and clean-shaven, and his attire was obviously tailor-made for his frame. April's eyes fell on the briefcase at his side.

"Good afternoon, ladies," he greeted, holding out his hand. "I'm Julian, Mr. Collier's attorney."

April's movements were labored with confusion as she accepted the hand. "Nice to meet you." Though she didn't anticipate anything nice from the meeting. Why was Warren sending in his lawyer?

Erika wasn't quite as cordial as she stared the man up and down with a knowing look of disgust. She didn't even bother shaking his hand.

Julian must not have noticed her demeanor because he didn't have a sense of urgency as he smiled. "You look amazing," he complimented with a nod to the wedding dress she wore. "Warren is an extremely lucky man."

April nodded but still didn't speak. It was clear he was setting up this conversation, and she was already cycling through a Rolodex of reasons for his presence, all of which were prompting a surge of light-headedness.

"You can skip all of the niceties," Erika snapped, crossing her arms over her breasts. "Get to why you're here. Because you being here tells me I'm about to be pissed."

Flustered, Julian cleared his throat and lifted his briefcase to rest across the sink. "Well, I won't disturb you for too long. I know you still have some things to do before the ceremony." The sharp hiss of the *zip* met her ears as he opened the bag, all the while murmuring more compliments and apologies for his intrusion. April ignored his words, instead focusing on the manila folder he pulled into view. ". . . in your best interest," he was saying as he flipped it open, revealing a stack of papers with small print etched from margin to margin. "You may not have time to read all of this, so I'll be happy to summarize it for you before you sign."

Before April had a chance to accept the papers, Erika snatched them from Julian. "Summarize what?"

"Are you familiar with a prenuptial agreement?"

"Oh, hell no! Where is he?" Erika yelled, her voice intimidating as it echoed off the stalls.

"Wait, Ms. Garrett, one moment please. Let me explain—"

"No, bring Warren in here. Now!"

Julian tried again. "I understand, but it's bad luck to see—" he paused as Erika cut a stare at him so sinister that he merely nodded and scurried from the room.

April's reaction felt like she was moving in slow motion. With limp fingers, she grabbed the papers from her mother's hand as the attorney's words played over again, seeming to brand in the recesses of her mind. Shock wiped her mind clean, as if someone had put an eraser to a dry-erase board. Then, just as quickly, anger colored her face so strong it burned. If he was serious about this, it would ruin everything.

Insult had Erika pacing like a caged tiger, stomping with such ferocity that her high heels nearly stabbed holes into the hardwood floor. "Can you believe him?" she was spewing. "He has the utter audacity. I'm not signing that shit and neither will you, understood?"

April nodded. She had no intention of signing anything that would keep her chained to Warren.

Within a few minutes, Warren entered the restroom, fully dressed in his groom's tux; crisp, debonair, and just as glossy as the pages of a *GQ* magazine. Erika clearly was fueled by adrenaline and well past rational as she marched up to him, reeled back, and let a satisfying slap connect with his cheek. Warren's eyes flared and if Erika wasn't there, April would've been afraid of what was going to happen next.

"You son of a bitch!" Erika was toe-to-toe with a man twice her size. "How *dare* you send your lawyer in here to make her sign a prenup right before the wedding? That wasn't at all what we discussed!"

Realization quickly extinguished the small flame of anger that danced in his eyes. His face fell and sorrow had him shaking his head. "It's not like that."

"Oh yeah? Well, how is it?"

Warren's silence only heightened her rage. April was glad Erika was the one to handle all of this. She wasn't going to get tied up with contractual strings.

"I can't believe you, Warren," Erika raced on. "What about trust? How can you claim you love her and want to marry her, but you don't trust her?"

"I do trust her."

Now they were talking as if she weren't standing right there. As if she didn't exist. No, not talking. *Arguing* was more like it.

"I'm *only* thinking of her."

"How?"

"Because it's protection," he insisted.

April maneuvered between them. "Guys, please! I can talk for my damn self."

That shut them up and both pursed their lips while silently staring at each other.

Warren turned passionate eyes to April, placing his hands on her shoulders. "Do you know how much I love you?"

April shook her head. She was going to have to take the theatrics up a notch. The man was too damn stubborn to get it. She shut her eyes, concentrating. Her face contorted into a pained expression and as if on cue, she felt the first few prickles of tears seep from her closed lids. "I don't see how you love me," she murmured, taking a step back to break their contact. "There is no way you can love me if you would do this to me. And on our wedding day." She continued shaking her head fiercely and raised a hand to stop Warren when he took a step in her direction. She lifted watery eyes to meet his gaze, keeping the hurt plastered on her face like a mask.

Warren sighed and nodded his understanding. "Okay," he relented. "Okay, you don't have to sign it."

April paused, counting the seconds in her head so the silence hung thick between them like a cloak. She could tell he was holding his breath as she kept her lips pressed shut. Finally, she nodded and Warren smiled before leaving.

She felt Erika's arm immediately drape across her shoulder. "That's my girl," she cheered. "An Oscar-winning performance if I've ever seen one. That's how I know you're my child."

Disgusted with herself, with Erika, with the whole thing, April didn't even bother responding.

The walk down the hall to the courtroom was torturous. Fortunately, all parties had decided a courthouse wedding was best. Quick, efficient, and, what April figured, secretive enough so everyone wouldn't know about the sickening arrangement.

The room fit her mood. The same array of seats that held convicts of DUIs and traffic tickets was going to hold, what was supposed to be her special day. Standing next to her mother, the justice of the peace, and Warren, she felt entirely overdressed in the white A-line wedding gown clutching the dahlia and rose bouquet.

The justice of the peace, an elderly white man, began the routine script of marrying them. April didn't hear a word. Instead, she ignored her mother's encouraging hand on her back and focused instead on her soon-to-be husband.

She had never thought Warren was all that good-looking. He was a heavyset man, very dark-skinned with one too many chins stuffed in the folds of his dress shirt collar. But she had always thought he had kind eyes and a charming smile due to the dimples that winked in each cheek when his lips peeled back. Now, as he gave her one of those infamous grins, he suddenly looked perverted.

When he flipped her veil and leaned in to kiss her, April cringed and instinctively snatched away so his juicy lips brushed her cheek. She winced as Erika pinched her forearm and she sighed and looked at his agitated frown, silent permission for him to try again. He did, this time his lips landing flat on hers and she even felt a stroke of his fleshy, pink tongue graze her mouth. Probably trying to coax it open. April turned away and gagged, swallowing the vomit that had now risen to simmer in her throat.

The justice didn't seem to notice, or care about the strange interaction between the couple. He merely smiled and said, "I now pronounce you Mr. and Mrs. Warren Collier."

Seven hours and seven hundred miles later, April Collier sat on a king sleigh bed in the Atlantis hotel of the Bahamas. Shopping bags were strewn at her wedge-sandaled feet, brimming with an entirely new wardrobe and anything else Warren had wanted her to have. The emerald stones of the tennis bracelet combined with the huge wedding ring set on her hand caught the sunlight spilling into the honeymoon suite. April's sigh was heavy as she closed her eyes.

She wished for her mother, but Erika was long gone. She had accompanied them on the honeymoon so she could "enjoy the

Bahamas" as well. But after the afternoon shopping trip, she had taken Warren's credit card and booked herself a spa treatment. Warren had even made sure to get Erika a hotel room a few floors down so as not to be disturbed. Her instructions had been clear before she left: *Make him happy. Stick to the plan.*

So that left them alone and April had to admit, she had never felt more abandoned than she did sitting amid all the things money could buy while waiting for her "husband" to come out of the bathroom.

As requested, April lay in the bed waiting, the satin white sheets pulled taut across her breasts and tucked under her armpits. Warren would want sex right after his shower and she was asked to wear some kind of black lace lingerie piece that would probably have that repulsive look glossing his eyes.

The water shut off and April turned her head from the bathroom door just as he emerged, bringing the warm steam and scent of Dove with him. She had never seen a naked man—well, in person. Sure, she had snuck and watched a few pornos from her mother's collection and had even felt compelled to please herself off of the explicit videos. But the man in her peripheral was nothing compared to the toned bodies she had witnessed. She didn't even feel herself getting turned on. Knowing perfectly well what was about to happen, April couldn't help the sobs that exploded.

"What is it, my girl?" Warren's voice held so much concern that it almost seemed genuine if he wasn't a pedophile. "What can daddy do to make it better?"

"Why me?" April croaked. She knew she wasn't supposed to question him. Erika had reminded her to shut up and go with the program now that everything was official, but it was agonizing trying to suppress the overwhelming emotions. "Why me?" she repeated. "Why not Erika?"

When he remained quiet, April risked throwing a pleading look in his direction. Tears clouded her vision, but she could still make out the pile of man standing in the doorway of the bathroom. And there was nothing desirable about his silhouette. She didn't want him to come near her, let alone touch her. The revolting thought of sex with him had even more tears drizzling down her face.

"I've always loved you, April," Warren said, his voice sympathetic. "I really have. I tried to deny my feelings for you. Throw all of them into your mother. But with Erika, I just didn't feel complete. Until I came around you. I know this is hard for you to understand because you're young. You'll sort out your feelings and you will grow to love me. I promise. But in the meantime, let me love you like you deserve and treat you like the princess you are. Can I do that?"

April didn't answer. She squeezed her eyes shut as he neared her, and she struggled to ignore the slimy feeling of his stubby fingers on her skin. Her first time would be with him. She wanted to die. But underneath the depression, the embers of a rage so fierce began to flicker and April already knew, even in her subconscious, she would be damned if she would settle for this relationship.

Chapter Fifteen

"Tell me, what did you think of Prez?"

April cringed as she raked some scrambled eggs on three separated dishes. One for her, one for Mama Edith, and of course Brynn, who had popped up earlier that morning with a chipper smile and full recount of the previous evening's experience at Red Velvet Bistro. According to her, it had been the best date ever. Which meant she hadn't noticed April's discomfort throughout the entire dinner.

"Why do you call him that anyway?" she asked. "His name's Jameson, right?" Her question was intended to keep her from having to answer Brynn. Thankfully, it worked.

Brynn shrugged. "Jameson is just too . . . I don't know. Formal for a first name. And the first time we talked, I joked that he had a president's name, so it just kinda stuck. Why? You don't like it?"

April lifted a shoulder in what she hoped would pass for an absent shrug. "Just doesn't seem to fit." No, what she really wanted to say was she wished Brynn had given him a more distinguishable nickname. Maybe then she would've realized who Jameson was and could've avoided the tense evening all together.

It was a blessing the night had been cut short anyway. Ramsey had insisted they get back so as not to be away from his mother too long. Whether it was true or an excuse, April hadn't cared. For all she knew, he could've been just as uncomfortable. She was just glad he was initiating some sort of respectful ending because she had been ready to leave ever since the date took such an unexpected turn.

"Well, he's nothing compared to Ram, I'm sure," Brynn teased with a wink. "But he's nice. And he makes me laugh. Plus, he's got a nice package."

Out of the side of her eye, April could see Brynn smirking in her direction. She turned from the counter. "You two—"

"Yes, girl! All night!" Brynn squealed, bubbling with excitement. "Girl, let me tell you. That man made my body feel things I've never felt before. Not even with Judge."

Another nickname for her deceased husband, April had always assumed, but never bothered asking. Brynn acted like saying someone's real name was painful.

"What does this mean then?"

"I guess I got a man now." Brynn hopped up and hugged April from behind, nearly spilling the breakfast. "And I have you to thank for it, girlie. I swear I was really feeling some kind of way after he was late, but you talked me through it so I wouldn't get so down on myself. And anyway, Prez made it up to me. All. Night. Long."

She was supposed to be a good friend right now. And a good friend would engage in some kind of agreeable banter. *That's what I'm talking about! You go, girl! Tell me about the sex, how was it?* April didn't have the energy to entertain that, or the answers. She mustered a smile and said, "I'm so glad it all worked out. Let me take Mama Edith her breakfast." And she hurried off down the hall before Brynn could object.

She was all too eager to dismiss herself from the conversation. Something about the way Brynn gloated about Jameson was unsettling, especially considering what he was up to. That was probably the only reason he'd pursued Brynn in the first place. A gateway to get to *her*. It was demented and April couldn't help feeling sorry for her friend. Brynn seemed genuinely happy about the relationship (or, at the very least, the sex part of it). Little did she know as soon as April confirmed what she already knew to be true, poor Brynn was going to lose the new man of her dreams.

Mama Edith was sitting up in bed this time, her injured leg propped on top of a pillow. She wasn't wearing the brace this time, which seemed to be an improvement. April entered carrying the plate of eggs, sausage, and toast with a glass of orange juice and Edith took her time turning from the TV.

"Oh, how sweet. Did my son send you?"

April's smile was polite as she sat the plate on the nightstand beside the bed. Ramsey had already warned that her mental condition would get progressively worse. *"She'll have her good days and not-so-good days,"* he'd said. *"We just have to be patient with her."*

Judging by the way Mama Edith was giving her that vacant look, today must be a not-so-good day. April eased on the edge of the bed, the mattress sinking a bit under her weight. "No, Mama Edith. I'm your daughter-in-law."

Edith's eyebrows creased together and she gave a slow nod, as if the pieces were there but wouldn't fit. It probably was for the best anyway. April found a little relief in the fact that Edith wouldn't remember the lies.

The woman took a sip of her juice and turned back to the TV. "Where is my son?" she asked.

"He went to work."

"I didn't know he was working again."

April took her time, absently fluffing the pillow underneath Edith's knee. "Yes, ma'am, he's at work. Remember the restaurant? Red Velvet Bistro."

"I thought he got rid of that place."

"Why would you think that?"

"Because he told me." Edith shifted uncomfortably and resettled against the headboard. "Didn't he?"

April felt sorry for her, but at the same time envied her. She wished she could forget sometimes herself. To be comforted in ignorance rather than knowledgeable in deceit.

"No, Mama Edith. He still has the restaurant. I went there last night."

Edith nodded, though her face still reflected a dubious expression. "I want to go. Is the food good?" She had gone before. Many, many times.

April nodded as she put her feet on the bed and settled next to the woman. "Yes, it is." And then because it sounded good, she added, "I'll have to make sure to take you so you can try it for yourself."

They sat in comfortable silence with the canned applause from the game show drifting around them. She didn't want to leave. Not even when Brynn appeared in the doorway with April's cell phone vibrating in her hand. She held it up to show the name flashing across the screen and mouthed *Ian* with a perplexed shrug.

April unfolded herself from the bed, shifted the breakfast closer so Edith could reach it, and accepted her phone. Brynn made her way back into the kitchen while April crossed the foyer into her bedroom for privacy. "Hello?"

"Hey, lil' sis."

April rolled her eyes. Now that Ian had crossed boundaries, his little nickname for her was revolting. She stifled a sigh. "What's up, Ian?"

"Aw, why you sound like that? You don't want to talk to me?"

"I'm busy."

His light chuckle glided through the receiver and grated her nerves even more. "Okay, well, I won't keep you. Will you be in town for Carter's surprise birthday party? It's next weekend."

"Sure." April didn't even care at that point. She just wanted him off the phone.

"Okay, cool. I'll text you the address for the hotel. It's in their ballroom. And do you happen to know a chef or somebody who could cater?"

The fact that Ramsey crossed her mind was almost laughable. Wouldn't that be the ultimate surprise?

"Not right offhand, but I'll ask around."

"Great, thanks, sis. Let me know what you find out."

The doorbell chime was a saving grace. April peered through the blinds, noting a black Cadillac parked against the curb. "Hey, look, I got to go. I'll talk to you later." And with that, she hung up.

Brynn was shutting the door just as April entered the foyer. She turned with an elaborate flower bouquet in her arms. Balloons that read *Thinking of You* bounced up from the arrangement. "Some-body brought these for you," Brynn piped with a wink as she handed over the flowers. "Oooohhhh, a gift from Ram, perhaps?"

No, it couldn't be. These were lilacs. Her favorite flower in her favorite color. Ramsey didn't know that. Only one person knew she loved lilacs. And he was dead. April stuffed her hand in the bouquet, searching for a card. Nothing. "Did a delivery driver bring these?"

"Yeah, he just left. Why?"

"Was he in a black Cadillac?"

Brynn blinked, flustered at the random question. "I—I'm not sure, I didn't—"

April shoved the flowers back in Brynn's arms and swept by her, swinging open the door.

Sun slapped her face as soon as she stepped onto the porch. It was unseasonably warm for January and a gentle breeze tickled April's bare arm as she glanced around. Sure enough, the car was gone. Brynn's Range Rover was parked in the driveway behind her car, and other than a neighbor strolling by walking her dog along the curb, the area was empty. Just to make sure, April walked to the edge of the front yard and looked both ways. Not a car on the street, whatsoever. Dejected, she turned and started the trek back toward the house.

Brynn met her on the porch, pressing the side of her hand against her forehead in a makeshift shade from the glaring light. "What did you want the driver for?" she asked.

"Just figured they could tell me who the flowers are from. There isn't a card," April added.

"Aren't they probably from Ramsey?" Brynn's forehead was wrinkled with her confusion. "Who else would send flowers and *thinking of you* balloons?"

Because she was waiting for an answer, April nodded, though she knew it couldn't be further from the truth. "Yeah, you're right. He knows how I feel about surprises, but I guess he's trying to be extra-sweet." She suddenly felt chilly despite the warm weather and she rubbed her arms. Or maybe it wasn't the temperature that was causing her goose bumps.

April started to head back in the house when something in the driveway caught her eye. Her tire. The sun's glare illuminated the jarring slash etched in the wheel, the flattened rubber pooling against the ground almost like Play-Doh.

She approached the car, mouth agape. No way that was an accident. Someone had intentionally slashed her tire. "Brynn, do you see this?"

Brynn moved closer, kneeling down in the driveway against the car. Her manicured nails pressed against the slit in the tire. "What the hell?"

April's head swiveled down the road once more, frustrated to see it empty. "Did you see anybody out here this morning?"

"No, just the delivery driver—"

"Brynn, please." Her voice was desperate. "I need you to think."

Brynn's eyes widened as she shook her head. "No, I swear. Just the flower guy, that's it." She rose with a wary gaze. "You don't think this was an accident." A statement, not a question and April could see the wheels spinning in her head as she looked from her, to the tire, then back to her again. Waiting.

April started back toward the house on shaky legs. The chills were gone. Now the heat felt excruciating. “Do you mind doing me a favor?”

“Of course, anything.”

“It’s too late notice to call Mama Edith’s aide, Tabitha. Do you mind watching her for me for a few hours?”

A pause. “Sure.”

“And can I borrow your car?”

Brynn looked like she wanted to object. “Where are you going?”

“I just need to run some errands and see about a new tire.” The lie sounded plausible and April was glad when Brynn didn’t push further, just nodded and fished in her pockets for her keys. She smiled gratefully, taking care to mask her troubled expression.

Back inside, with Brynn settled on mommy-sitting duty, April quietly snuck a text: **We should meet. Now.**

She still looked like the egotistical, self-centered bitch that she was. But tell Erika that and she would thank you for the compliment.

From her seat in the diner booth, April watched her mother emerge from a truck—a Maserati this time—the candy apple red of the vehicle matching the lapel and cuffs of the designer pantsuit that hugged her body like latex. Huge glasses shielded her face from view, but April knew, even with the obstruction, Erika’s makeup was just as gorgeous and pristine as her own. She would never leave the house without a full face reminiscent of a glamor photo shoot.

Erika sailed into the restaurant and promptly looked around. April waited and watched, not bothering to wave the woman over. Her mother was definitely a handful and she needed those few extra seconds to gather her strength. She hadn’t wanted to call her. April tried her best to avoid her altogether. But at this point, she had no other choice. She was desperate.

Erika didn't hug, didn't kiss, didn't do anything remotely affectionate. She just slid into the booth across from her daughter with the hint of a frown creasing her face. "Girl, you couldn't have us meet at a nicer place?" Her eyes darted around the quaint diner. "Or a spa or something to get pedicures?" Her citrus perfume beckoned from across the ratty table.

"This isn't exactly a courtesy call," April admitted.

Erika gave a half-hearted shrug. "Yeah, I figured that." Did she sound disappointed? She slid the laminated menu toward her, trailing her acrylic nail down the list of menu platters and specials. "What's good here, anyway?" She didn't really care, nor did she bother hiding it. Still, she kept her gaze laser-focused on that damn menu, probably to keep from looking at her daughter. At least that's what it felt like.

April lowered her eyes with a sigh and scanned the picture collage of entrées. Truth be told, she'd never even been to this place. But it was tucked off the main road in a country town a few miles from Columbus. And it meant no one would know her, or Erika. Discretion. She needed it now more than ever before.

A waitress in an oversized uniform and wrinkles marring her face, shuffled over with a notepad and pen in hand. "I'm Barbie," she recited with a low voice clouded with all of the weariness she was probably feeling. "What can I get you two?"

Erika tossed a pointed look across the table.

"We'll have two of the turkey sandwich plates," April piped up. "Fries and Cokes, please."

"Actually, I'll have a salad," Erika corrected with casual arrogance. "Add chicken strips and onions. Do you have balsamic vinaigrette dressing?"

April shifted, embarrassed for Barbie, who was visibly rattled with the request.

"Um, no, ma'am. We have ranch, Thousand Island, honey mustard—"

"Fine. Let me get ranch. And a sweet tea with a lime. Not a

lemon." The statement was dismissive and Erika was already turning back to April as Barbie hurried off to place their orders.

"Do you always have to be so difficult?"

Erika rolled her eyes at the question. "And how am I being difficult? Because I'm trying to order a damn salad?"

She studied her mother, so similar yet vastly different from her, which was karmically ironic.

Erika fished in her purse and pulled out a cigarette. She lit it, exhaling a plume of smoke into the air. "Alright, what is it?" she started, using the cigarette to gesture in April's direction. "I've been trying to catch up with you for weeks. You always act like you don't want to be bothered. Now all of a sudden, you're campaining for the *world's best daughter* award. You must be in trouble . . . wait, what's the name you're going by nowadays?"

April released an exasperated breath. Her chest felt tight, as it always did when she was in her mother's presence, but still she kept the annoyance from her voice. "Mom, please—"

"Oh, I'm 'Mom' now? Not just Erika?"

A pause. *Breathe. Breathe.*

"Is it Carter?" Erika asked.

"No."

"How is he anyway? You still milking that one, I see."

April kept her eyes level and tried again. "I'm not here to talk about Carter. Someone is after me."

Erika's eyebrows lifted, disappearing underneath the razor-cut bangs on her forehead. "What the hell are you talking about?"

It was late afternoon, so the lunch rush was over. Habit had April glancing around to make sure no one was within earshot. "I got something in the mail," she went on. "Addressed to April."

Erika's gaze was wary and for a moment, April couldn't tell whether she believed there was a problem. But the wrinkles in her forehead were more pronounced coming through the Botox. "It probably was just a mistake with the delivery."

April shook her head. "It wasn't a mistake. It was the necklace." She made sure to emphasize that last comment. That it wasn't just a random piece of jewelry.

Erika caught it and took a deep drag from her cigarette. "Shit, I told you to get rid of that."

"I did. It was put away in my storage."

"Is it even the same one?"

April shrugged. The truth was, she was even more scared to find out.

Barbie returned, setting two glasses and straws on the checkered table. She eyed Erika's cigarette as if she wanted to say something, but didn't.

Erika waited until they were alone once more. "It's probably a prank or something," she offered. "Somebody toying with you."

"Who would do that?"

"I don't know, *Michelle.* You haven't exactly made a lot of friends."

April stabbed her Coke with the straw and took a greedy sip. Her throat felt like the Sahara.

"I don't think you have anything to worry about," Erika said, her tone flippant.

"That's not all," April added with a shudder. "I also got some flowers. And earlier my tire was slashed in the driveway. I don't think any of this is a coincidence."

"Who would be doing this to you? Who would even know anything about you?"

April swallowed the name hanging from her lips, threatening to leave a sour taste on her tongue. It couldn't be Warren. He was officially dead. She blinked, struggling to keep the sordid images at bay. "I don't know," she said. "I was hoping you could help me."

For some reason, Erika found the comment amusing. She shook her head with a smirk and stabbed her cigarette out on the place mat. "You're kidding right?"

April shook her head. It just didn't make sense. Her mind

trailed back to the double date. Jameson. But as crazy as that was, how could he know?

Barbie returned this time with their lunch, which didn't look that appetizing at all. She sat April's sandwich down in front of her, but she couldn't bring herself to eat. Not when her stomach was tied in knots. She took another sip of her soda, letting the carbonation stir in her belly. Or were those nerves?

Erika was picking at her own salad with a frown of disgust. "I'm not eating this mess," she grumbled, poking a piece of lettuce that hung over her bowl. "It looks nasty. Why don't we get out of here and get some real food? My treat, because you're clearly acting like you don't have any money." She had moved on just that quick, all thoughts of their conversation replaced with her bougie attitude and luxurious appetite. It was appalling.

"What about your friend?" April asked. "The guy who helps get you ID's and stuff. He knows who I am."

"Sure, he does."

"What if he has something to do with this?"

Now, Erika did laugh out loud. "And why the hell would he be bothering you?"

"I don't know. Who is he? Maybe if you gave me his number—"

Erika blew an annoyed breath as she began shifting from the booth. "Look, let's go have a girl's day and forget all of this nonsense."

"I can't. I'm busy."

"Fine. Whatever. Call me when you're *un*busy." And with that, she swooped from the restaurant, her salad, and apparently her concern, left untouched.

Chapter Sixteen

"You want to tell me what's going on?"

April's head snapped up from her cell phone screen to Ramsey, with narrowed eyes glaring at her from across the dinner table. It was taking everything in her to resist looking at the phone again, to her bank account transactions. That would have to wait for a moment. Her husband's quiet demeanor was enough to give him her undivided attention for the time being.

He gestured to the food on her plate. Untouched from the neat placement he had arranged about an hour before. Her wineglass, however, was empty. Again. She didn't even remember refilling it the second time.

Feeling guilty, April picked up her fork and scooped some garlic mashed potatoes on the utensil. Still, she couldn't bring herself to lift the food to her lips. "Sorry, I'm not really hungry," she admitted. Something about being possibly haunted by a dead man and stalked by the ex she tried to steal from was enough to curb her appetite, that's for sure.

"It's not just the meal." Ramsey picked up his own wineglass and took a generous swig. He nodded toward the flowers sitting on the counter. Dammit, why hadn't she remembered to throw those out? "Who are those from?"

"I'm not sure. Brynn had them when I left." April did her best to make her shrug look nonchalant. "I'll make sure to ask her tomorrow."

"Did they come here?"

"Yeah, but they didn't have a card or anything, so I figured it was a mistake."

"A mistake?" The word dripped with indignation as Ramsey took one more look at the bouquet. He shook his head. "I guess there's a lot of that going around."

"What's that supposed to mean?"

"It's just that, I feel like . . . I don't know. That you haven't been here mentally since you got back. Like you're just going through the motions."

"It's just work stuff." Hadn't she used that same excuse with Carter? Had it worked?

"I didn't know your job was that stressful."

"It can be."

He wasn't satisfied, but he nodded anyway. "You sure it's not something else?"

"Like what?"

"Brynn told me what happened earlier with your tire. Said it was slashed and you seemed to be freaking out. Why didn't you tell me?"

"Because it's not a big deal." Not true. It was because she had gotten it fixed and had hoped he wouldn't find out. Thanks a lot, Brynn.

Ramsey's voice heightened with his rising frustration. He was losing patience. "If someone slashes your tire, it is a big deal, Erin."

"I'm sorry, but why are you mad?"

"Because I feel like my wife is hiding things from me." He was on his feet then, pacing the length of the dining room. April could only watch him quietly, trying to see how best to mitigate the situation. "She also said you were gone damn near all day. Said you wouldn't tell her where you were going, and you left her here with Mom. I thought we agreed you were going to help out with her."

"I did—I am," she corrected. "Mama Edith was fine, and I just needed to run some errands. I didn't think any of this was worth mentioning because it's never been a problem before."

"Don't you think that looks weird?" Ramsey leaned against the counter, gesturing toward the hall where his mother rested in her room. "You're out all day, won't tell anyone where you went, and Brynn had to watch my mom. I was embarrassed, honestly. I don't ever want anyone to feel like I'm burdening them with my mother."

April bit back a smart-aleck comment. "I'm sorry, sweetie," she said, her tone gentle. "It won't happen again."

"You're not lying to me, are you, Erin? I don't want there to be any secrets between us."

Her mind flashed back to that night when he got the strange phone call. He, conveniently, hadn't even mentioned that. "We can trust each other, right?" she asked instead. "I mean, you would tell me if there was something going on I needed to know about?"

Ramsey nodded. "Of course. I don't have anything to hide."

Guess they were both lying, then. But April kept that thought to herself as she rose and took both of Ramsey's hands in hers. She squeezed, prompting him to meet her direct gaze. And with all of the conviction she could emote with a straight face, she said, "I didn't mean to worry you about the tire. I think it was either a nail or something I ran over. And I promise to do better with Mama Edith."

As if to prove her point, she pressed her lips to his and hoped he would be satisfied with that answer.

"I love you, Erin," he whispered, breathless.

"I love you too." April broke away to head to the kitchen. She needed to think and the only thing she was craving at the moment was alcohol. That would have to do.

A phone buzzed, the vibration clattering loudly on the table. April turned from the refrigerator, bottle in hand, just as Ramsey picked up her phone and looked to the screen.

"Work?" He lifted questioning eyes in her direction and held the phone up for her to see. As if she needed confirmation.

April kept her face neutral as she reached for her phone. "My supervisor," she said with an exaggerated roll of her eye. Ramsey nodded and resumed his seat at the table while April turned to answer the call. She would have to keep it short and discreet.

"Hello?"

"Hey, babe," Carter greeted.

"Hey, I'm surprised you're calling. It's a little late."

"I know, I hadn't talked to you in a few days, so just was checking on. I miss you."

April snuck a glance at Ramsey. He was preoccupied with his phone; at least that's what it looked like. She really couldn't be sure. But she knew, whether he was pretending or not, he was certainly within earshot. "Same here, but now is not really a good time. I'm having dinner."

"Oh sorry, babe. Call me before you go to bed."

"Of course." And she hung up before he could pepper her with the intimacies. She took her seat back at the table and poured herself another glass of wine.

"Everything okay?" Ramsey asked.

"Everything is great, babe."

Ramsey nodded, chewing pensively on his steak. "Work is calling kind of late, isn't it?"

April shrugged. "Well, I work late sometimes." *Why was he acting so suspicious all of a sudden?*

She didn't eat much, but she managed to push her food around on the plate enough to appease Ramsey. After he'd cleaned the kitchen and left her alone, she slipped into his art studio. It wouldn't be long before he came in. But Ramsey was a creature of habit. He'd shower first. About fifteen minutes. Then he'd iron his outfit for work tomorrow. He would maybe lay in bed for thirty minutes willing sleep to come but knowing it wouldn't. Not until he painted for a few hours. Which would lead him here.

April hurried along to the privacy lock file that he kept on a bottom shelf near the window, behind paint cans and brushes stiffened with one too many uses. He kept the key on him and, having previously made a copy, April dug her own out of her pocket. She'd done this a few times because she knew what he stored in the box. But he usually kept track of the jumble of bills he stashed, so after one time, she never dared take the cash again for fear he would realize some was missing. No, this time she had another purpose in mind. She sifted past the money to the organized paperwork for Red Velvet Bistro.

Ramsey kept all of his employee documents and onboarding forms arranged alphabetically by last name. Each of their folders had their application, along with their background check, copies of identity documents, Social Security cards, and the like. April zeroed in on the person she was looking for: *Ashford, Kimberly*, little miss pretty hostess with the attitude problem. Who, April remembered, certainly didn't mind flirting with the boss right in front of his wife.

April narrowed her eyes at the photocopy of the woman's driver's license. She wasn't too much younger. A little makeup would do the trick. April touched her fingers to her wig. Yes, she would do just fine. Satisfied, she used her cell to take pictures of all the woman's pertinent information. She would need it for later.

Chapter Seventeen

What the hell was she doing?

April glanced in the rearview mirror for the tenth time, her bones quivering in anguish. It was one thing to drive by the neighborhood. She'd done it too many times to count. But what she was planning to do was another thing entirely.

It would be a short visit, she promised herself, her grip tightening on the steering wheel as yet another car drove past the road. She was already farther from Columbus than she should've been, but thankfully Tabitha was sitting with Mama Edith. Now April had a few hours to spare.

Ms. Walsh lived across the street from the house she'd shared with Warren. They didn't speak much after she had moved in, all things considered, but they'd been polite enough that the impromptu visit didn't seem too outlandish. At least, April hoped. It was risky to even engage with her, but if anyone knew anything about what had, or had not, happened after April left in the middle of the night those years ago, it would be Ms. Walsh. April could only hope that enough time had passed so the older woman wouldn't question her about her whereabouts. But not too much time where her return raised suspicion.

The muffled chime of her cell phone rang and had April glancing down in her lap. One look at the screen and she rolled her eyes. She paused then, deciding whether she wanted to answer. One ring, two rings. She really didn't have time to talk to Carter right now. She needed to remain alert and focused. And she didn't want to risk being distracted that she would miss her opportunity to talk to Ms. Walsh.

At the last minute, April swiped the screen to reject the call, surprised when only a few seconds later it rang again. This time, the number was blocked. She had to shake her head. That was certainly a new level of persistence, even for her husband.

She watched it ring in her hand a couple more times before she went ahead and answered it. She didn't know why he was so insistent on speaking with her, but her curiosity outweighed her stubbornness. It must have been important.

"Hey," she answered, intentionally keeping her voice flat and nonchalant. She was met with silence, and her face crinkled in a frown. "Hello? Carter?" April pulled the phone from her ear to eye the screen and saw the clock ticking away the seconds, indicating the call was still connected. Well, he hadn't hung up. "Hello?" she tried again.

"Hi, how are you?"

The voice sounded muffled, as if someone was talking into their palm. April couldn't even tell if the voice was male or female. Her frown deepened. Something about the call, about the caller, wasn't right.

"Who is this?" She didn't realize she was whispering.

"Is this April?" the caller repeated, followed by a weighted pause.

April's heart felt like it had been jolted into hyperdrive with bolts of electricity. Not knowing what else to do, she hung up, half-expecting another mysterious call to follow. Thankfully, her phone remained silent. But now, her head was reeling.

The familiar PT Cruiser turned on the street and April took a steadying breath. For strength. For serenity. Or both. She'd been parked against the curb for an hour, comforted in the vibration of the engine's dull roar as she nervously drummed her fingers on the console and watched the luminescent numbers from the dashboard tick the time away. She hoped she didn't look too anxious as the Cruiser wheeled by and turned into the driveway.

"Ms. Walsh," she greeted with a wave, rushing to the old woman's side as she struggled to nudge open the heavy car door. She gripped her arm and helped her to her feet. Ms. Walsh squinted at her through her small-framed rims, the generic smile already warming her face, though the eyes showed she clearly didn't recognize her.

"How are you doing, sweetie?" she said, patting April's hand.

"I'm fine." April noticed the grocery bags in the back seat and realized why it had taken her so long to get home. "Here, I can get these for you. I'll meet you inside."

"Oh, you don't have to—"

"Please. I insist. It's the least I can do for dropping by unannounced."

Ms. Walsh looked like she wanted to object, but instead relaxed into a grateful smile. She carried only her purse as she padded into the house.

The nostalgic smell of fudge brownies and coffee beans welcomed April when she stepped through the kitchen, sitting the plastic bags on the counter. Ms. Walsh was already pulling mugs from the cabinet. "Are you thirsty, dear?"

"No, ma'am. But thank you." April began unpacking the bags. She turned and stifled a grin when the mug of coffee was shoved in her hands anyway. "Ms. Walsh, you don't remember me?"

The woman sipped her own drink on a stumped frown. "I'm sorry, dear. My mind's not as good as it used to be. Half the time I can't even remember who I am."

April swallowed. "April." Her biological name almost sounded foreign to her ears. She cleared her throat. "I'm April," she tried again with a little more vigor. "I used to be your neighbor."

Ms. Walsh nodded, but her expression remained blank. "That's nice, dear. Have a seat. How have you been?"

"I've been good. Just working." Obediently, April lowered herself in a nearby chair. She wasn't sure how productive this visit would be with the woman's ailing mental state. Why she'd even considered returning to the neighborhood with all of its horrid memories—well, she'd badgered herself about that during the drive over. But she'd figured it couldn't hurt. At least it could give her something regarding her uncertainties. Which was more than she could say for Erika or anything else at this point.

"And what about your husband?" April's body frosted with the nonchalant question. There was no way Ms. Walsh could know about Ramsey or Carter. Which meant she was referring to Warren. And the fact that she was asking meant she didn't know, or remember, that he was dead. *Or should've been.*

"I'm . . . not married." April decided the lie was the safest way to deflect from the topic.

"Oh, I thought you were with that big fella . . . what was his name? Started with a W or M or something. Matthew?"

April shook her head to further dispel the old lady's accuracy. "I had a few boyfriends here and there, but nothing serious." She couldn't be sure if she sounded believable.

Ms. Walsh shook her head, her lips pursed in a grim frown. She looked like she wanted to delve deeper but covered her intrusive questions with an embarrassed smile. "Forgive me," she said simply, lifting her mug to her lips. "I get confused easily. So anyway, what brings you around here, April?"

"I was in the neighborhood. Haven't been back since I moved, and I thought it would be fun to drive by my old place."

Ms. Walsh kicked her feet out of her baby doll flats and took another sip from her mug. "Yes, a lot has changed, that's for sure. At one point, I thought we were gentrifying, but I think they gave up on that when they realized that most of us weren't going anywhere."

"You see a lot of the same people around?" April pressed.

"For the most part. Nothing too out of the ordinary."

April started to power forward, decided she better tread lightly on the subject. "Ms. Walsh, can I have a brownie? They smell delicious."

The comment hit the perfect chord. Ms. Walsh's eyes nearly disappeared behind the folds of her smile as she stood and shuffled to the oven. "Of course, darling." She reached in and pulled out a flowered plate overflowing with moist, chocolate squares. Saran Wrap kept the dessert packed tight against the plate as she brought it to the breakfast table.

April folded back the plastic and plucked one from the top of the bunch. She'd polished off two brownies, debated on a third, before she continued. "I was curious if you'd seen anybody over next door. I don't think anyone has bought the house since I moved out."

"No, I don't think so. But you know, I mostly stay to myself around here. Watching the soaps and collecting dust, as my grandkids say."

"It's been abandoned the whole time?"

"Except for when the police were out there."

The aftertaste of the brownie suddenly tasted like acid. April took a healthy swig of her coffee. The police? How did she not know the police had come snooping?

"Do you know what for?"

Ms. Walsh made some sort of a noise that passed between a snort and a chuckle. "No idea. But they came for a few weeks straight. Poking and prodding and whatnot. Had the cars lined up all outside. Then all of a sudden, they just stopped. Guess they found what they were looking for."

April's head ached with dread. That's what she was afraid of.

Chapter Eighteen

Fear was beginning to set in. April felt it inch its way up her spine, and her grip tightened on the steering wheel. Calming down didn't seem possible at the moment. *Someone was following her.*

Her eyes cut from the red light to her rearview mirror for the fifth time. The black Cadillac looked sleek like a bullet with its tinted windows. It had maintained a steady three-car distance for the past twenty minutes and it hadn't taken April long to see it expertly dodging in and out of traffic. She recognized it as the same vehicle that had been parked outside of her house when those dreaded flowers came.

It was best to detour. Instead of heading to her original destination, April turned right toward Red Velvet Bistro. She wouldn't tell Ramsey why she was there. That would require too much explaining. She would just make up an excuse that she'd been in the area and wanted to drop by to see him, which she was certain would suffice. He appreciated those kinds of gestures.

Just as she expected, the Cadillac eased into the restaurant behind her and maneuvered to an available parking space across the lot. April watched it for a minute. It didn't move and in no way made a point to cut off the car, nor get out. It was clear that whoever it was didn't seem to notice or care about discretion anymore.

She moved quickly; sliding from the car and hiking toward the building on legs that felt like bricks. Not that it mattered, but she kept her head down and pretended to be focused on the task at hand. It was another day where it was too warm to be January, and the heat was violent against her jacket and denim jeans, or maybe it was the heat of eyes bearing into her like daggers. Either way, it only amplified her panic as she quickened her pace.

It looked like the lunch rush was still pretty busy, April noticed, as she breezed into the restaurant with its dense group of patrons. A cool air tickled her slick skin in what should have felt good, but only peppered goose bumps that sent chills grating against her forearms. The hostess, Kimberly Ashford in fact, glanced up from the stand where she'd been stacking menus. April wasn't sure but it looked like the woman's eyes rolled just before a tight smile stretched the skin around her mouth.

"Good afternoon. Table for one?"

April caught the subtle disdain licking her words and normally, she would have called her on it. But not today. No, today she needed her husband. She needed safety. She flicked a glance through the window where the Cadillac was still waiting.

"I'd like to see Ramsey Duncan."

Kimberly's fake smile fell a few degrees. "I'm sorry, he's not here."

April blinked. Once, then twice. No way she could've heard correctly. "I'm sorry," she clarified. "I meant my husband, Ramsey. I'm his wife."

"Yes, I know who you are. And I know who Ramsey is. Like I said, he's not here."

"Well, what time will he be in?"

"Probably for the dinner shift."

Kimberly tossed her ponytail over her shoulder and turned her back to April, the gesture blatantly dismissive.

An incredulous frown etched April's face as she thought back to that morning. Of course, she hadn't had much rest. That was always thanks to the nightmares. But was she so out of it that she was confusing even the simplest of things? Hadn't Ramsey distinctly gotten up and gotten dressed? Hadn't he made mention of how busy it was supposed to be because of a convention that was in town? Or was that tomorrow? He'd called Tabitha to care for Edith, that much she remembered for certain. But everything else felt like a blur. One big agonizing blur where she didn't know what side of the lie she was on.

She was mistaken. That's what it was. Ramsey must have clearly said he needed to leave the house early to run errands or go to the bank or something before he went into work. She'd been so engrossed with her own issues she hadn't been listening.

The logic had relief swelling through her stomach. And because Kimberly was pretending to be too busy to acknowledge her further, April didn't bother responding. Instead, she left, stepping back out into the humidity. Even though her rationale made perfect sense, there was still something unsettling about the mix-up that splintered April's chest. So much so that she wasn't paying attention to see the Cadillac was no longer in the parking lot.

As soon as she wheeled away from the restaurant, April reached for her phone to dial Ramsey. She needed to hear him confirm what she knew had to be true. She needed to hear his voice. "Please leave your message for . . ." the voice mail prompt chirped. April hung up, not bothering to leave a message. There had to be an explanation for Ramsey's absence. And she would ask him about it. Later. She turned into the storage unit just as the first few sprinkles of rain splattered across her windshield.

The disk lock was beginning to rust. April couldn't remember the last time she'd been to her storage. She hadn't needed to. Or maybe she'd wanted to forget this part of her past. The key went in with minimal effort and the door rattled up with an echoing clang. She could make out the shape of boxes piled in makeshift towers, none of them labeled. A cloud of dust had her eyes watering as she squinted into the darkened unit. She wasn't sure exactly what she expected to find by coming here. *Proof, maybe?*

There was a pungent smell in the air, a stench of stale blankets and nicotine mothballs. It was a scent memory that took April back to when she was little, before Warren, before marriage, just before. When she was just *April* and the worst thing she'd had to struggle with was one- bedroom apartments with dingy carpets and roaches to distract her from the hunger pangs. And, of course, Erika's temper. Somehow, that was better.

April flipped a switch and an overhead head light flickered on with a steady buzz. The last time she was here, she'd been with Erika. She didn't remember ever coming by herself. There was something disturbing about sitting here alone with the weight of the memories, knowing what she knew now. She shuddered and pulled open a flap to a nearby box. It was withered with age, but the contents were just as fresh.

She hadn't had much growing up. But what she did have had been compartmentalized into this 12-by-12 cardboard. A cluster of plush animals with blanched colors on their soiled fur had been stuffed inside. April pulled one out, swallowing the longing that burned in the back of her throat. It was a blue elephant; well, it used to be blue. Now it was a sour gray color with matted stuffing protruding from under its trunk. One of Erika's boyfriends, she didn't remember who, had given her this one, thus sparking her collection.

April sat the toy on her lap, peering inside the box through the remaining assortment of cotton. The rest were a mix of animals and colors and time periods. Erika had probably given her a few, but the one in particular she was looking for was the purple teddy bear. That one had been her favorite. She hadn't wanted to keep the necklace Warren had given her, nor could she bring herself to give it away. That's why she'd wrapped it around the neck of the purple teddy bear he'd given her on their last Christmas together. As far as she knew, it should've been there with all the others, and that would be the telltale sign that someone was messing with her. It didn't take her long, or maybe she knew before she even opened the box, there was no sign of the bear. Which only left her even more confused. Someone had snuck into her garage, rifled through her belongings, taken a very specific stuffed animal with a very specific necklace around its neck, and dropped the necklace off at her doorstep? It just didn't make sense.

A noise from somewhere outside had April's ears perking. She held her breath, listening to the subsequent silence. It had sounded like footsteps, though she couldn't be entirely sure. No, correction. A footstep and then quiet as if the person had stopped to listen just as hard as she was. Panic vibrated around her in a tiny falsetto and had April struggling to her feet, inching toward the open doorway. Her car sat mere feet away, but otherwise there didn't appear to be anyone else nearby. An image of the Cadillac flashed in her mind. Had she seen it after she left the restaurant? It was a gated storage unit so if there was someone else present, they would need a code to get in, then know which unit was hers. Stop it, she scolded herself as she stepped back into the garage. She scolded her paranoia but kept her eyes peeled, just in case.

April kneeled to re-tuck the flaps on the box, once again sealing all of those memories inside. She hefted it to her trunk. Then, she went back in and grabbed one more box in particular that she dreaded but would go through later when she had more time. And privacy.

That last thought had something coiling in her bones, something tight and raw. Again, she angled her head to look down both ways at the empty aisle. She reached up to slam the trunk closed.

Just as she turned, she stopped in her tracks. The passenger-side door of her car was hanging wide open on its hinges. She froze, afraid to move closer, or away from the terrifying sight.

April didn't have time to let out a scream as a knife slid under her chin to nick the flesh at her neck. The cut was more startling than anything and she felt the first few trickles of blood wet her skin. Then a hand shoved her down. April gasped as she hit the trunk of her car first, the metal biting into her stomach. She rolled and landed with a thud on the pavement. Pain ricocheted through the left side of her body like a lightning bolt. Dazed, she could only lay there squinting against the harsh sunlight as footsteps echoed their hasty retreat.

PART IV: DEPRESSION

The stage of grief where sadness sets in as you begin to understand the loss and its effect on your life.

Chapter Nineteen

Before

She was a prisoner. The only difference was that she wasn't in a jail cell. She was in a lavish 8000-square-foot mini-mansion on Lake Spivey. But the good thing was, she had managed to memorize every inch of it, and she'd yet to get caught. There were more rooms than she knew what to do with, most of them with doors closed and strict orders not to investigate. Warren had moved Erika in as well and she occupied a mother-in-law suite on the ground floor, just off the gourmet kitchen. And the basement: Oh, the basement was a huge no-no and April knew that was where his office was. She was planning to see for herself. And there was a library that April spent a great deal in, pouring over criminal justice books like the gospel.

It was one such time when Erika barged in, not bothering to knock. "We need to talk," she announced.

April didn't bother looking up from the law book spread open on the table in front of her. "About?"

Erika's sigh was irritated as she eased onto a nearby chaise. Her expensive perfume mingled with the subtle smell of dust and leather from the abundance of books that lined each shelf. She looked out of place, sitting in the middle of the library with her crisp, white capris, wedge sandals, and billowing floral print blouse that scrunched at the waist and the elbows of the three-quarter-length sleeves. As always, her makeup was flawless. Once upon a time, her mother had wanted to be a makeup artist. April was sure that dream had flown out the window since the inception of their new life.

"You need to speed up the process," Erika said.

Now it was April's turn to sigh. "Damn, Erika, let me just start robbing the place then."

"You know what I mean."

She rolled her eyes. "You must not care if we get caught. I have to be smart about this whole thing."

"Well, what else is there to drag your feet about?" Erika glanced toward the French doors to make sure no one was around, though they both knew Warren had left the house a few hours ago. "Come on, April. You know where everything is, right? You know his office is in the basement. How long is it going to take you?"

April would never admit to Erika the truth: That she was scared and she didn't want to do it. She regretted even agreeing to this stupid idea. "I'm working on a plan," she said. That part was true. She feared going anywhere near Warren's basement, afraid of what she would find. Or worse, what would find her.

Erika groaned. "Well, you need to work harder. You said you were on board with this. Don't back out now. Warren deserves everything that's coming to him, so get the shit done."

April turned her attention back to her book in a mock dismissal, not surprised when Erika didn't take the hint.

"I think you should have his baby."

April's chest tightened with the words. She snapped back as if she'd been punched in the mouth. "What?"

Erika didn't bother repeating herself. Just barreled on without a care in the world. As if she'd proposed something as simple as having salmon for dinner. "I know this is a lot to ask, but why else would Warren choose you over me? But it makes sense. You're young and fertile. Just think of how set we would be if you give him a child." Erika's voice carried a sickening excitement that was reflected in her eyes. "That baby will be a definite meal ticket. Even a bargaining chip. Warren will give you anything your precious heart desires."

"Even a divorce?" April's voice cracked at the gravity of what she probably had to do. It wasn't supposed to be like this. None of it.

Erika's shoulder lifted in a half shrug. "I don't know. Probably. But think if he does, he would have to pay you child support."

April shook her head fiercely. The sideswept bangs of her bone-straight weave slapped her in the forehead with the gesture. She couldn't do this. She just couldn't. "You're sick," she muttered, her voice barely audible or recognizable to herself.

"No, I'm smart." Erika stood with the finality of her words. "For some reason, that man loves you. Now, I'm trying to help you capitalize on that. Sacrifice. I told you from the beginning life isn't fair. But you do what is necessary to survive. So, stop acting childish like you don't know the things we've had to do to live. Hell, do you even have sex with the man?"

Not willingly. April shuddered. Just picturing herself trying to fight Warren's big body off hers some nights made her feel filthy all over again. But that didn't seem to stop him. And apparently when he didn't have the urge to fight her, he found comfort in Erika's bed anyway. She had heard them plenty of times, the moans from the mother-in-law suite loud enough to carry through the massive house. What the hell did she care? Warren had his cake and was eating it too. And her mother, she had everything she could ask for at the degradation of her teenage daughter.

She wasn't stupid. They thought she was, but she never went anywhere and that afforded her a lot of time to think. Aside from mapping out her exit strategy, April picked up on a lot that most people didn't think she noticed. Like how Warren was an attorney, but he didn't make enough money for the luxurious lifestyle he led people to believe. It hadn't taken a lot of snooping for April to realize it was because he was on the wrong side of the law; defending high-level criminals and cartels and the people who others knew of but shuddered to speak their names. The ones who ran the cities from underground or skyscraper offices, and only came out to get their hands dirty when it was absolutely necessary. And she overheard his whispered conversations in the middle of the night, and she saw the random visits with his clients that usually left him shaken and sometimes bruised. More recently, a dead fish that had shown up on the doorstep that April deduced was a death threat. When she had asked the maid, Carlita, about it, she had responded in broken English that Mr. Warren was a lawyer for some "bad people" and he didn't really do what he was supposed to do, whatever that meant.

But Erika had made it clear to play her position. And part of her position was not to ask too many questions which was why April kept her thoughts to herself. She turned a blind eye to the conference calls and frequent meetings with his so-called "partners" and instead, poured her energy into learning everything she could on her own, so she could use it to her advantage. But she knew that her little cushy lifestyle was only an image and within these walls lay something far more dangerous.

Chapter Twenty

An intense throbbing pain at her temples snatched April from her drug-induced sleep. She winced and opened her mouth to cry out, not surprised when a throaty moan escaped from her parted lips. She opened her eyes and blinked to clear the blurriness from her vision.

It took a moment for the harsh memory of the events to materialize in her mind. She half-expected to still be lying outside by her car, the blood from her neck pooling on the gravel. A quick scan of the room told her otherwise.

The pastel blue hospital room was empty and carried a hint of latex and antiseptics. She lay now under the starched sheets of the bed, an IV hooked up to her arm. Buzzes and whirrs from the monitor quietly echoed to a steady rhythm that harmonized with her heart. She was weak but at least she was alive. She wondered how much damage had been done for her to end up in the hospital. Who had found her?

The door creaked open and a nurse entered, carrying a tray of food. She seemed surprised when April's eyes met hers. "Oh, you're awake," she said with a smile. "I'm glad. The pain meds definitely kept you knocked out."

April winced again at the throbbing pain that was now a dull aching with enough intensity to wrinkle her forehead. Sensing her discomfort, the nurse quickly set the tray on a nearby table and crossed the room to assist.

"You hurting?" she asked and April simply nodded. "On a pain scale of one to ten."

"Twenty."

"Oh, dear, let me turn some of this up."

The nurse, which April was able to make out the name Greta on her name tag, busied herself with the IV drip. "Who brought me in here?" she asked, closing her eyes and waiting for the meds to kick in.

"Some nice-looking gentleman." Greta began pulling things from the cabinets as she spoke. "He left for a bit, though. I'm not sure if he'll be back. Oh, and some cops came by."

April's eyes snapped open. "Cops?"

Greta continued absently fiddling with the needles and medications. "Yes, but I think they had the wrong room. They were looking for some April or other. I'm not really sure. Your gentleman friend got everything straightened out."

Worry creased April's forehead, but rather than inquire further, she opted to remain quiet. She didn't want to mess around and say something she didn't need to say. And who was her gentleman friend? Ramsey?

April felt the drugs beginning to take effect and she welcomed the feeling. Like she was almost floating. Even the pain had begun to fade. She felt her eyes get heavy and she didn't bother fighting the urge to sleep.

Somewhere far off, it sounded like a door opened and footsteps echoed closer.

"How is she?" Ramsey's voice was clear but sounded distant and fuzzy.

"I've given her some more medication because she woke up in pain," Greta was saying. "The doctor will probably want to keep her for another day for observation, but she's healing just fine. It was a surface cut, thank God, so no serious damage. She just may have to deal with the emotional pain more than the physical."

"Yeah."

"If there is anything else you need for her, just let me know."

"Thanks."

More steps, a door opened and shut, and April felt the bed sink under some added weight as apparently Ramsey sat down. She felt his hand touch hers and heard his relieved sigh.

She heard him murmuring something inaudible just as she dozed off.

When she woke up after what she assumed was a few hours later, Ramsey had moved to a chair beside the bed. He was wide awake, watching as if he had been patiently waiting for her to get up. April's eyelids fluttered and she winced, that familiar feeling of pain slowly intensifying once more. She was better off just staying asleep if she had to deal with this every waking moment.

Ramsey was up and beside her bed in an instant. "Hey," he said. "How are you feeling? Do you need me to call the nurse?"

"No, I'm okay." Though she wished like hell they would up the dosage of her medication.

Ramsey touched her arm. "What happened, babe?"

"I—I don't know, honestly." She shut her eyes against the memory of the knife against her throat, struggling to will the image away. "Who found you?"

"I don't know. The hospital called me and told me you had been brought in. Where were you? What were you doing?"

It was best to lie. She couldn't tell him the truth. "The last thing I remember is stopping by the gas station, and then before I pulled off . . ." she trailed, holding up her hands helplessly.

Ramsey leaned down and attempted to hug her as best as he could, despite the awkward position. "Babe, I am so sorry I wasn't there. Work was crazy and . . . shit, now I just feel bad that this happened."

Work . . . April's mind flashed back to the black Cadillac, stopping by the restaurant, Kimberly's smug smile as she relayed how he was indeed, *not* at work. He was standing there lying straight to her face.

"Ramsey, where were you?" she asked, keeping her gaze level with his. When he didn't immediately respond, she went on. "I stopped by your job while I was out just before all of this happened, and Kimberly said you weren't there."

Ramsey's lips turned down in a considering frown. He shook his head, running his hand over his beard. His face had seemed to age with stress. And if April was honest with herself, he actually looked fearful. "She must have been mistaken," he said.

"I called you," April tossed back, with a pointed glare. "You didn't even answer your phone."

"That's because I was working, sweetie."

He was lying. The question was, why?

Silence stretched between them. April wasn't sure what Ramsey was thinking, but she knew her mind was reeling with the events that had taken place. There was an uneasiness about the situation and both of them felt it.

Greta reentered moments later, breaking up the silent tension between them. "Look who I found for you, Ms. Duncan," she declared with a dramatic sweep of her hand. Jameson stepped through the doorway and April nearly fell out of the bed. *What the hell was he doing there?*

Then, right behind him was Brynn and April had to force herself to relax. "Oh, girl, are you okay?" Brynn being the drama queen that she was rushed to the side of the bed and grabbed both of April's hands. "Ram told us what happened. Who would do such a thing?"

April didn't know how to respond. She shifted in the bed, the springs seeming to bite into her back. Across the room Jameson stood with his hands shoved in his pockets. Watching her.

Brynn followed April's gaze. "I hope you don't mind that I brought Prez," she said with a chuckle. "I was headed to pick him up anyway when we got the call."

"We're glad you're here," Ramsey said. He was talking to Brynn but, for some reason, April noticed he was giving Jameson a menacing stare that heightened the already thick tension. What was that about?

Brynn pulled one of the chairs closer to the bed so she could sit while she talked. "Do they know what happened?" she asked, glancing from April to Ramsey.

April shook her head.

"It's so scary nowadays." Brynn went on. "You could be walking around minding your own business, then—" she snapped with a dramatic flair. "Crazy how unsafe the world is. But what matters is that you're okay."

"I appreciate that, Brynn."

"Glad you're okay, Erin," Jameson chimed in. It was something about the way he said it that had April's stomach twisting. And when she risked glancing over at him again, she caught the cryptic smile on his face. Then, it vanished just as quickly as if it were never there.

Chapter Twenty-one

"Are you sure you should be traveling right now?"

April stifled an eye roll as she tucked another pair of pants in her suitcase. "Yes, I'm fine, sweetie. Promise."

Ramsey leaned against the doorjamb with crossed arms, watching her pack with a restrained urgency. "I just don't see what the rush is."

"Who says I'm rushing?"

"Come on, Erin, you were just released two days ago. And you're jumping right back to work like you weren't attacked."

April pursed her lips to keep from commenting. He was concerned. She couldn't blame him. Hell, she would've been herself if she wasn't so terrified. She was tempted to rub the small cut on her neck. It was thin, about the size of a paper cut and unless you knew what had happened, it almost looked invisible to the naked eye. Still, it seemed to sting when she thought about it too long, or when she remembered the prick of the knife on her skin. The emotional damage was far greater. Therefore yes; to Ramsey she was rushing back to work. To herself, she was running away from her killer. Because that's what it had grown to in her mind. A killer. Someone who could've dug that knife in just a little deeper and literally sliced her throat. The thought had April's fingers trembling as she flipped the bag closed and zipped it tight.

Ramsey had reiterated again that it must've been a mugging. Sure, the assailant had taken her purse, but April knew better. It wasn't random, nor a typical burglary. Not when her wallet contained a fake driver's license and a collection of maxed credit cards in various names. Which brought her back to wondering: Who were the cops that Greta mentioned had come by? Whoever they were, they hadn't returned. April didn't know if that was a good or bad thing.

"I'll be back in a couple weeks," she said, feigning a smile for reassurance she didn't feel. "You won't even realize I'm gone."

Ramsey looked like he wanted to say something else but decided against it. "What time are you leaving?" he asked. "Are you able to stay with Mom until I get off work? I can get someone to cover the dinner shift for me, but I have to be there for lunch. And her aide has classes today so she can't get here until after five."

April nodded, quickly calculating in her head. "I can stay until then so you can work. Hey, have you worked the lunch shift all week?" she added, keeping her voice light.

Ramsey frowned. "Of course. Why would you ask that?"

April paused long enough to eye him from across the room.

One similarity between her two husbands, she could usually tell when both of them were lying. They just showed it in completely different ways. Carter had a timidity about him that manifested when he averted his eyes and gave this sheepish grin that, April guessed, was supposed to distract her while he tried to come up with a lie. It never worked. At least not with her. Thankfully, Carter was also the more compliant spouse, so it wasn't often he felt led to lie that she knew of. If only that mindset was reciprocal.

Ramsey, on the other hand, was a little bit harder to pinpoint sometimes, not that it kept her from figuring him out. She noticed that his pattern was restlessness, whether he was fidgeting with his clothes or rubbing his neck. Like the deception was making him uncomfortable, so he had to move. Which, she noticed, was what he was doing now at that moment. She remembered showing up at his job before going to the storage unit. And calling him repeatedly. He had yet to justify his absence or mention the missed calls altogether. With everything else going on, had it really just slipped his mind?

And it was more than obvious he was upset, considering he left her alone in the bedroom and didn't bother offering to take her suitcase to her car.

April lowered herself to the bed and logged into one of her accounts. She knew the balance all the way down to the penny, but it appeased her to see the dollar figure. Plus, it solidified the real reason why she was leaving so quickly. It was time to disappear. And as much as she had to ignore the guilt, she didn't mind staying as long as she needed to tonight. Because she knew it was her last night. A year ago, Erin didn't exist. And tomorrow she wouldn't anymore. The assault had only expedited the inevitable. She would spend her last night with Ramsey and Mama Edith. She would get things tidied up back home in Atlanta, then she would finish up with Carter. By next week, she would be rid of both men, both identities, and both issues.

The laptop screen glowed to life, illuminating her blank page. April pecked in her log-in information and watched the page load. The balance flickered onto the screen, prompting her eyes to widen at the glaring red digits singed against the white page. Negative. Her account was negative. Which meant it was about 100,000 dollars short of what it had been earlier that week. A surge of panic had the headache gathering at her forehead. It was a mistake. Had to be.

April clicked on the account to open the recent activity, scanning the transactions until the figured blurred together. There had been multiple Zelle transactions, siphoning all of the money from the account. Thousands spread through various distributions to about eight recipients she didn't recognize. April's heart plummeted to her stomach. She'd been in the hospital and had quickly reported her cards as stolen to keep anyone from using them. Never did she think someone would have access to her account. It would be a nightmare to dispute.

She couldn't let herself wallow too long. Quickly, she logged into her remaining bank accounts. All but one reflected a lower balance. Her fingers were numb as she changed her username and passwords. Her mind was in a fog.

A voice floated through her subconscious, one she didn't quite recognize. *April.* It called her name with such conviction it startled a gasp from her lips. She squeezed her eyes shut to block it out. It was getting louder, more demanding. More aggressive. No, no. She wasn't April. April was gone. April was—

The hand on her shoulder had April screaming and lunging backwards from the touch. She blinked, surprised to see Edith standing on the side of the bed. A worried look creased her face. "Are you okay, sweetie?"

"I—" April's head whipped around the room. She had to keep it together. "I must have dozed off, Mama Edith. I apologize."

The woman's head bobbed with a half-nod. "Would you like me to make you something to eat, dear?"

"No, ma'am." April climbed to her feet and put her arms around the woman's frail shoulders. "Were you calling my name just now?" She didn't want to believe Edith was saying the name "April." But she had heard it loud and clear, hadn't she? But Edith wouldn't have known that. There was no way.

Edith's eyes met hers, completely kind and blank. "No, I don't think so." That's what she figured.

April steered the woman back to her room and helped her back into the bed. She tried to keep her movements casual, even as her mind was spinning elsewhere.

She needed to call the bank to see if she could get this mess sorted out with her money without causing too much suspicion. She sat with Edith a moment longer, satisfied when her eyes fluttered closed. Good, she was napping. That would give her a little privacy.

April tiptoed from the room and took care to pull the door closed behind her. She heard the faint vibration of her phone and jogged back to her room, snatching it up without bothering to check the caller ID.

"Hello?"

"Hi, Brenda Drummond?" The professional voice had April hesitating. She hadn't expected to hear that name. Her mind flipped through her mental Rolodex. She had her condo in Atlanta as Brenda. Of course.

"Yes?"

"This is Janet with RTech Monitoring and Security. We received an alert that the burglar alarm was triggered on your front door. Is everything okay?"

April steeled. No, it wasn't okay. Now someone had tried to break in. She couldn't have the police at her place.

"Um, yes, everything is fine," she lied.

"What is your passcode, please?"

April rattled off the passcode and hung up, pinching the bridge of her nose. She had to get home. It wasn't enough to be attacked and have her purse stolen, but someone was obviously hell- bent on breaking her mentally and emotionally.

April started to dial Edith's aide, Tabitha, then remembered Ramsey said the young lady was in class and wouldn't be available until the evening. She dialed Brynn, praying she would answer.

"Hi, you've reached Brynn . . ." She hung up again, determined to remain calm. She couldn't very well call Ramsey because then she would have to explain more than she was willing to.

She poked her head into Edith's room, saw the woman was still sleeping soundly. She would be quick. If she left right then, she could get back in time to beat Ramsey home. Edith would be okay until then. April hurried for her keys. She knew if she stopped to think about it more, she would talk herself out of going. And she couldn't afford that.

Chapter Twenty-two

April noticed the car as soon as she turned onto her street. It wasn't like it looked out of place or anything. It was that same glistening black Cadillac, an older model by the looks of it. The windows were tinted black, obscuring the inside completely. It was parked against the curb leading up to her building.

April started to wheel her car into her building's lot but quickly thought better of it. Instead, she pulled to the side of the curb and cut off the ignition. She didn't know what she was waiting for. It wasn't like cars parked on the side of the road were uncommon. But she just felt compelled to wait a few moments longer before pulling into her condo. She didn't even know what the hell she was expecting to happen. But something about that blacked-out car brought on a swell of panic. *Was the car there for her?*

As if on cue, the Cadillac peeled away from the curb in the opposite direction. Even after the car disappeared down the street, April counted an additional ten minutes before she braved pulling into her parking space.

Her phone buzzed in her cup holder and April shrieked at the interruption. Brynn's name was displayed on the screen and April allowed herself to relax. A little. *Get it together, girl.* She started not to pick up, but then thought better of it. She could use Brynn to establish her alibi in case word got back to Ramsey. Her eyes darted around before venturing to pick it up. "Hello?"

"Hey, girlie," Brynn chirped. "I came by the house looking for you. I'm headed to work a little later, but I thought we could grab something to eat. You close by?"

April paused, her eyes darting to her condo looming in front of her. "Oh, I ran out to the grocery store for a second." She would have to find a way to stall because she knew she wouldn't be back in Columbus for another couple of hours.

"Oh, okay, I get it. Doing your wifey thing. Girl, I have to show you this new Parmesan-crusted chicken recipe I tried—"

"Brynn, I don't mean to rush you, but I have to go."

"I'm sorry, girlie. I didn't mean to hold you up. Is Mama Edith with you or is she with Tabitha at the house?"

April winced. Ramsey would piss a diamond if he knew she had left his mother home alone. "She's out with Tabitha," she said. "I think they went to the community center or something." It was a weak excuse, but an excuse, nonetheless. And it was the best she could do under pressure. Now if she could just get off the phone, then she could hurry back before anyone noticed she was gone.

After April promised she would call later that evening, she hung up and edged from the car, tossing another glance around to make sure the coast was clear. Most of the residents were probably still at work, which could account for the meager number of cars sprinkled throughout the lot. A sudden breeze tickled her face and at the same time, an echo of a thought floated in her ear. *Someone is stalking me.* April shuddered.

April locked her door and broke out in a run to her building. The area was nearly empty with the exception of a few pedestrians walking by on the sidewalk. Somewhere a siren wailed, and the shrill laughter of children danced in the distance. She knew she looked silly dashing like a madwoman as if she were being chased by a ghost. But that was honestly what it felt like to a degree. And it frightened her just the same.

She fumbled with her front door and slammed it closed, leaning up against it to catch her breath. Then, as an afterthought, April turned and flipped the locks into place. That was when she heard a noise. She held her breath, craning her neck to listen. She couldn't be 100 percent certain, but that sounded like footsteps muffled against carpet.

April's eyes scanned the living room, the neat placement of her expensive sectional and big screen with abstract art pieces adorning her walls. The ceiling fan whirred overhead, setting a slight chill to the air. Other than that, silence.

She took a quick peek into the galley kitchen. Nothing seemed out of place. Except the cup on the granite countertop. Had she left that there? Then she heard it, clear as day. A sniffle. She couldn't be sure if it was coming from inside the apartment, but fear gripped her throat as she reached for the knife in the drainboard. A butter knife, but it was better than nothing.

April took her time, walking carefully toward her master bedroom so she didn't make a noise. Her chest was tight as she struggled to level her breathing. Again, she thought of the Cadillac she'd seen, and the man at the mall in the black hoodie, not to mention the robbery in front of her storage unit. If she thought long and hard about it, she really had to scold herself for continuing to venture off alone. And without protection. She would get a gun as soon as possible.

April stood at the door of her bedroom, afraid to go in, all the while her eyes sweeping the room. Her bed was still neatly made, with decorative pillows and stuffed animals lining the headboard; her lotions and makeup were scattered across the nightstand, just like she'd left them. A few Styrofoam heads were lined on a dresser, undisturbed, donning her wigs in various colors and styles. Not even a strand of hair appeared out of place.

April took a step in the direction of the bathroom. Her heart was beating so hard it felt like it would jump out of her chest and lie throbbing at her toes. She lifted her knife, gripping it like a lifeline as she inched closer to the ensuite.

The figure entered the doorway and April's scream split the air. Without thinking, she wielded the knife, her eyes squeezed shut as she swung senselessly at the unknown assailant.

"Girl, what the hell are you doing?"

April opened her eyes and stood face-to-face with Erika. She looked like she had just emerged from the shower as she clutched a towel to her chest, her mouth rounded in disturbed shock. Her eyes were zeroed in on the knife April still clutched in her sweaty palm.

As if she just realized she was still holding the weapon, April loosened her grip and let the metal slip from her grasp to clank loudly on the bathroom linoleum. Her breath came out in a heavy *whoosh* that nearly stung her lungs. "Erika, what the hell?" She hadn't meant to shout, but the adrenaline elevated her voice.

"What the hell are you doing with a knife, April? Damn!" Erika lowered her gaze to the weapon before lifting stunned eyes back to her daughter in a questioning stare.

"How did you get in here?"

"My key!"

"Shit!" April took a staggering breath to calm herself down. "You can't just show up uninvited—"

"You mean after you knew I was in town?"

"You didn't say anything about staying here."

"Well, I certainly didn't think I was going to die for it." Erika's look was incredulous as she reached down to pick up the knife with a shake of her head. "What is wrong with you?"

"I . . . thought someone had broken in. The alarm person called and said it went off."

"Yeah, it took me a minute to turn it off." She was still shaking her head as she dropped the knife on the dresser and moved to the closet. "Honestly, girl, get yourself a gun like a normal person. What were you going to do with a butter knife? Make him a sandwich?"

April touched her forehead and felt the beads of sweat pearling on her brow. She let out another grateful sigh as she watched her mother rummage through her suitcase. "I never thought I'd say this, but I'm glad it's you."

"As opposed to who?" Erika blew an exasperated breath at her daughter's continued silence. "You want to tell me what's got you so shook up?"

April shrugged. "It's nothing," she said.

"Right." Sarcasm laced the solitary word. "You sure it's not anything else? Anything you need to tell me?"

April lifted an eyebrow, but she kept her face neutral. "What do you mean?"

Erika emerged, now in some leggings and an oversized T-shirt. She crossed to the dresser to begin fiddling with her hair. "I'm just checking with you, that's all," she commented absently. "Especially after that guy came by earlier."

April's head snapped over at the comment. "What do you mean, *came by*? What guy?" It was a stupid question meant to stall for a few additional seconds as her mind kicked into fight-or-flight mode. Someone had come *here?*

Erika was pulling her hair into a high ponytail. She met April's eyes in the mirror. "Now do you want to tell me what the hell is going on? Or do you want to keep on trying to handle whatever it is alone?"

April's eyes slid to the window as if someone would still be standing on the other side. Her mind flipped back to the black Cadillac she had seen too many times now. "Who did he ask for?"

Erika rolled her eyes and ignored the question, resuming the task with her hair.

"Erika, please. This is important."

"Is it? But not important enough to tell me."

"What do you mean? I tried to talk to you at the diner and you didn't believe me. You told me it was probably a prank or something."

"Yeah, and that was before you had random folks strolling up to your doorstep. Obviously, you didn't realize it was that serious either." She had whirled around now, anger spiking her voice. She gestured wildly to nothing in particular. "I'm the one who has always had your back, April. Always! You didn't always agree with me, but you could *never* say I wasn't there for you or that I didn't sacrifice so you could have a better life. All of this—" her arm swept the bedroom "—is because of me. I made a way for you and you have the nerve to push me out like you got all the answers."

April felt horrible. Erika had a way of doing that to her.

"So," Erika pressed, crossing her arms over her chest. "Are you going to tell me what's going on?"

"I'll tell you."

At her hesitation, Erika threw up her arms. "Is this about that whole necklace thing?"

April debated telling. Decided it was best. Maybe then she would acknowledge the severity of the situation. "Erika, I was attacked the other day."

Erika's head jerked up. "What do you mean, *attacked*?"

"I mean, I was getting some things out of storage and somebody came up and pulled a knife on me." Even now as she relayed the traumatic story, her throat clogged with the weight of the emotion. And the fear.

Erika's mouth was agape. "Why didn't you tell me this before, April?"

"I—I don't know."

"Did they find out who did it?"

"No."

Erika muttered something under her breath as she stalked to

her suitcase, dug around, and pulled a pack of cigarettes from a side zipper pocket. "I can't believe this."

April opened her mouth to request that she didn't smoke in the house, then decided to ignore it. She knew the best way to tolerate Erika was to be as conciliatory as possible. She could've sworn she saw Erika's hands shake as she cupped a hand around the tip and touched it with the flame from her lighter. Slowly, as if it were her first breath from underwater, Erika took a deep drag and exhaled, sending a wave of smoke fanning around the room.

"So now you see," April went on. "That's why I need to know who this guy was."

Erika nodded. "I didn't open the door," she admitted. "He didn't even knock. Just walked by and stood there staring at the door. I wasn't even sure if he was here for you, but then I saw his shadow in the window when he kept walking by. He must've did it like five or six times and then he would always pause at your door."

It felt like her skin was slithering with something, cold and unforgiving. She shuddered. The smothered sound of her cell phone ringing carried from her pocket. April ignored it, her mind focused on her mother's recount of the mystery visitor. "Okay, did you get a good look at him?"

Erika shook her head and cast a frown at the window. "All I saw was his shadow."

So that did absolutely nothing to help. It could be anyone. Her phone was ringing again and this time, April took it out and spared the caller ID a distracted glance. Brynn. Lord, that girl could be bothersome. But she would have to wait. Without hesitation, April powered down her phone so as not to keep being disturbed.

Her thoughts then turned to Jameson, with his enigmatic looks and his comments with its double meanings. And how he was, not surprisingly, everywhere. But something else crossed her mind then. Something she hadn't considered before. "Warren was in with some bad people," she voiced. "His clients were criminals, crime bosses, men like that."

Erika's eyebrows lifted as if she wanted to ask how April knew that. But she didn't comment.

"Do you think . . . I don't know. Could they have something to do with all of this to maybe get back at him for something?"

"I don't think so. But it can't hurt. I'll look into it. In the meantime, where are you going to be?"

April started to say *Ramsey* but stopped when she remembered she hadn't told Erika about him yet. Then, she jumped to her feet as she remembered. *Mama Edith.* "I'll be somewhere safe," she said evasively as she headed for the door. "But I got to go. Call me if you find out something."

"And April." She waited until April's eyes found hers. "Get yourself a gun."

The thought wasn't such a bad one. April left and broke out into a run back to her car. She hadn't meant to leave Mama Edith at home for so long by herself. She should probably call Brynn back and have her run by the house, just to check on her. Make up some excuse about car trouble and Tabitha having to get to class or something. She sped out of the neighborhood as she powered her phone back on.

To April's surprise, she had not only several missed calls from Brynn, but Ramsey too. There was even one from Tabitha. It felt like the life had been vacuumed out of her. She slammed a foot on the gas, watching the speedometer inch up to 80 . . . 85 . . . 90. She had to get back. Something had happened. She just knew it. Why else would they all be looking for her when she should've been home?

She couldn't bring herself to look at the text messages. Or listen to the voicemails. Not yet. Not until she had a logical explanation for her absence and then, ignoring their calls. April turned her phone on silent, tightened her hold on the steering wheel, and focused on speeding the rest of the way back to Columbus without getting pulled over by the police.

Dusk was beginning to settle as April whipped into Westmoore Oaks. She'd returned in half the time, and she just prayed that everyone was okay and it had been nothing serious. If she was lucky, it'd be another one of Brynn's surprise parties because it was the anniversary of when she'd purchased her first piece of furniture, or something stupid like that. She could only hope.

April saw the glaring red sirens spilling across the trees and her heart picked up speed. Her street was congested with police cars. Neighbors who had been blocked from their homes packed the sidewalks, all standing and waiting. For what, she didn't know.

April followed suit and pulled to the curb, where a line of cars were illegally parallel parked. A new wash of terror crept through her spine as she climbed out and made her way to the crowd.

She happened upon an elderly couple first, long coats over robes shielding them from the chilly air as they huddled together to watch from the lawn. "Excuse me," she called. "What's going on?"

"A fire, I believe," the old man said. "The ambulance just came by, so looks like someone's hurt."

April nodded and moved faster, weaving through the assembly of neighbors and trying to peer through to see where the activity was coming from. She spotted Brynn through the chaos, cradled in Jameson's arms with a blanket wrapped around her limp shoulders. As April neared, she could tell the woman was most certainly crying. No, bawling was more like it. "Brynn," she called.

Brynn lifted tearstained eyes to April before rushing over to collapse in her arms. "Erin," was all she could croak before she dissolved in another fitful of sobs. But her own panic was rising.

"What happened?"

"There was a fire," she sniffled. "Mama Edith, she—she . . ."

Brynn could only shake her head. She was hyperventilating. But April didn't need to hear anymore. The fire trucks and ambulances told her everything she needed to know. And if that wasn't enough, her house—or the plot of land where her house once stood—was now nothing but charred pieces of wood; embers of the extinguished fire rippling sparkles that split like open wounds against the sky.

Chapter Twenty-three

She felt dead. Her body had gone limp with exhaustion, but more than that she had been sitting there agonizing over what happened to Edith so much that her head hurt. How could she have been so stupid to think Edith could stay home alone, especially after what happened last time. She was riddled with guilt and she'd cried all she could. Now, fresh into the third hour of waiting in the hospital lobby, her nervousness had surpassed worry. She felt like she was having a full-blown panic attack.

Ramsey looked like he'd just risen from a stretcher in the morgue. His face was sunken with worry; all his color had left him ashen and a shell of himself. He must've paced the length of the room over a hundred times, and she could see him jostling with his own anxiety with the way his leg shook, and he'd rub the back of his neck.

Across the room, Brynn sat with her face buried in her hands. April only knew she was crying by the muffled sniffles and the slight tremble of her shoulders. To April's distress, Jameson was also there, but thankfully he'd left them alone for a while to fetch

Brynn some food from the cafeteria. No one had asked her any questions. *Yet.* Everyone was too busy worrying about Edith's outcome. She'd been inside the house when it caught fire, but no one knew the extent of the damage.

Everyone just sat wallowing in their own angst, which had an uncomfortable, nearly painful, mood settling across the lobby like an ominous cloud. As much as it pained her, April appreciated the time alone. To think. To regret. To suffer.

A patient in a wheelchair was trundled by on their way to triage. Nurse and doctor calls echoed over the loudspeaker, disrupting the otherwise empty silence. April hated hospitals. They always smelled of medicine and the halls reeked of death. Not to mention, the medical staff always seemed to have that solemn expression on their faces, like they all knew a secret that had to remain inside the desolate walls.

"Ram . . ." It was Brynn who broke the silence, her voice a hoarse whisper corroded with tears. "You should sit down."

Ramsey didn't answer, nor did he stop his pacing. She might as well have been talking to herself. April wanted to hug him, but she knew it wouldn't be received. She rubbed warmth back into her arms and felt compelled to cross the aisle to sit next to Brynn. Poor woman looked like she was about to shatter.

"How you holding up?" April asked.

Brynn sighed. "I'm just worried about her, Erin."

"I know. We all are."

Brynn steepled her fingers and rested her chin on her hands. "Ram was at the house crying, girl. I've never felt so bad in my life."

"Did they . . . did they say what happened?"

"The fire started from inside," Brynn whispered. "I heard them say in the kitchen. Ram was afraid she may have been trying to cook."

April's assumption was bad enough. But hearing the cold, hard truth was agonizing.

"I tried to call you," Brynn went on, casting her a sideways look. "Ram got the call and when he couldn't find you, he called me." She didn't press further, but her eyes were full of questions. Accusations. Everything left unsaid.

"I got caught up," April evaded, unable to hold Brynn's gaze. "Not sure why I didn't hear my phone ringing. None of this should have happened."

"You're right. You know, I couldn't find Jameson either." Brynn's comment came out slow, as if she were pondering her words before speaking them out loud. "I just hate I couldn't get in touch with either one of you. Then, he just showed up right before you got there . . ." she trailed off, letting the words hang suspended for a moment.

April wanted to tell her it was because he was probably trailing her and had been the one Erika had seen walking outside of her condo. But how could she mention that without looking even more guilty? So, she didn't say anything. And neither did Brynn.

April caught a glimpse of movement out of the corner of her eye and her head snapped up as Jameson approached with to-go containers in hand. His shadow dropped over their hovered frames, shrouding them in a veil that shaded them from the brightened hospital lights overhead.

They had opposite reactions: April slinked backwards against the plastic seat, while Brynn seemed to perk up at her boyfriend's intrusion. She was reaching for the food and drink he brought with him. "Thank you, Prez," she said with a drowsy smile. "I appreciate you. Erin, you hungry?"

Just thinking of food brought on a surge of nausea. She shook her head.

With that, Brynn rose and carted her meal over to Ramsey, who had found a seat alone in a corner of the lobby. If April didn't think it would look strange, she would've followed. Anything to get away from Jameson.

"You sure you're not hungry," he asked as soon as they were

alone. The nerve of him to act innocent. When he'd probably been the one stalking her for the past few days.

April averted her eyes. "I'm good," she mumbled.

"Suit yourself." He sat down next to her, entirely too close, their thighs nearly touching in the adjacent chairs. "But you should probably eat anyway, Erin. I'm sure you worked up an appetite doing all of that running around today." She didn't respond immediately, just watched that little smirk of his spread across his face, like a cat that had caught the canary. Then his tone turned accusatory. "You had Ramsey and Brynn worried. They were wondering why you weren't home and they couldn't get in touch with you. Just thought you should know in case you needed to come up with some kind of . . . excuse."

She was losing her patience. "What the hell do you want, Jameson?" He had the nerve to widen his eyes in mock surprise. "Don't think I haven't caught on to you."

"No, don't think I haven't caught on to *you*," he retorted. Then he lowered his voice. "If I were you, I'd be careful how you talked to me. Wouldn't want Ramsey to find out the truth of why you really left Edith alone." And with that, he winked at her and rose to his feet.

April looked over to see Ramsey looking at them with his eyes weary but narrowed in suspicion. Had he heard any of their interaction?

Her phone vibrated, snatching April's attention. She looked down and sighed at the caller ID. Now wasn't really a good time but ignoring him would prompt him to call repeatedly. She rose from her chair and padded down the hall for privacy, fully aware that Ramsey was probably still watching her.

"Hey Ian," she answered, her voice weary.

"Hey, where have you been? I've tried to call you a few times."

"I know, I just . . . it's been a rough few days." That much was true.

Ian sighed. "Yeah, I figured that when you never got back to me about the caterer and helping out with the party."

Shit. She had honestly forgotten about that. "I'm sorry."

"It's okay. We're working it out. But listen, I wanted to make sure you would be able to make it to the party."

"I . . ." April glanced around the hospital. "I can't. I'm sorry."

Ian groaned. "What do you mean, you can't, Michelle? It's your husband's birthday. And I've been telling you about it so why didn't you make arrangements?"

"I'm sorry. Something came up."

"More important than my brother's birthday, huh?" He was pissed. Understandably so. But at that point, there was nothing she could do about it. She couldn't leave Ramsey.

"Look, I'll make it up to him," April said. And then because she saw Ramsey storming toward her, she added, "I got to go. I'll call him later. Bye." She hung up before he had a chance to respond. Carter would probably be just as upset, but she really couldn't worry about that now.

Needing something to do, April turned to the vending machine against the wall and popped in a dollar bill. Her mind was running through all kinds of scenarios, but she knew there was nothing she could say to make this better.

"Who was that, Erin?" Ramsey asked as soon as he was at her side.

April blinked. She hadn't expected that question. She thought fast. "Just a friend of mine. She was calling to check in on Mama Edith."

"A friend?" It was clear he didn't believe her. "Where were you, then?"

April turned back to the vending machine. She could feel Ramsey's eyes burning a hole in the side of her face. He wasn't bothering with any kind of subtlety as he stood, blocking the hallway so she had no choice but to face him. She'd been craving some carbonation to hopefully settle her stomach. But now, as her canned drink fell from its rack in the machine, she wished for something stronger.

Ramsey waited as April took her time, stooping down to retrieve her drink from the bin.

She'd had all evening to think of the perfect lie, but now, she was afraid it didn't sound convincing. But she went with it anyway, spinning the same story she'd told Brynn. "I went to the grocery store."

"You left my mom alone, so you could go to the grocery store?"

April swallowed. "Yeah. I didn't plan on being gone long. Then I had some car trouble."

"Car trouble." He was shaking his head and she could tell he was struggling to restrain his rage. She'd seen that look before. She willed her breath to remain steady. He was quiet for a minute. Then two.

His swing had her flinching and she let loose a startled gasp. But he wasn't aiming for her. Instead, his fist rammed into the side of the vending machine with such a force it rattled all of the food and beverage items inside. He jabbed his finger in her face. "If something happens to my mom—" And he shut his mouth on the rest of the threat. Just stood there giving her this menacing stare that was so intense it set her body quivering. He wouldn't do anything to her, would he? At that moment, she really couldn't be sure.

She didn't release her breath until he whirled around and stormed off down the hall. Her legs felt like putty. April waited an extra few minutes until she was sure she could walk without needing the wall's support. She then followed him back to the lobby.

Just as she took a seat, a doctor strolled through the double doors, his footsteps brisk, his eyes compassionate. "Family of

Edith Duncan," he called. Ramsey and Brynn were the first to rush forward. April lingered behind, afraid to get too close. Afraid of what she might hear. Afraid of the reactions.

"I'm Dr. Opry. I've been working on your mother since she was brought in."

"How is she?" Ramsey's voice trembled over the words.

Dr. Opry sighed and that's when April knew. Even before he uttered any words. Even before the screams and the cries rang like alarms in her ears. She didn't realize until she had collapsed to the floor that those noises were her own.

Chapter Twenty-four

It was sickeningly beautiful. The sun shone, entirely too cheerful, through the car window as if denouncing there was a tragedy. It was perfect park weather, conducive to playgrounds and picnics and bike rides. A funeral, on such a pretty day, seemed like a mockery.

April rode in weighted silence so thick, it felt suffocating. She felt hollow. Nausea was beginning to simmer as the car carried them closer to the church. Not that it mattered, but she risked peeking over at Ramsey as he drove. Even though her vision was obstructed through the black birdcage veil, it was more than evident he was visibly distraught. He hadn't so much as spoken to her in the past week and his pain only added to the insurmountable guilt. He didn't have to say it, but he faulted her. She couldn't blame him. Hell, she faulted herself.

The tears had long since dried up, leaving in their place a heavy feeling of dread and regret at the tragedy. She'd only seen a dead body one other time, but nothing could prepare anyone for the image of death or those lingering images that clung to the recesses of your mind and spontaneously popped into view like one of those old-school View-Masters toys. And the smell—God, she would never be able to forget that stench of soot and smoke. April shut her eyes against the image, struggled to ignore the crackling that echoed in her ears. She just had to get through the day without losing her sanity.

The driver circled the car and opened the door, letting Ramsey out first. He didn't wait, nor attempt to help her from the seat, already making his way through the dense crowd of mourners peppering the sidewalk. April shielded her eyes from the bright sun as she followed him up the stairs of the church, stopping briefly to nod her appreciation for the polite condolences and hugs and handshakes.

In the lobby of the church, she paused again as Brynn materialized through the procession and glided forward to fold Ramsey in a hug. Makeup streaked her face and she clutched a soiled tissue in her hand. "Ram, I'm so incredibly sorry," she sobbed, clutching Ramsey as if she would crumble under the weight of her agony. She looked absolutely pitiful and for a moment, April had to scold herself for despising the woman displaying her theatrics. But no, Brynn seemed absolutely devastated and April couldn't be mad that she was more visibly emotional with her duress. Even if she had gotten used to masking hers really well. And, by the looks of the hug Ramsey reciprocated, he was appreciative of her sentiments. April swallowed a bubble of envy at their shared grief.

They lingered in the hug for a few extra seconds, just as April caught sight of someone out the corner of her eye. She turned, hardening at the sight of Jameson standing quietly in the crowd. He wasn't watching Brynn. He was watching *her* with intense scrutiny that had April pivoting to hide behind a few funeralgoers. What was he doing here? Okay, maybe that wasn't too far-fetched, considering he was technically Brynn's boyfriend of sorts, but he sure as hell didn't seem to be playing the best support system at the moment. Not with the deviant way he was staring, or that knowing smirk that made April uncomfortable. He was plotting. She could see that clear as day, even from across the room.

Brynn released Ramsey to tuck her arm through Jameson's and fell into step beside April. They wordlessly led the way into the sanctuary.

It was a closed casket, for obvious reasons. According to the reports April remembered, the degree of burns covering Edith's body had done extensive damage. Too disturbing for anyone else to see outside of Ramsey. But a huge picture of a smiling, younger, more vibrant Edith during happier times had been stationed on an easel in front of the casket, along with an array of flowers that reminded April of a garden. The faint instrumental of "His Eye Is on the Sparrow" wafted like a melodic hum throughout the church, punctuated with the quiet sniffles and hushed whispers as they walked up the aisle.

April took a seat in the front pew, Brynn and Jameson piling in beside her. Ramsey stopped at the altar with his head bent low. He was either crying or praying or both. He placed a hand on the glistening ivory enamel of the casket and even from her perch, April could see his knuckles white with his tight grip. She knew she probably should go up there, if only to stand beside him, give him a shoulder, a hug, some display of consolation. But she didn't know what to do, so she did nothing. Finally, Ramsey sat down on the other side of Jameson and buried his face in his hands.

April kept her eyes trained on him, even as she felt Jameson sneaking looks her way. He wasn't bothering with subtlety anymore, that much was clear, and April jockeyed between sorrow and anxiety at the heightened tension. She didn't know which was more palpable.

⇒⊶⊷⇐

"I'm so sorry this happened." Tabitha, Edith's aide, shook April's hand with a grip moist with stress. "I'm still in shock."

"I think we all are." She cast a look toward Ramsey across the church lawn, mingling politely.

"Please let me know if there is anything I can do. For you or Mr. Duncan."

April nodded, her lips pulled tight in a grim smile as the sweet medical student turned to trudge away. She wished there was something she could do as well.

"That's really sweet of you."

April whirled around, nearly stumbling back as she came face-to-face with Jameson. He was standing so close that she could see the first few beads of sweat pearling around the collar of his shirt. But still, he merely smiled at April's obvious discomfort. "For a moment, it really seems like you care."

"Of course, I care."

He scoffed. "Come on now, Lisa. You don't care about anyone but your damn self."

He still thought she was Lisa. Not April. It was an alias she'd used with him before she'd disappeared, but the fact that he was acting like he didn't know who she really was; well, that was puzzling. What kind of game was he playing?

"What do you want, Jameson?" she asked, folding her arms across her chest. "Clearly you know more than you're letting on."

"What would make you think I want something?"

"Because you need something to hold over my head," she snapped. "Otherwise, you would've told Brynn or even Ramsey what you know already. You've been following me," she added with a glare. "You tried to kill me. You're lucky I don't go to the police."

Jameson chuckled. "The police? You wouldn't do that because you would be in a lot more trouble than you could stand."

"You admit it was you?"

"If someone is trying to kill you, I'm sure you deserve it for all the shit you've been doing." To her surprise, Jameson grabbed April's arm to steer her further away from the clusters of people.

She didn't want to make a scene, not at Ramsey's mother's funeral, so April plastered on her best smile and fell into step beside him. She didn't need to draw any unnecessary attention.

As soon as they were out of earshot, she snatched from his grasp. "You may think you have some kind of control over me, but you don't." She stepped closer to meet his menacing stare. "You don't scare me, Jameson. It's your word against mine."

"Oh, is it? Because I have proof."

"Of what?"

"That you're clearly not who you say you are." He leaned closer, his breath just a whisper in her ear. "And you're going to pay for everything you took from me."

April's legs felt like putty as she took a step backwards, her heels sinking into the moist soil. "Look, I didn't take your money—"

"This is not just about money. I want you to admit to Ramsey and Brynn who you really are."

She paused, her lips quivering over the words. "And if I don't?"

"Then I will." He was past serious. She could hear the restrained hatred in each word. He wanted to not just hurt her. He wanted to destroy her. As if to prove his point, his eyes dropped to April's stomach and her throat constricted as she watched the awareness wash over his face. "By the way, what happened to the baby?"

A surge of panic stung April's body. How did he know? How could he possibly know? Muted terror subdued her movements, even as footsteps stomped across the gravel walkway, sounding like gunshots. They were approaching fast. April put distance between them, not caring how suspicious it appeared. The look on Ramsey's face told her he was borderline angry. No, perhaps downright pissed. She couldn't be sure why. Had he heard what was going on?

"Is this it, Erin?" A crowd had followed him and were now gathering in a circle.

"Ramsey, what—"

"Is this why you snuck off and left my mom alone? For him?" He bit off each venomous word as his head swiveled between her and Jameson.

April was stunned speechless. He had it wrong, so very wrong. She watched in horror as Ramsey turned on Jameson, getting so close in his face that she could see the spittle flying from his lips. He jammed a finger in Jameson's chest. "Don't think I didn't see all the sneaky looks you've been giving my wife."

To Ramsey's outrage, Jameson laughed. Loud. "Your wife? I think you need to have a little talk with your *wife*."

"No, I need to talk to you. I saw how you two were meeting during the double date. Couldn't keep your eyes off of her during my mama's funeral!"

April inserted herself between the jostling bodies, both feeling like they were closing in on her. She struggled to break them apart. "Ramsey, please! This isn't what you think!"

"Oh, it's exactly what I think."

"Ram!" It was Brynn this time, her pleas deafening as she pulled desperately on Ramsey's arm. "Stop it, please!"

They were nearly nose to nose. April didn't know who exactly threw the first punch. All she knew was that she heard a scream, maybe hers, maybe Brynn's, as both men flung themselves to the ground in a flurry of jabs and punches. Someone from the crowd tried, in vain, to pull them off of each other. Someone else had pulled out a cell phone and was recording the chaos. Still, a crescendo of shouts and cries and pleas lifted above their grunts and curses.

Finally, several burly men, who April had never seen, managed to pry the fight apart. Ramsey was out of breath, his black suit ripped and disheveled. Jameson's face was flushed and he was massaging an obviously injured hand. Someone was bleeding. April didn't know who, but she spotted the crimson blood flecked across the gravel.

"What is wrong with you?" It was an elderly woman with a cane who piped up with a voice too strong for her feeble frame. Edith's best friend, Maggie, April remembered from the eulogy. She stood now with eyes in slits and a scowl etched on her face. She popped Ramsey's arm. "Boy, don't you know your mama is rolling over in her grave right now?"

Ramsey either didn't hear or didn't care to acknowledge the reprimand. He kept enraged eyes narrowed on Jameson. "Stay the fuck away from my wife," he muttered.

Jameson inhaled sharply. "You don't even know your wife," he retorted. "If you did, you damn sure wouldn't be fighting over her." And with that, he turned, gave April a prolonged stare, and then stalked off across the lawn with Brynn on his heels.

April couldn't bring herself to look in Ramsey's direction, but she could feel his and everyone else's gaze on her, watching. Wondering.

Chapter Twenty-five

Before

It didn't surprise April to turn over and see that Warren wasn't in the bed. He had started spending more and more time in Erika's room, which was perfectly fine with her. Anything where she didn't have to sleep with him.

April crept down the grand staircase, her hands gliding on the banister to guide her steps in the darkened area. Her only source of light was a glimmer of moonlight peeking through the skylight. Well, that and her memory. She knew which floorboards creaked, which doors squeaked, and which blind spots kept her concealed from the countless surveillance cameras that swept the expansive estate. The home was absolutely majestic and under any other circumstances, April would have relished in the amenities; the maid service, infinity pool, movie theater, gourmet kitchen, and huge bedrooms with carpets that felt like velour. But the gorgeous amenities were nothing more than a reminder of her captivity.

April tiptoed across the glistening hardwood floor, keeping her ears perked for any type of noise. But the house was dead silent, as if it too were sleeping at the early morning hour. She blended easily into the dark as she scaled the back wall out of the camera's lens. She knew she had to hurry. Because as much as he wanted Erika physically, he claimed his heart was with April. Which meant he would be back upstairs in a few hours because he hated not waking up next to her.

Which was why that despite her gut telling her she probably shouldn't, she was tiptoeing downstairs to Warren's office. She knew the quicker she siphoned enough money, the quicker she and Erika could leave. It had been hard trying to steal from Warren because he was smart and kept everything under a closely guarded eye. It wasn't until Erika began to flirt that he began to let up on April, clearly distracted by Erika. They just needed a little bit more money and they could leave. Erika already had their game plan in motion so as soon as she gave the go-ahead, they would walk out of the door with the clothes on their backs and hundreds of thousands in their account, never looking back. April couldn't wait for that day.

Warren's office spanned the entire finished basement. He'd chosen an industrial theme, with exposed brick walls and ceiling beams to create a raw, rustic aesthetic. It certainly suited him. He'd accented the minimalistic space with functional pieces and splashes of black and military green.

April passed a bathroom first, then entered an open space with plenty of seating and bookshelves. A coffee table with a stack of magazines was positioned beside an L-shaped sectional and a mounted TV dominated one whole wall, with a bar off to one side. French doors to the right led into what looked like a conference room. Those same French doors were mirrored to the left and that's where April headed.

He'd decorated his personal office in all black; sleek, dark and sophisticated. A huge desk dominated the room with two chevron chairs situated in front. Behind the desk, floating shelves carried the only personal items she'd seen so far in the basement, a glass balance scale of justice paperweight and some architectural pieces serving as bookends for some law books. The room carried his scent, a musky vanilla that April had grown to recognize. And hate.

Expertly, April stepped over the threshold and shifted to the side to keep the automatic sensors from detecting her entry. She paused, her back pressed against the wall. Waiting. Sure enough, it remained dark. She relaxed into a smile. It had taken her a few times to perfect the little trick and sometimes, she wasn't quick enough to keep the recess lighting from automatically lifting. Not that it mattered too much because there were no cameras in the basement, for the privacy of his clients and partners. And himself, she had deduced. But it still didn't stop her panic from rising if those lights came on. She preferred to avoid them altogether. It was better to work in stealth mode.

Quickly, she rounded the large desk and kneeled to the drawers. There were three, with the bottom being the largest. She dug in the pocket of her shorts and her fingers wrapped around the small piece of metal. Eager, she pulled the stolen key into view. She moved quicker now. It wouldn't be too long before Warren returned to the bedroom, and she still had to put the key back in its place and get into bed before he noticed she was missing. April inserted the key into the lock and turned, the resounding *click* like music to her ears. She tugged on the drawer and it slid open with ease, revealing a lockbox.

April was pulling out the lockbox, quietly, carefully, when something faint had her freezing. Her head was pounding as she strained to hear any type of movement. Nothing. She risked peeking over the desk, squinting through the darkness. But all was still. She lowered her head and popped the key into the lockbox to lift the lid.

Warren usually kept about $100,000 in this little safe. April took her time, meticulously peeling off hundred-dollar bills until she counted $2,500. She usually varied her amounts, sometimes $500, sometimes $1,000. Never more than $5,000. Any more than that and she was afraid he would get too suspicious.

The lights rose and the sudden illumination had April shutting her eyes against the brightness, even as fear vaulted into her chest.

"What the hell are you doing?"

April squinted against the harsh light. Warren stood at the door, his face horror-stricken, rage reddening his face to a crimson hue that had the veins bulging from his forehead. *Oh my God.*

Her chest rattled with heavy, panicked breaths as he took a step into the office. She noticed his hands balled into fists at his side. And judging by the almost demonic look in his eye, she would never forget this night.

April shrunk back in fear and began scooting to the corner to put some distance between them. She opened her mouth, but the words caught in her throat—she couldn't breathe or speak. Or scream.

Chapter Twenty-six

Hey, can we meet?

April read and reread those four words with an apprehensive breath. The text had come as a surprise, considering she was expecting to have heard from Ramsey after the funeral showdown. But to open the message and see that Brynn was the sender . . . well, she was still trying to decide how to feel about that. Not that Brynn didn't have reason to demand an explanation. She did watch her boyfriend fight her friend's husband. April had been so caught up in the embarrassment she hadn't even stopped to think how bad it had looked from Brynn's perspective. Everyone had left in such a hurry afterwards, so now after reading the text for the fifth time, April realized she really didn't know how Brynn was feeling. Was she as pissed as Ramsey? Was she trying to blindside so April would walk into an ass-kicking of her own? Could she really be mad at the karma?

April took a bottled water out of the refrigerator and rested a hip on the counter with a pensive stare. She knew she needed to leave for good. It was probably wrong, but since their house was gone and Ramsey wasn't speaking to her, there wasn't any reason to stay.

April swallowed a swell of guilt as she deleted the message and hesitated only briefly before blocking Brynn's number altogether. It was best to get out while she still could. She didn't owe anyone an explanation. Especially Brynn.

This was the part that she had become desensitized to. Having to leave the life she'd made for herself and forget the what-ifs. Ignore the nagging guilt and distract herself from wondering what ever happened in the aftermath of her disappearance.

"It's easy to have more than one life. You just have to know how to balance them." Erika's words came back to haunt her like a twisted lullaby. Part of the balancing act, April knew from experience, was leaving the past where it was and remaining focused on the task at hand. For her, that was now Carter and only Carter. Erin Duncan was as gone as Mama Edith at this point.

April willed herself not to look at her phone again and instead, crossed into the hotel bedroom. The suite felt even bigger and even more lonely, since Ramsey no longer shared it with her. Hell, if she could be honest, it wasn't much better when he was there, and the tension was so thick it had been smothering her. When he didn't come back to their room after the funeral, and the night crept to morning with still no sign of him, April was appreciative for the break. That had been her cue to sever ties. She would have to be more careful next time. April shuddered at the thought. She wanted to say *if* there was a next time, but she honestly couldn't be sure where things were settling right now. After Ramsey, then Carter, what was next? *Who* was next? The uncertainty was scaring her. What she needed now was a strategy.

Her cell rang and April snatched it up from the bed. She frowned when she saw the unknown number and promptly swiped the screen to reject the call. Not even a few seconds later, the hotel phone's shrill ring echoed in the quiet room and had

April freezing. Who the hell could be calling her at the hotel? Other than Ramsey, who else knew she was even here?

April sat on the edge of the bed. The mattress sank under her weight as she tentatively lifted the phone to her ear. "Hello?"

"Hi, Ms. Duncan?" The man's voice was crisp and professional.

April hesitated. "Yes," she answered.

"I apologize for disturbing you. This is the front desk. Just letting you know that you have a visitor."

April's heart skipped a beat. "I don't know who the visitor is," she stammered. "But I'm not expecting anyone."

"Would you like me to ask his name?"

His?

She shifted uneasily. "Is it my husband?"

There was a muffled sound and some inaudible dialogue that had her straining to hear. Then the representative came back on the phone. "No, this isn't your husband. He says he's an old friend."

Jameson, maybe? Someone else? April's grip tightened on the receiver. "Please tell him I'm not accepting visitors. Thank you." She slammed the phone back in its cradle. She wasn't exactly sure who was waiting downstairs, but the chances of them looking for Erin Duncan were slim. Which meant they were looking for April. The *real* April. A chilling thought crossed her mind. What if it was her attacker? Had he somehow tracked her down?

April picked up her phone and dialed Ramsey's number. She still didn't know where he was, but she knew she would feel much safer if he were around. She shouldn't have been surprised when her call went straight to voicemail. She cursed under her breath, snatching the device from her ear. *Now what?* It was taking everything in her not to call Erika. She didn't want that woman involved because it would be yet another thing for her to hold over her head. She quickly grabbed her purse and started for the door.

The front desk had rung her room, so whoever it was could possibly know exactly where she was. She needed to get to safety.

April was only on the third floor, so she opted to take the stairs down to the lobby instead of the elevator. The stairwell was off to one side, so it would give a clear view of the front desk in case her "visitor" was still waiting. Plus, she could exit without being seen.

The lobby was just as elegant as the rest of the hotel, which could account for the high sticker price and the two-night minimum requirement. The floor was tiled in diagonal marble sheets of rich cream and burgundy. An elaborate chandelier embellished with Venetian crystal and black diamonds dominated the domed ceiling, casting an array of glittering twinkles on the numerous patrons below. People were either scattered on the embroidered silk sofas, wheeling luggage through the revolving doors, or clustered against the amber-colored wooden front desk with the etched clear-glass waterfall display cascading behind the attendants.

April pushed out of the stairwell and stood briefly against the wall, taking in the scene. Though she wasn't sure whom she should be looking for, she scanned the crowd for anyone who looked suspect. Satisfied when she saw no one, April tried to appear as casual as possible as she started toward the front door.

"Erin."

April ignored the voice, keeping her head down and quickening her pace. She just had to get to her car, then she could—

The sudden hand on her forearm had her snatching backwards with a jolt, nearly colliding with another patron in the lobby. Brynn looked just as shocked at the reaction, but kept her grip firmly on April's arm, as if she were afraid the woman may run away.

"Erin, you didn't hear me calling?" she asked, knitting her eyebrows together.

April collected herself with a smile to hide her discomfort. "Sorry, my head was elsewhere."

"I understand." Now, Brynn did let go and shoved her hands in the pockets of her denim jacket.

She looked like death, April noticed immediately, taking in Brynn's sunken appearance and oversized clothes. A far cry from the woman she'd gotten used to with the bright eyes and sunny disposition. No, this Brynn looked like she was on the verge of passing out any second. Her eyes were swollen and even her skin looked ashen with the weight of her grief. She didn't appear angry. Just . . . empty.

"Brynn, what are you doing here?"

Brynn shifted, readjusting the strap on her purse. "I . . . came to check on you and Ram. No one was answering my calls, so I thought . . ." She trailed off, like she'd lost the willpower to justify her visit. Her shoulders sagged and when she looked back to April, her eyes were glassy. "Listen, can we talk?"

"I was kind of on my way out."

"It won't take long," Brynn insisted, taking a desperate step closer. "I just know everyone was upset about what happened yesterday and I just feel so confused . . ." Again, she quieted down and tossed up her hands helplessly. "Is Ram around?" Her head whipped around, as if she expected to see him among the lobby guests.

April debated telling Brynn the truth, that she hadn't seen him and nor had she heard from him. "No, he stepped out," she decided, simply.

Brynn nodded her understanding. "Yeah, I get that. Can we go have a drink at the bar?"

She probably should've said no. It would've been less complicated. But April found herself following Brynn.

Windows adorned one whole wall of the adjoining restaurant with morning light intruding through the sheer curtains. An assortment of breakfast was being served in a buffet-style procession with the sweet smell of maple and fresh-steamed coffee suffusing the air.

Brynn bypassed the line and took a seat at one of the two-seater tables. She looked anxious, April noted, as she slid into the chair across from her. The way she was fidgeting and brushing invisible lint from the white tablecloth, it was obvious she had everything and nothing to say.

A waitress wandered over with a pitcher of iced water and two glasses. "Can I get you any coffee or juice?" She asked, her words nearly lost in the thick Hispanic accent.

Though she was desperately craving some, April shook her head. "No thanks."

"Coffee for me," Brynn said. "No cream or sugar."

The waitress nodded and threaded back through the tables toward the kitchen.

"How are you feeling?" Brynn started.

What did she want her to say? Scared. Paranoid. Ashamed. Guilty. April took her time answering, making sure to keep her expression calm. It seemed like Brynn needed that more than she did. "I'm worried, honestly," she admitted, which wasn't far from the truth. "About Ramsey. I know this is such a tragic loss for him."

"Yeah, yesterday was just awful." Brynn cast a dejected look toward the window. "It's just a lot to deal with."

"It is."

The waitress returned and set a steaming mug of coffee between them. "You can go to the bar," she offered, gesturing to the buffet.

April nodded her acknowledgement. When the woman left once more, she watched Brynn's fingers fold around the handle of the mug, clutching it like an anchor. But still, she didn't drink. Just stared into the black liquid as if it had the strength she needed.

Heat rose to color her face as she met April's gaze through the steam. "I tried calling Ram, but he didn't answer," she spoke again. "I know you both are dealing with a lot right now, but I wanted you to know that if you needed a place to stay, my home is always open."

"Thank you. We appreciate that."

"Have you . . ." An agonizing pause. "Have you talked to Prez?"

There it was. The cushion on the chair suddenly felt like concrete and April shifted and cleared her throat. "No, I haven't."

"Just seemed like you two would've spoken after yesterday." She was no longer gripping the handle. Now, she was tapping her fingers on the side of the mug, her nails making a metronomic clicking noise as it hit the porcelain. She was waiting. If she were still nervous, she was no longer showing it.

April's face remained neutral. Innocent. She knew not to give anything away. "Nope. Haven't talked to him."

"That was crazy, huh? That fight, I mean. "

"It was."

"I don't even know what they were fighting about. Do you?" Pause. *Click, click, click.*

"No."

Skepticism washed over Brynn's face. She didn't even try to hide it. "Did you know Prez? Before?"

April didn't miss a beat. "No. Maybe in passing or something."

"In passing," she mused. "Just seems weird. He was acting like he knew you.

"Perhaps you should talk to him about it."

"I would, but strangest thing. He's not answering my calls either." When her eyes flickered to the ceiling, April caught the insinuation. Did she really think Jameson was there at the hotel? With her?

"Look, Brynn. I am just as confused as you." She didn't know why she felt the need to pacify Brynn, but she did anyway. If only to leave the woman with some sort of peace. "I don't want Jameson. At all. I couldn't do that to you."

Brynn stared. Just when April wasn't sure what she was about to do or whether she believed her or not, Brynn's shoulders went slack and her face fell. "Oh my God, I'm so sorry, Erin." Her hand shot out across the table to grab April's apologetically. "What am I thinking? Of course, I know you wouldn't do that. I think Mama Edith's death has just gotten to me so I'm thinking crazy. I know you wouldn't do anything to hurt me or Ramsey."

April grimaced and watched her blow on her coffee before taking a generous sip. "Prez was supposed to come by before he left town but . . ." she shrugged. "Oh well. I guess it wasn't meant to be with him anyway. I really didn't like how he acted at the funeral anyway." April could see she was struggling to appear nonchalant. But it was obvious Jameson's behavior was upsetting her. Finally, Brynn unfolded herself from the chair and rose. "I guess I'll let you go then. Want to come by the house later? You can crash with me instead of the hotel."

April's smile bloomed as the lie fell from her lips. "Sounds great. I'll call you."

Brynn's hug was tight, desperate even, and April almost regretted letting her go. Aside from her little neighborhood acquaintances, she couldn't even be sure Brynn had any real friends. When she pulled away, putting distance between them, the sudden void hung like a stale blanket in the air. April watched her leave and she couldn't help the subsequent envelope of sadness. It wasn't like she had any real friends either. In a distorted sort of way, the loss was mutual.

Chapter Twenty-seven

The gun felt surprisingly light.

April's hand was taut on the grip, twisting her wrist to observe the firearm from all sides. It was compact, just what she needed. And the sleek, purple metal made it feel more personable. Like it was tailor-made just for her.

She expected the gun to feel intimidating. Maybe even scary. But April was surprisingly calm. No, *empowered* was the right word. The thought of having this within reach when she had been assaulted dispelled all traces of anxiety she'd had about that situation. Why hadn't she purchased one of these sooner?

"So?" Molly, the store associate with spiky, jet-black hair and bulky metallic jewelry, popped her gum as she leaned tattoo-covered arms on the glass encasement. "What do you think of this one?"

"I . . ." April closed her eyes and imagined pulling the trigger. It was only for protection, she forced herself to remember. And she needed plenty of that. But something about the possibility of having to use it, had a surge of adrenaline coursing through her fingertips.

"You can try it out if you want. We have a range in the back."
Molly gave her gum another excited *pop* as she gestured toward
the back of the building. April couldn't tell what was twinkling
more: Molly's eyes or the numerous piercings puncturing her
face. It was like the eager employee couldn't wait to put a weapon
in another person's hands, whether it be an assailant or a victim.

April nodded. "Yes, let's try it out."

Molly pulled a waiver form from the drawer and slid it across
the counter. "I'm just going to need some ID," she said.

April hesitated only briefly before digging in her purse for her
wallet, all the while thinking if she wanted to purchase the
weapon in her real name. It was better not to. Not with her true
identity floating around for the world to see. April grabbed her
Michelle Evans driver's license and handed it over. If Carter
found out . . . well, it wouldn't even matter. She would have disappeared by then.

Molly began removing items from the shelves behind her, am-
munition, eye goggles, and earmuffs. She was rambling on about
proper range safety and etiquette as she stuffed the rental supplies
in a duffle bag monogrammed with the store's name, Girls Just
Wanna Have Guns. "You ever did this before?" she asked with a
raised eyebrow.

"No, not really."

Molly grinned. "Great. This will be fun then. Let's go." She motioned for April to follow her toward a door in the back of the store.

The ricochet of gunshots was nearly deafening as Molly led her
to lane four. It was a somewhat narrow booth, with just enough
space for the two of them to stand between the two panes of bullet-
proof glass. Directly in front was a bench as well as a target hooked
to an automatic rail that slid back and forth downrange.

Molly set the bag on the bench and began unpacking the firearm, checking the magazine and chamber with the ease of a woman
completely comfortable with weapons. Her hands moved quickly,
but she made sure to speak carefully so April wouldn't miss the

importance of her briefing. April watched her, soaking up the information like a sponge. Whether it came in handy or not, she planned on being prepared.

With everything loaded and ready and April in her safety gear, Molly guided her into the proper stance, then pushed the button to send the target gliding down the lane.

April's finger trembled on the trigger, as she squinted through the foggy goggles. The target, a human silhouette with markings to indicate zones and bull's-eyes, seemed to be taunting her. She blew a breath, forced her eyes to remain open, and discharged.

She gasped as she nearly catapulted backwards under the force of the shot. Her arms tingled, her hands were sweaty, but she had to admit, the release felt good. Too good. She didn't even know if she hit the target.

Energized, April stepped back into position, doing her best to duplicate Molly's instructions. Then she fired again. And again. She fired until she heard the click of the empty magazine, and she knew she needed to reload.

"You got the hang of that quick, huh?" Molly chuckled as she helped April put the weapon in a safe spot.

"Did I hit the target?"

"Let's see."

Molly pushed the button to bring the target flying back toward them on the overhead rail. Now with the paper up close, April could see it was riddled with bullet holes, most of them shockingly close to the center.

"Damn, girl. I would hate to be the person you were thinking about."

Pride had April grinning. She tossed a glance to the duffle bag. "How many rounds you got in there?"

———◆———

She should've known something was wrong. It was entirely too dark and too quiet. April sat up in the bed, her eyes struggling to make out the silhouettes of the furniture in the bedroom. The ceiling fan hummed and caused a light breeze to tickle her arms and the back of her neck. On a sigh, April ran her hand through her short crop of spiked hair. The sheets pooled at her waist did nothing to warm her skin, which was exposed by the tank top and cheerleader shorts of her pajamas. Her eyes landed on the bathroom door of the master ensuite. It was dark, but she could see the glint of the mirror from the crack. April frowned. Why was the door cracked? Hadn't she closed it the night before?

April tossed a hesitant leg over the side of the bed and rose to her feet, all the while keeping her eyes trained on the door. Her quiet steps were muffled against the carpet as she made her way toward the bathroom. She hesitated at the door, her hand on the knob, before giving it a slight nudge.

The door swung open, revealing the darkened bathroom: the double vanity sinks, the jetted tub, the half-enclosed walk-in shower with brown marble–tiled wall . . . nothing seemed out of place. Her peripheral vision caught a shadow of a movement, and April's head whipped around to the mirror. Her own reflection stood frozen in place, her chest heaving with the first few prickles of fear. She didn't know what she was expecting, but April's hand gravitated toward the light switch.

A flick of her wrist and light from the four fluorescent bulbs hanging over the mirror spilled out. She blinked, waiting for her eyes to adjust to the brightness.

"I always did like the lights on."

April heard the voice and her eyes ballooned as she met his in the mirror. The faceless figure stood directly behind her; his large frame so close that she could feel the hot breath stinging the back of her neck. He was dressed in black, and what looked like blood was streaming from under a baseball cap and down his cheek. His lips peeled back into a sinister grin as he lifted his hand into view. April's breath caught in her throat as she felt the barrel of the gun crush her skull.

"Your turn, sweetheart," he said and his finger snapped back to pull the trigger.

April's scream erupted and snatched her from the nightmare. She yanked her body up from the sofa, tumbling onto the carpet with the force of her abrupt movements. Pain immediately seared her arms as she hit the ground. But at least she was alive. At least it wasn't real. April lifted her hand to her head. It was as if she still felt the barrel of the gun. Still felt the explosion of the bullet as it shattered her skull. Still felt the hole in her head and the warm blood as it mixed to stain her hair. But there was nothing. She sighed, either in relief or with the remnants of fear, and climbed to her feet.

She didn't even realize she had been sleepwalking again. She had gone to sleep snuggled in bed but had somehow made it out to the sofa. A strong feeling of uneasiness had settled in her, and it was taking all of her energy just to deal with the insomnia. Then, when she finally did fall asleep, her patterns were sporadic, and now the nightmares and sleepwalking had become more and more frequent. And the fact that she was dreaming about *him* all of a sudden was chilling.

She needed to do something productive. April threw on a sweatsuit and went downstairs to her car.

They were right where she left them. April peered into the trunk with slight apprehension as she stared at the two boxes she'd packed from her storage unit. A brief flashback of the assault had April's vision blurring. She braced against her car, momentarily losing her breath. Then slowly, the nauseous feeling subsided and April took her time hoisting the boxes into her arms. She shifted to rest them on her hip and pushed the button to close her trunk. She wouldn't go through them, she promised herself as she carried them up the stairs to her condo. She just needed them out of the way.

In the morning, she was planning to abandon her car—well, *Erin's* car—in a parking lot somewhere, catch a rideshare to the airport, and have Carter pick her up. But tonight, she would relax and spend the evening erasing Erin Duncan from the face of the earth. For good. That meant cleaning the car of everything and leaving no trace of herself behind.

April dropped the boxes in the middle of the living room while double- and triple-checking that her front door was locked. So far, she hadn't had any other scares with break-ins or burglar alarms, but she knew she could never be too careful. As soon as she wrapped things up with Carter, she planned to abandon the condo as well. Maybe move out to the west. Somewhere she could start over entirely without the risk of her past catching up with her. She and Erika had run the gamut up and down the East Coast anyway. It was time for a fresh start. Well overdue.

She reentered the living room and stared down at the two boxes with a frown. One of them she knew was her box of stuffed animals. The other she'd marked simply with a scribble on the side: *W*. Warren's stuff that she managed to salvage. She couldn't even be sure why she had taken the little trinkets. Maybe because part of her felt it contained sentimental value for him, so it contained stuff she could use as leverage should anyone ever try to come for her. Thankfully, she hadn't been given the opportunity to use any of it.

April's cell phone sat charging on the kitchen counter. She scooped it up to send Carter a quick message: **Hey, babe. My flight arrives around noon. Will you still be able to pick me up? If not, I can catch a ride home.**

His three-word answer popped up within minutes: **I got you.** That was it. She could feel his attitude through the phone as clear as if he had been standing right beside her. He was still pissed about the birthday party thing. April's thumbs hovered over the digital keyboard to type a response, excuse, or something to soothe him, but she rolled her eyes.

She couldn't say she didn't understand his anger, but what did he actually expect her to do? Miss the funeral? She knew there would come a time when she would have to make a decision between lives, and she figured neither choice would be necessarily the "right" one. She would have to go back to Carter and do damage control as best she could. At least appease him enough to buy herself some time. A week longer. Maybe two. That was all she needed.

April put her phone down without replying to him and opened her laptop instead to check her accounts. She'd been more meticulous about confirming and reconfirming her funds as of late. Ever since she realized someone had managed to hack into one to steal some. She had long since decided the stolen money was a lost cause (it was easier not having to deal with logistics of claiming fraud). After changing passcodes and usernames, then opening other accounts to transfer the money so new account numbers were listed, it was the best she could do given the circumstances.

April went into the second bedroom to paint. This was an idea she had gotten from Ramsey, setting up a makeshift studio in this room. She had several paintings and sketches already completed and they had been set to the side, exposing her raw talent.

She added detailed brushstrokes to her picture and sat back with a heavy sigh. She was nowhere near an expert, but she was passionate about the craft, and it showed. This one was a rough outline of a woman, the background glossed with lurid hues of orange and red. Flames. A single tear trailed down April's cheek before she realized she was crying. She hadn't meant this to be symbolic of Mama Edith, but her art was her heart. Ramsey once told her it was like bleeding onto the canvas. She now saw what he meant. It probably didn't help that her room contributed to her sullen mood.

She'd never bothered to fix it up. When she had moved in, she had merely discarded her stuff in here for a few weeks before pushing everything aside to make room for some beginner paint sets. A gray table burdened by sketches and papers dominated the room, encompassed by brown moving boxes containing blank canvases she'd yet to put up. Shelves lined the walls containing her paints, brushes, cups, pencils, pens, and other art supplies. Along another wall was a sterling silver sink stained with old paint, embedded in a countertop the color of a faded peach. No, it was nothing like Ramsey's had been, nor was any of her artwork as beautiful or as fluid as his, but it was her outlet, and something she could be proud of.

The ache in her heart wouldn't let her finish the picture of Mama Edith. April abandoned it on the easel and headed back to the kitchen. She made herself a bowl of cereal and sat eating at the bar as the boxes, once again, caught her attention. She probably shouldn't open them. Too many memories. Too much she'd tried to forget that would only spiral her back into a dark place.

Ignoring her better judgement, April left her bowl on the counter and sat down cross-legged on the floor. This time, she pulled the W-marked box toward her and snatched the flaps open. Dust wafted up to clog in her nose and she sneezed, fanning the particles with a wave of her hand. The air felt stale inside. She hadn't gone through the items. It had been Erika who had brought the box to her a few days after the incident, instructing her to put it somewhere for safekeeping. "What is it?" she'd inquired.

"Just some of Warren's stuff," she said. "Didn't want to leave anything to chance if they ever find him."

Erika hadn't offered more of an explanation and April hadn't asked. It was better to not know.

T-shirts had been thrown on top. April knew Warren's scent was still in the fibers. Vanilla cigars. The man had loved them like the air he breathed. April reached in and nudged the garments to the side. Warren loved to read, so there were a few books with tattered covers also thrown in. Stephen King. He was a huge horror buff.

Absently, April flipped through the worn pages of *Carrie*, startled when one of the pages fluttered from the spine to rest in her lap. She reached down to tuck the page back in the book, frowning when she noticed what it was. Not a book page. A picture. Perhaps burrowed in the book as a placeholder or bookmark. But it was the image that had April's eyes ballooning. Warren looked to be in his thirties in this picture. Those same eyes boring into hers through the lens and sending a prickle of fear up her spine.

He was dressed in a formal, monochromatic look with his ivory tuxedo and matching bow tie. Even though it was slightly blurred, she could tell the background had all the trimmings for a wedding decor that she didn't recognize. Most certainly not hers. But what was even more shocking were the men standing around him in formal black tuxedos with their arms draped protectively around each other's shoulders. One man stood out from the rest. Jameson.

April dropped the picture as if it burned and it fell face down on the rug. That's when she saw the inscription on the back that tightened around her throat and ignited her brain's panic sensors: *Warren and groomsmen from left to right: Paul—best friend, Marcus—friend, Liam—brother, and Jameson—nephew.*

Chapter Twenty-eight

April walked into the nail salon and was met with a blast of cool air and the smell of nail polish remover. Erika was already situated at a pedicure station with her feet soaking in the bowl. April bypassed the wall of polishes and made her way to the adjacent chair.

"You want a pedicure too?" the technician asked and April shook her head.

"No, thanks. Not today."

The technician nodded and eased onto a tiny stool to get to work on her client's toenails.

Erika shook her head as April sat down and placed her purse on her lap. "You really should do something for yourself," she said with a smirk. "You've been so tense lately."

"I don't have time. I need to talk to you."

Erika gestured vaguely to the salon. "Okay, that's why I told you to meet me up here. What is it?"

April paused, glancing around at the scant patrons. Everyone appeared to be immersed in their cell phones or getting their services. The technicians spoke in hushed whispers in their native tongue. A comedy movie played on a TV mounted to the wall. No one seemed to be paying any attention to her. She shifted closer in her seat, the uncomfortable plastic biting into the back of her thighs. "Was Warren married?"

If Erika was surprised at the mention of him, she didn't show it. "Of course," she said absently. "To you."

"No, not to me. To someone else."

"How would I know?"

But her nonchalant demeanor told April everything she needed to know. Warren had been married. And Erika knew about it. She tucked that revelation away for the moment. They would most certainly revisit that.

"I found a picture of him with his nephew," she went on. "Jameson. Did you know about him?"

Irritation laced Erika's voice as she rolled her eyes. "What's with the sudden interest in him all of a sudden?"

The technician finished Erika's toes, black with white tips, and lifted Erika's feet in the air for her to see. "You like?"

Erika nodded her approval. She didn't so much as part her lips for a "thank you."

The technician helped her into a pair of paper-thin flip-flops and stuffed Erika's red-bottom heels into a grocery bag for her to carry with her. Of course, she would wear luxury stilettos to a nail salon. She climbed from the massage chair and did a shuffle-type waddle to the front of the salon with April following close behind. She knew something. She was too quiet and not as readily dismissive of April's allegation, which only heightened her dread.

Erika didn't speak again until after she'd paid with a credit card, Hilary Teague by the name etched on the plastic, and they were outside in the afternoon sun. "Where did all of this come from?"

April had known she would ask, so she was already snatching the picture from her pocket and shoving it in her face.

Her mother's eyes narrowed at the picture and one arched eyebrow vaulted above the other. "Shit," she mumbled and fished in her purse for a cigarette.

"What is it?"

"Yeah, that's his nephew all right." Erika lit the stick and blew smoke into the air.

April felt like she'd been punched in the chest. "Why didn't you tell me?"

"To be fair, I didn't realize it was the same guy you were dating until after y'all broke up," she said. "Okay Warren was his uncle. What difference does it make?"

"I think he's been stalking me."

"Who? Warren?" She chuckled. "I seriously doubt that."

"No, not him. Jameson."

That had Erika's head whipping around. "What?"

Flustered, April pinched the bridge of her nose and took a steadying breath. "He's dating a girl I know, but I think he's using her to get to me. He found out who I really was. What I did to his uncle."

Erika was taking urgent drags on her cigarette now as she spoke. "Okay, okay, um . . . shit. Okay. Are you sure it's him?"

"I'm sure." April said, wrapping her arms around her waist. "I was at a funeral and he basically admitted it to me. All this time, I figured it was because I stole some money from him. When really it was because of Warren."

"What the hell does he want? Money?"

April shook her head. She wished it were that easy. "He wants me to confess to . . . everything."

"Well, he can forget that." Erika tossed the stub to the ground and extinguished it with the bottom of her flip-flop. "Here's what we're going to do. We're going to disappear together."

"I can't. Not yet." She paused, debating if she wanted to reveal the next part. "He . . . stole some money from me."

"Dammit, girl." Now Erika was pissed. "What have I told you about stashing your money properly?"

"I didn't think he would have access. So now I just have to stay with Carter for a couple weeks to get myself situated."

Erika nodded, her mind working through the pieces. "Okay,

good. Yes. That works. Get some more out of him to get yourself secured."

"And what about Jameson?"

Erika tapped her acrylic nail against her chin in consideration. "I know somebody who can track him down. Get some answers. See what his price is to make all of this go away."

"Do you think he knows about what happened to Warren?"

"No, he can't. It was an accident." She shook her head as if to affirm her assumption. "Look," she stared April in the eye. "Don't be worried. I got you now, okay? You know we always have each other's back and this ain't no different. I'll take care of it." She held her pinky in April's direction, just like they used to do. Appreciative, April locked their fingers. "Where are you keeping all of your stuff?"

"I have a storage unit."

"We need to move it."

"Now?"

"Yes. If he's been following you like you say, he probably knows about it."

April shuddered as she thought again about the assault that happened right outside of her unit. In broad daylight. Erika was right.

<hr />

They made it to the storage unit in record time. April swiped her key card to let her mother's car drive through first, then swiped it again so she could follow behind in her own vehicle. They both turned on the aisle and then expertly navigated to back their trunks close to the garage of her unit to make transport easier.

"There's not too much," April said as she got out, fiddling with her keys.

"Okay, but it's best if we err on the side of caution and still take what's there." Erika waited as April inserted the key into the lock and flicked it open. "What name is this in?"

"Erin Duncan."

"You need to—"

"I've already taken care of all that," April said, anticipating her list of instructions. "Erin is no more. This will be the last thing."

April stooped to grip the handle and lifted up the door with an amplified rattle of the aluminum as it slid up on its rails. Immediately, the putrid smell of decay assaulted April's nostrils. She and Erika both staggered back against the sickening aroma.

"Oh my God. What the hell is that?" It was Erika who spoke through the hand cupping her nose.

April blinked as her eyes adjusted to the dark interior. From behind her, sunlight intruded through the entryway, casting light on a heavily inflated trash bag that wasn't there before. April's hand shot out to squeeze Erika's arm, drawing the woman's gaze to the bag as well. "What is that?" Erika asked. But somehow, some way, they both knew. The telltale odor was excruciating.

Erika inched closer and used the toe of her flip-flop to nudge the bag. It rolled slightly, weighed down by something heavy. "Shit," she whispered. She stooped down to where the top of the bag had been fastened with a zip tie. She used napkins from her purse to work it open, twisting and twisting as the stench intensified, flooding the unit with a crippling thickness that had April's legs buckling. It was a familiar feeling. The same one that she'd felt before with Warren. The same one that had plagued her for the last eight years.

The trash bag rustled as Erika snatched it down to reveal its contents.

April let out a gasp with the realization of the body, that face. Not again. She turned to stumble out of the unit, the vomit searing her throat as it came up and out to splatter on the ground. But she would never be able to erase that look from her mind or those empty eyes wooden with death from the body in that trash bag. *Who would do this to Ramsey?*

Chapter Twenty-nine

"Is he—" April couldn't bring herself to utter the words out loud. Not with the confirmation of her husband's demise spread out in front of her like a museum display. She swallowed, though that was a mistake because the taste of death suddenly felt clogged in her throat.

"Who the hell is this?" Erika was gesturing toward the body, a mix between shock and anger coloring her inflection.

"Ramsey. My husband."

"I thought . . ." Erika shook her head, a desperate attempt to put her thoughts together. "Never mind. We got to get out of here. Now." She stepped over the bag as if it were garbage and stalked toward the car with urgency.

April hurriedly pulled the garage door down and took a greedy gulp of fresh air. Her vision wavered and she braced on the door for support. Her mind was in shambles and the fear was, once again, beginning to take over. So as much as she didn't like her mother's tactics, she was grateful one of them could take charge of the situation. She certainly wasn't capable of logic at the moment.

"Oh, no you don't. You are not about to pass out," Erika spat vehemently, her fingers circling April's forearm to pull her upright. "You need to explain what the hell I was just looking at. What did you do?"

"I didn't do anything. I haven't seen Ramsey in two days."

"What happened to Carter?"

"He's still around."

"Then who is *that*?" Erika cut a finger to the storage unit. "And how the hell did he get in there?"

"I don't know!" April had to struggle to keep herself from hyperventilating. Someone had killed Ramsey. Her mind was trying to wrap around the facts, but it felt like another one of her nightmares. And she was desperate to wake up.

Erika slapped her hands on her hips as she tossed a considering frown to the storage unit. "Okay, you've apparently left me out of the loop for a lot of shit you've been doing. As far as I'm concerned, this is your problem to handle."

April was grabbing her mother's arm before she had a chance to walk off. "Erika, please. I need your help. Please." She knew she sounded as desperate as she felt, but she couldn't do this alone. Erika hadn't always been the best mother, or hell, the best person for that matter, but April appreciated how she could always count on her to have her back. As if to remind her, April used her pinky and hooked it on Erika's. "Help me, Mom."

The label had Erika blinking. They both knew April never called her that. Slowly, she nodded. "I can help you. But first, you need to tell me the truth." She nodded toward the unit with the body sealed inside. "Did you kill your husband?"

"No." April was shaking her head, fiercely. "No, I wouldn't do that."

Erika's gaze narrowed as she pulled out a crumpled cigarette. She was thinking what they both knew to be true. That April had done it before.

April was silent as she watched Erika pat her pockets again, cursing when she couldn't immediately locate her lighter. She gave up and just stuck the stick between her lips, momentarily satisfied with the subtle hint of nicotine.

"I know it looks bad," April tried again, this time calmer as she leveled her eyes with Erika's. "But I promise you, I have no idea what happened to Ramsey. The last time I saw him was at his mother's funeral and—" She stopped, remembering what had transpired during that event. Her heart quickened with the revelation. "Jameson," she said.

"Jameson? He did this?"

"He had a fight with Ramsey at the funeral." April's words were coming out in a quick jumble as the pieces began to fit together. "Ramsey thought we had been cheating and they got into it. Jameson was pissed and we thought he left town since no one could get in touch with him." April began to pace, an anxiety-induced headache drumming at her forehead. If Jameson did this to Ramsey, what was stopping him from coming after her next? Was this a warning?

She stopped by her car, suddenly feeling exposed and vulnerable. Was he here watching her now? Was it only a matter of time now before he came back to finish the job?

"We need to get somewhere safe." Erika's voice was startling. She had nearly forgotten she was there.

"But what about Ramsey?"

"Does he have any friends? Family or anyone who would be looking for him?"

April shook her head. "No, he's an only child. And his mom just died in a—" April bit back the words and the swell of guilt that threatened to erupt. "She died," she said, instead. "We just had the funeral. No father or anything that I'm aware of."

"I'm trying to see if there would be anyone looking for him," Erika clarified.

April thought for a moment. "He owns a restaurant," she said. "Red Velvet Bistro. Not sure if he'd taken some time off work or anything because of what happened to his mom, but if he doesn't show up or call or anything, I'm sure it would look suspicious."

"Got it." Erika nodded, taking her phone from her pocket to dial a number. "Go back to your place and I'll be along as soon as I handle this here."

April started to object, but decided it was best to follow instructions. Besides, she didn't know how much longer she could stand outside knowing there was a dead body only a few feet away. Truth was, she was scared to be alone, now that she knew Jameson was coming for her. But Erika was now on the phone barking orders into the receiver at someone and April knew she needed to get the hell out of there. She already looked guilty enough.

She and Erika had pulled some scams over the years, ever since she was little, if she could be honest. "They are rich," Erika had said many times. "They aren't doing anything but hoarding their wealth, after making their money by relentlessly exploiting the working class." It was all part of their survival. Take, or be taken from. But out of all the cons, from check fraud to shoplifting, April had never experienced anything of this magnitude. No, *murder* was something she was not properly equipped to handle alone. Thank God for Erika's composure.

The thought of starting over should have been thrilling, but for some reason, there was an uneasiness about the situation. That maybe, just maybe, she had somehow dived into something that was way over her head. And she had no idea how to prepare for what was to come.

⸺⸻◦⸺

She didn't remember the drive back to her condo. Just looked up and realized she was sitting in the parking lot, staring up at the building in a daze. She texted Erika the address and, not caring how crazy she looked, broke out into a run to get to her unit.

How much longer did she have? Two days? Two hours? Was she even safe here?

April clicked all four of her locks into place and immediately swept the apartment, closing blinds and shutting curtains, even though it didn't help quell that weird, acute sensation that she was being watched.

Her movements were jittery as she sat on the sofa and cradled her head in her hands. She had lost all control, she knew. Just thinking about everything that had happened brought about this burning sensation in her lungs, as if she were drowning and couldn't catch her breath. It was tempting to call Erika and see what was going on. Had she gotten the body removed? Where was she going to put it? April cringed, her own thoughts leaving a sour taste in her mouth. *That body* was a person, Ramsey. Her husband. A man she had made a life with. A man who had loved her despite everything. Her breath caught in her throat, that burning sensation intensifying. She couldn't think about it too long or she would fall apart. And she couldn't afford that right now.

She wouldn't call Erika. Not right now. As much as she wanted to, she didn't want to let her curiosity get the best of her. Disturbing her right now would only belabor the process, because whatever her mother was doing with whomever, they were cleaning up *her* mess. Again.

It was best to be patient. Easier said than done.

April got up, intent on making something to eat. Or drink. Any kind of distraction would suffice right about now. But she could only stare inside the refrigerator, scanning its meager contents, not really looking at any of the items on the shelves. All she could think about was Ramsey and she felt guilty all over again. Because just like with Edith, April hadn't done anything to help him, nor stop his death. She was to blame for both of them by pulling them into her mess, and the guilt was eating at her like a disease.

April closed the refrigerator and stood in the middle of the room. She needed to do something, or she would make herself crazy with waiting. Painting was out of the question. Yet another reminder of Ramsey. Hot, sticky tears stung her cheeks, and she quickly brushed them away. But they were flowing now like a faucet. April sank to the floor and clutched her knees to her chest, succumbing to the urge to let the tears fall. She heaved, grateful for the cleansing. God, it felt good to let it go. Therapeutic.

A brisk knock at the door interrupted the silence and she scurried to her feet. Without thinking, she grabbed her pistol case and popped open the snap locks. And there it was, her new purple handgun nestled in the polyurethane foam, just like Molly had packed it. No, it wasn't loaded, but she pulled it out anyway. Hopefully, she wouldn't need to use it.

She inched to the door with fearful steps. Another knock, this time more persistent. It couldn't be Jameson. He wouldn't knock, right? Just break in. It could be Erika, but she hadn't announced herself yet and April surely wasn't about to assume. It was better to err on the side of caution.

April peered into the peephole and instantly relaxing, flipped the locks and pulled open the door. Erika hurried inside and closed it behind her. Her eyes fell to the gun in April's hand. "I see you took my advice."

"Yeah."

"Good. Now put that thing down before you kill us both."

Obediently, April put the weapon back in its case. "Well?" she asked.

"Don't worry about it. He's gone."

April hated how cold it sounded, but she shouldn't have expected her mother to exercise sensitivity. Had she ever?

Erika was rummaging around in the kitchen, opening cabinets and pulling down glasses. "You got anything to drink in here?"

April ignored the question. "Now what?"

"This is what I need you to do." Erika found some remaining wine in a bottle toward the back of the refrigerator and poured some into her cup. "Go back to Carter while I try to track down Jameson. It's safer for you there."

"I don't want to put anyone else in danger. Especially Carter."

"What are you going to do, stay here by yourself and—" she gestured toward the gun case—"shoot whoever comes to your door?" She was right. It sounded ridiculous. And completely unsafe.

April considered the alternative as she sat down on the couch. "What if Jameson follows me there?"

"Is there any way you could get Carter to take you away for the weekend or something?"

April thought. That didn't sound like a bad idea. "I'll ask him."

"Good. Don't tell him anything. Just stay with him. I don't know how much Jameson knows, but I think that's best. At least until we can locate him."

In a weird sort of way, there was something comforting about Erika's presence. She felt herself relaxing inch by glorious inch. Maybe, just maybe this would be okay. But then she thought about poor Ramsey and couldn't help getting choked up all over again.

"Hey, calm down." Erika brought the wineglasses to the living room as she ushered April onto the couch. "I can't afford to have you break down right now. You understand me?"

April nodded. She was right. She accepted the cup and knocked back the liquor, welcoming the bitter taste.

"What else do you need?" Erika was asking, taking sips of her own wine.

"I have to get rid of the car. I can't have anything else in Erin's name."

"Done."

"And after all of this is over, I think I'm done with everything, too, Erika." She hadn't realized the thought had been festering until she heard it from her own mouth.

Even Erika blinked in surprise. "Really?"

"Yeah. With everything that's been going on, I'm realizing I can't live the rest of my life scared and looking over my shoulder. I don't deserve that."

Her mother nodded. "You do deserve your happily ever after."

April chuckled at the familiar slogan she'd heard Erika quote. "Why do you always say that?"

"Because it's true. Life is not a fucking fairy tale, so we deserve to make our own." Erika lifted her glass in a mock toast and April raised hers as well. She wished it were that easy.

Later on, Erika had dozed off in the bedroom and April was painting once again in her studio. That was when she saw it. A shadow fell across the blinds as someone walked right outside of her door. Then, it stopped, the dark silhouette like a statue against the backdrop of the settling dusk.

April climbed to her feet, taking care to keep her movements quiet. Whoever it was seemed to be waiting for something. She flattened her back next to the window and squinted through the blinds. Someone was definitely there. But looking past the figure, her breath stilled when she saw the black Cadillac parked right next to her vehicle in the parking lot.

April rushed out of the room, once again pulling her weapon from its case. Maybe if she hurried, she could catch the culprit. And do what, she needed to know. But now she felt more protected with her firearm.

April swung open the door and nearly screamed when she came face-to-face with Deuce.

Deuce had done some work for her in the past. A certified tracker, he was called upon to help locate a person. Some off-the-record black-market stuff that April had found useful before.

And by the looks of it, the same man who April had seen following her when she was in the mall with Brynn.

He'd cut his locs into a low-cut and he reeked of weed. He stood on her porch giving her that signature cocky grin of his. "Hey, April," he said with all the casualness of a companionable relationship. "Long time no see."

"Deuce, what the hell are you doing here?"

"Looking for you."

"Does someone have you tracking me?"

"Something like that." He wasn't making any move to continue his dialogue, which was only angering April more.

"Who hired you?"

"I can't say."

"Deuce?" It was Erika this time, appearing in the living room as she blinked the sleep from her eyes.

April looked between Deuce and Erika. "You know him?"

"Yeah, he's been the one helping me."

Deuce took the opportunity to step into the room and nudged the door closed behind him.

April shook her head. "Wait, I don't understand. He's a tracker. Why is he—" a thought popped into her head. "Have you been having him track me, Erika? Is he the one tailing me all the damn time in the black Cadillac?"

Erika lifted her shoulder in an absent shrug. "Not track you, girl. *Protect* you. He's been keeping an eye on you for me. Plus, I told him about Jameson. He'll be able to locate him for us. And obviously I'm glad he's around because he's helping me clean up your shit. I suggest you be grateful."

April shook her head in apparent disgust as Erika waved Deuce into the kitchen. "I had him stop by since he took care of our little storage problem. You know he's always been a greedy bastard when it comes to his money."

Something like amusement danced in Deuce's eye.

April frowned. She didn't know whether to be angry or glad. It was great to know that Deuce was looking out for her, but why did Erika have to keep that secret? April would've liked to think she would've understood if she'd at least mentioned it.

Erika trotted to the bedroom to get some money for Deuce. Now alone, April took a deep breath. "Sorry for giving you a hard time," she said. "I didn't know Erika was the one you were working for. I thought it was . . ." she trailed off, not wanting to verbalize her thoughts.

Thankfully, Deuce didn't seem to care. "No problem," he said.

As he stood there, a thought crossed April's mind. She glanced back to her bedroom to see if Erika was around before stepping closer and lowering her voice. "Hey, do you have time to locate someone for me?"

"If you got the money for it, I'll make time."

April nodded. "Actually, it's two people," she amended, the idea causing a bubble of excitement to simmer in her belly. Thanks to Deuce, she would be able to end this once and for all.

PART V: TESTING

A stage where a person tries to experiment with different ways to manage grief.

Chapter Thirty

Before

Warren was going to die tonight. She would make sure of it.

April woke up with the thought fresh on her mind. The events from the prior three weeks were like a dark cloud looming overhead. Knowing what he was saying, what he was doing to her in the privacy of their bedroom where no one could help. Knowing what she had to do in return. If she went through with it, she would have to live with the consequences for the rest of her life. But if she didn't . . . well, she didn't even know if that was an option. The choice had been made for her the moment she'd entered into this arrangement and the bad decisions in life it fostered. She was a prisoner in his home, but then again, she'd always been a prisoner in her own body. She knew she couldn't react on impulse. She had to be patient and strategic to pull this off. So, she watched, waited, and planned. But tonight, tonight this would be her opportunity to be somewhat free.

April clung to that last thought with desperation as she moved about her day like she was on autopilot. On death row. She showered and got dressed in warm, comfortable clothes. The chef, Maurice, had prepared a lavish brunch that April didn't attempt to eat. Her stomach wasn't settled, and she knew she wouldn't be able to keep it down, even if she tried. She nibbled on toast and orange juice that tasted stale as she went over her plan again and again until her head ached.

"What's your problem?" Erika strolled into the kitchen and caught her daughter staring off in a daze. She looked sun-kissed in her ritzy maxi dress and new blond wig. Of course, her makeup, as always, was immaculate so even if April thought her mother had a night as bad as her, she definitely wouldn't show it.

Erika began piling food onto a china plate and poured herself some of the freshly prepped mimosa Maurice had stuck in the fridge.

April chewed silently, her mouth as dry as the remnants of toast. "Just tired," she admitted.

"Did you stay up late?"

It was Erika's code phrase asking if she'd been able to sneak down and take some more of Warren's money. But April couldn't admit what had really happened. It would ruin everything, and she wouldn't be able to carry out her task. Erika would just be in the way.

Not this time. Her mother couldn't help her. She would have to fix her own mess.

"Yes, I did," April said and left it at that.

Erika nodded with a satisfied smirk. "That's my girl. Hopefully not too much longer. This is it. I can feel it." She clapped her hands emphatically and there was another sickening feeling of dread that ballooned in April's stomach. *If only she knew.*

Warren would be working from home today, which meant he would be holed up in the basement with his clients. Erika would probably go shopping or to the spa or whatever it was she did to occupy her time. That would leave April to herself, for the most part. She just needed to take care of the witnesses.

When the afternoon rolled around, April began methodically

sending the staff home. She had gained a positive rapport with everyone, so she was met with little resistance to the proposition. After they were gone, April snuck upstairs to make a call.

Erika picked up on the first ring, the background noise nearly drowning out her voice. She sounded like she was at some kind of party. "Yeah girl, what's up?"

"Great news. Warren said he was treating us to a night in the city." April piled the enthusiasm in her voice to really coat the lie. "He went ahead and got us a hotel for the night and reservations at Pipe City Steakhouse for seven o'clock."

"Good. He knows how to treat you and I'm certainly not mad at that."

"Go ahead and check in and I'll meet you out there."

"I know he's going to give me some money for shopping, right?"

April rolled her eyes and at the same time, reached in the nightstand drawer for one of Warren's credit cards. "Of course. I'm going to text you a picture of the card and the reservation confirmation for the hotel." She hung up and did just that, sending Erika a screenshot of the hotel reservation she had made the previous night. The setup was necessary. April was already energized with the fact that this was going to be her last night in this prison. With Warren. And even with her mother. After the dust settled, she knew it would probably be the end of their relationship as well. There probably was a piece of her that would miss Erika, but that piece was long buried with the part of her that was already dead. April wondered how she would start over and where. Would she be alone? Would she be able to pull all of this off and escape unscathed?

The time now read 4:34. Her heart was picking up speed as all of the pieces were beginning to fall into place. She couldn't afford to mess this up. Her life was depending on it at this point.

With Erika occupied and the staff gone for the evening, April began picking through the house, shoveling everything of value into large duffle bags for later. She'd been sneaking time over the past few days digging holes in the backyard and now she carried everything outside, along with stashes of money.

Finally, she grabbed a gun and pressed the intercom to call down to Warren in his office in the basement. "What?" he barked.

"Can you come up here, please?" she asked, her voice quivering. "I—uh—need to show you something." When he hung up and she heard him stomping up the stairs, she aimed the gun and waited. She was going to end this once and for all. She just hoped she could live with the consequences.

Chapter Thirty-one

"What are you doing here?"

April frowned as she wheeled her bags toward Ian. She'd just emerged from the airport and, expecting to see Carter, her brother-in-law leaning against his car wasn't a pleasant surprise.

Ian unfolded himself from his lazy waiting position and skirted the trunk, popping it open as he passed by. "Carter sent me. Come on. I got something to do." He hadn't even offered to help with her luggage.

April kept her attitude at bay as she loaded her stuff and slid into the front seat. He barely waited for her to close the door before he peeled away from the curb.

"Where's Carter?" she grumbled once they hit the expressway.

"Busy."

"Busy doing what?"

"How am I supposed to know? He just asked me if I could pick you up and drop you off at the house. That's your husband, so why don't you tell me what he's busy doing." He smirked at what he knew was a slick comment.

April swallowed her own retort and ignored the remark, as derisive and rude as it was. She didn't dare voice the truth; that she hadn't spoken to Carter. He hadn't answered when she called, nor had he responded to her text messages other than to assure her she would have a ride from the airport. She didn't realize he'd pushed the task off to his brother.

A stifled silence lingered between them, not relieved by music or noise of any kind. It was tormenting because she knew she needed to lighten the tension with a conversation. But she couldn't push the recent events out of her mind, nor stomach the energy to engage with Ian. Still, April forced herself to initiate small talk. Anything to ease the discomfort.

"How was the birthday party?"

"Good." His reply was intentionally terse. "Had a great time. Especially when Chloe stopped by."

April tensed at that last comment. She didn't need him to expound on that to know exactly who Chloe was. And he seemed to be gloating at the fact that Carter's ex-girlfriend had shown up to the event. Which let April know that Ian, or probably his sister Valerie, had decided to extend the invitation. Was that why Carter was ignoring her? He was occupied with his precious Chloe? It probably was ridiculous to even allow the assumption to upset her, but she couldn't help feeling the brunt of the blatant disrespect. It was infuriating.

April shifted in her seat. "Ian, do you get off on being an asshole?"

He laughed at that. "How am I an asshole?"

"Well, let's see. You try to kiss me, which you're lucky I didn't tell your brother, then when I had a family emergency and couldn't make his party, you invite his ex?"

"For the record, I didn't invite Chloe. You should talk to your husband about that. And the only reason that happened was because I figured you would give in."

"You were testing me?"

"Yeah. Did you think I actually liked you, Michelle?" He tossed an incredulous look out of the side of his eye.

April blinked, shocked at his admission. "What were you trying to prove? That I would entertain my brother-in-law?"

"Actually, yes."

"Why?"

"Because I know you're not serious about Carter." There it was. April rolled her eyes. She couldn't even bring herself to waste her energy. Ian used the silence as his springboard to continue his rant. "I didn't think nothing of it at first. Then I started listening to Valerie and realizing that we really didn't know much about you. That you just came in and now you've got my brother's nose wide open."

She crossed her arms over her chest. "Sounds to me like you're just jealous," she snapped. "You and your sister. You would think you'd be happy that your brother is in love."

"We are. But note what you said. That *my brother* is in love. You didn't mention your love for him. And that's my issue with you."

April shook her head in annoyance. Did the technicalities really matter? "Are you serious, Ian? I miss one birthday party and now you're questioning my feelings for Carter?"

"I did some digging." He let the words hang between them. April could tell he was analyzing how she would react, so she intentionally kept her composure, even though she was bracing inside.

"Okay, and?" she tossed with a flippant shrug. "What did you find?"

"Nothing."

"Exactly."

"No, nothing," Ian said again with a suspicious frown. "No high school records, no social media, no background stuff, nothing. And that's pretty strange, don't you think?"

April rolled her eyes. He didn't have anything. Just trying to scare her or bait her with his outlandish assumptions. At least, she hoped.

But she kept quiet as she turned to look out the window, watching the city whizz by in a blur. It had been a mistake to make niceties with Ian. She had more important things to focus on. Like Ian not blabbing his suspicions to his brother. And this ex-girlfriend Chloe not stepping in and ruining what she was so close to finishing.

Ian dropped her off at the high-rise without so much as a good-bye. She was thankful he didn't bother being a gentleman and escorting her upstairs. She'd had enough of him and clearly the feeling was mutual.

* * *

The warm water felt relaxing as it dribbled along her back and down the muscles in her legs. It seemed to beat the tension out of her shoulders and her mind became clear, her troubles seeming to wash away like the soap on her body. She sighed in luxury, turning to allow the water to tickle her breasts and stomach. Her stomach. April looked down and laid her palm on her navel. She felt the sudden pull of sorrow, as if the baby were still inside her.

A loud crash had her nearly jumping clear out of the tub. Fear inched up her spine and tension drew her shoulders up. Her fingers trembled as she drew back the shower curtain just wide enough for her to peek out into the empty bathroom. She glanced around, squinting through the steam that enveloped the room like a damp fog. The door to the bedroom was left ajar, the adjoining bedroom's light off. Hadn't she left it on? Trapped. The realization hit her on a punch that had a frightened gasp whispering from her parted lips. Naked in the shower, her gun seemingly miles away. She could almost taste the fear on her tongue as her heart seemed to trip and stumble in her chest and she withdrew into the shower.

April fumbled with the nozzle and the warm spray cut off. Her breathing was roaring in her ears as she strained to listen. All was quiet. She was reaching for her towel when she saw the shadow. Her heart stopped and almost habitually, April lunged out for a weapon of defense, knocking her soap to the tub in the process. There was nothing to protect her. She plastered her back against the cold wall of the shower, shuddering more from the fear than from the wall's temperature.

April saw the silhouette of something in his hand and her eyes rounded as she saw the length of the blade. A knife? As if on cue to some nineties horror film, the smell of blood and sweat dampened the air. A stubborn scream was locked in her throat, refusing to come out. "How did he find me?" her mind coiled around the thought. A hand came up and grasped the shower curtain, his fingers long and slender, and her worst fears were confirmed. He had found her.

Squeezing her eyes shut, April let out a hoarse plea as the curtain was snatched back and the first thing she saw was the blade glistening in the light, ready to be jammed into her heaving chest. April let out a shrill scream and lunged out to protect herself.

"Michelle, what the hell?"

Carter was standing in the bathroom with steam clouding around him, giving her a dubious look.

"Carter, what are you—" April clamped her mouth shut on the question. Of course, his presence in his own home shouldn't have been a surprise. But since he was "busy" or at least too busy to pick her up from the airport, she hadn't expected to see him for a few more hours. "I meant," she tried again, this time calmer, "I didn't expect you back so soon."

"I kept calling your name."

Had he? Instinctively, her gaze lowered to his hand, where he was clutching a razor, not a knife. She released the breath that had tightened in her chest.

He crossed out of the bathroom and April turned off the

shower and stepped out. She grabbed her terrycloth robe from the back of the door and belted it at the waist as she joined him in the bedroom.

Carter had set up the ironing board and he was now pulling a pastel blue, button-up shirt from the closet. "How was your flight?" he asked.

She glanced around, noticing the suit he had spread out across the bed. *Where was he going?* "It was fine. How are you?"

"I'm good."

Quiet. No kiss, no hug, no warmth whatsoever. April had to admit, it made her feel lonely. She sank to a chair and watched him go about his business like she wasn't even there. "I tried to call you a few times."

"Yeah, sorry about that." Not even an explanation.

She waited until he had begun ironing before she spoke again. "Look, I'm sorry about the party thing. I know you're probably upset I couldn't be there."

"Yeah. We had a good time anyway, though."

She knew. With his ex.

April sighed. Now that her mind was clear, she knew what she had to do. "Carter, I was thinking," she started, mustering as much sincerity as she could. "Before I left, we were talking about spending more time together. And I believe you're right. I'm going to take a little time off work."

Carter's eyebrows shot up in surprise. "Really? Where is this coming from?"

"I understand what you meant, and I certainly don't want my job to put any type of strain on our marriage. I love you," she added with a smile. It was a manipulative tactic, but she couldn't have him being so distant. Nor distracted with Chloe. Not now. If that meant she needed to layer on some extra affection, so be it.

He had stopped ironing, but he hadn't made a move to cross the room yet, as if he were conflicted. Or trying to see if he believed her. "Is this about Chloe?" he asked finally.

April's face creased in feigned confusion. "Who?"

"My ex. I'm pretty sure you found out she was at the birthday party."

Now, April did get up and close the distance between them. She wrapped her arms around his waist. "Yeah, I heard, but I don't care about that," she said. "I'm secure enough and I trust you completely. Like I hope you trust me."

"I do, it's just that . . ." Carter sighed as he put his hands on her shoulders. "I just didn't like that you were so evasive about not coming. It was a huge surprise and I'm glad my siblings threw me a party. But the biggest letdown was that you weren't there to share it with me. And to know that you keep talking about some *family emergency*, but you won't tell me with who or what happened. Like you're shutting me out with that part of your life. That hurts, Michelle."

April leaned into him, resting her cheek on his chest. She could hear his heartbeat thundering against his ribs. Beating for her. Loving her. She felt horrible. "I'm sorry," she murmured. And that was probably the most truthful thing she had ever said to him. Because she was sorry. Sorry that she couldn't be the woman he loved, the woman he deserved, sorry that she was such a disastrous person with a messed-up childhood. She was sorry she wasn't—couldn't be a better person.

He lifted her face to his and caught the glimmer of tears on her cheeks. His face crumbled. "Hey, it's okay," he said. His lips felt like liquid on her skin as he attempted to kiss her sadness away. "I love you and I'm glad you're willing to work on us. That's all I can ask. I was worried this whole time that you were upset at me for bringing that up. And whatever happened with your family, I hope everything is okay."

She took a grateful inhale of his scent and relaxed in his arms, soothed by the compassion she knew she wasn't worthy of. "You know what," she said, her voice muffled against his shirt. "Why don't we go away together?"

"I think that's a great idea. I'll be wrapping up this project in the next couple of months, so how about we plan something for March?"

April's face fell. "Well, I was thinking something sooner," she offered. "Like this weekend."

"Damn, babe, I wish, but I can't. We have a function this evening and I'll be working all weekend." Of course. That explained the suit and tie attire.

"What type of function? Babe, I just got home and I was hoping we could stay in and spend some quality time." Really, she was too scared to be seen out in public.

Carter rubbed her back. "I'm sorry, sweetie. This is a charity event I can't miss. I would love for you to go with me, but you can stay home if you prefer. I know you just got off work, so if you're tired, I understand."

"No, I'll go. It'll be fun." April forced a smile, struggling to mask her disappointment. As much as she would rather hide out in the penthouse, there was no way in hell she was going to be left alone. Not after everything she had just witnessed. It was better for her to stay with Carter, for her safety. *And his.*

Chapter Thirty-two

She hated the calm before the storm. But that's exactly what tonight felt like.

April held out her hand as Carter helped her from the car. By looking at her from the outside, no one would be able to tell anxiety had a churning feeling in the pit of her stomach.

Carter had picked out one of her favorite dresses to wear tonight, a slinky chiffon material that clung to her curves with a thigh-high slit that swayed to expose inviting pieces of her leg. The gorgeous silver material seemed to glitter off of her tanned complexion, wrapping around her neck and disappearing under the loose curls of her hair. She smiled, prompting Carter's lips to curve at the casual gesture.

"You look breathtaking," he complimented with a wink.

April flicked a manicured finger across the lapel of his jacket. "You don't look so bad yourself."

"I'm so glad you're home." He then leaned closer to whisper in her ear. "I can't wait to explore you more in detail later. Hopefully after tonight's surprise, you'll let me."

April felt her insides twist. She paused on the sidewalk. "Carter, I don't think that's a good idea."

"I promise you'll love it, babe."

"Maybe, I should—"

But he was already placing his hand on the small of her back and gently guiding her to the building.

As usual, Atlanta was lit up like Christmas. Virtual billboards flashed commercials and ads to city-goers illuminated by bright neon lights. Rideshares and a variety of vehicles stuffed the roads, and the sound of car horns rang out in a harmonizing chorus. Pedestrians were so cluttered on the sidewalk that it looked as if the concrete had been replaced with boots, sneakers, and heels. No matter if it were 3:00 in the afternoon or the early brushes of dawn, the city was always awake.

Carter's company had rented out one of the ballrooms in the Marriott Marquis and even went so far as to reserve rooms in case employees got a little carried away with the alcohol. The futuristic-themed room was predominately white with pub tables and swivel stools. White, leather circular couches were sprinkled throughout the room to allow for leisure resting from the upbeat music that blared through the speakers. An entire accent wall had been decorated to look like a starry night sky and massive screens displayed the company logo and party slogan *Our employees are the future.* The party was already in the throes of entertained laughter when they stepped into the ballroom. Carter grabbed April's hand and propelled her through the throng of formal gowns and alcohol-induced laughter.

They found a vacant pub table and April took a seat. Carter immediately whisked away and returned with punch, and April was disappointed he hadn't bothered with an alcoholic beverage. Lord knows she needed it to calm her nerves.

"I got you something," Carter said as he reached into his pocket. He pulled a long jewelry box into view. As she watched, he lifted the lid to reveal a diamond and emerald encrusted tennis bracelet. She gasped as the delicate stones caught the light and seemed to cast a glittering array of light across his fingers when he lifted it into view.

"What is this for?"

Carter draped the bracelet over her wrist and hooked the clasp together. "I just missed you," he said. "I missed us. And I just wanted to see you smile. Like, *really* smile. I feel like I haven't seen that in a minute." He didn't know how right he was.

"I don't know what to say." April's voice was throaty and breathless as she looked down at the bracelet. "I really love it, babe. Thank you."

"There he is!" A burly man made his way over and gave Carter a friendly squeeze on the shoulder. "Good to see you, Carter."

"Always good to see you, Jake." Carter turned to April to make introductions. "Michelle, this is one of my clients, Jake Pram. Jake, my lovely wife, Michelle."

Jake's smile was a mile wide. "Carter, why didn't you tell me your wife was so beautiful?"

April felt herself blush at the compliment.

Carter laughed. "Because you're a ladies' man and would probably try to steal her from me," he teased.

Jake playfully cupped April's hand in both of his. "Don't listen to him," he said, giving her hand an elaborate kiss while keeping his eyes on Carter. "He's just jealous because every woman he talks to wants me instead."

April laughed. "Okay, thank you. I'll keep that in mind."

" I guess congratulations are in order?" Jake said, lifting a glass in April's direction.

Confused, April turned in time to catch Carter shaking his head. "What is he talking about?" she asked, glancing between the two men who were, not so obviously, exchanging pointed looks.

Jake covered his mouth. "Oh, you haven't told her yet. Sorry about that." He smiled again at April. "It was nice to meet you." With that, he strolled off.

April turned to her husband. "Carter, is there something I need to know?"

Sighing, Carter took a seat on the stool. "It's kind of a surprise," he said.

"I told you I don't like surprises." Something he had clearly ignored. It was upsetting and she felt her face wrinkling in restrained anger as she got to her feet. "I think I need to go." Her eyes darted around the room as she spoke.

Carter rose in confusion. "Babe, why do you look scared?"

"I don't like surprises, Carter. I told you this." April couldn't keep the pleading tone out of her voice and she hated how vulnerable she was at the moment. "Just tell me what you've done. Why do I need to be congratulated?"

"It's good, April. I promise you'll love it."

"Then tell me."

Carter relented with a sigh. "Well, you know how you mentioned—"

The lights began to flicker, halting his words. April turned worried eyes to the stage as the music faded and a hush fell over the crowd. A woman in a gorgeous sequin gown with a mass of curls piled on top of her head took to the stage with a microphone in hand.

"Good evening, everyone," the woman greeted with a smile. "I'm Stephanie Parrish and I want to welcome you all to the employee appreciation party for Evans Architectural Designs. We would, of course, like to thank Carter Evans as the owner for taking this opportunity to show his appreciation for the hard work and dedication of each one of you. Now eat, drink, enjoy, and remember how essential you are to the success of this company." She paused to allow for the appreciative claps and cheers from the audience. "Also, I would like to make a special announcement. On behalf of Evans Architectural Designs, we would like to extend a heartfelt welcome to Mr. Evans's wife, Michelle, as our newest partner. Where is Mrs. Evans?"

April's eyes rounded as the thunderous applause lifted in a crescendo around her. A spotlight panned the crowd as she looked to Carter, who was smiling so big, his eyes had nearly disappeared into his cheeks. "Surprise," he mouthed.

She couldn't even feel her limbs as he took hold of her hand and lifted her arm in the air. *What had he done?*

"Oh, there she is." Stephanie gestured toward them with a wave of her hand. "Mrs. Evans, we couldn't be more thrilled to welcome you to the team." More cheers and even a few back pats from people within reaching distance. April was utterly stunned, and her face warmed underneath the attention.

"All right, now let's party!" Stephanie announced. The music rose once more and so did the crowd.

April felt Carter give her arm a light squeeze. "Well, what do you think?" he prompted.

She narrowed her eyes. "What exactly just happened?"

"So good to meet you, Mrs. Evans," Stephanie gushed, appearing at the table and immediately pulling April into a welcoming hug. "We're so happy to have you with us. Carter here has done nothing but rave about your talent and experience."

April was clearly at a loss for words and could only smile. "Oh, well thank you," she murmured.

Stephanie patted Carter's shoulder as she spoke. "Carter has already set everything up for you. We'll just need your stuff for your personnel file. Driver's license, Social Security card, resume, references, etc. Again, it's just technicalities to have your information on file. Congrats again," Stephanie added, "Carter, show my girl a good time." And she breezed away.

Carter turned to April, who had dropped her head in her hands. "What's the matter?"

April wasn't sure how to feel. On one hand, she was irritated because Carter had, unintentionally, opened up her personal life and forged documentation for scrutiny. She had gone so long under the radar that she didn't know what to expect with this type of exposure. On the other hand, she was honored that Carter would give her a percentage of his business. It demonstrated his love, his trust. It showed she was his future. Which was probably why she felt so terrible. "Carter, how could you do this without consulting me?"

He was clearly taken aback by her reaction. "I thought you would be happy, Michelle. We talked about wanting to spend more time together. Plus, this was something I thought long and hard about. It was a big decision for me because you know my business is my life. But so are you." He paused, frowning when she didn't immediately respond. "Babe, I don't get it. Are you mad about this?"

"I'm . . . not mad . . ." How could she explain? This isn't what she wanted to do. This isn't what she wanted from him. "I just wish we had discussed something this big before you went and made the decision for me."

"Honestly, I thought you would appreciate the gesture." He was struggling to restrain his rising anger. She could see that clear as day. "I damn sure didn't think you would piss on this."

April shook her head. She pressed her fingers to her closed eyes, staving off the impending headache. "What about my job? I can't just up and quit." She was grasping at straws. Anything to make him see.

"Michelle . . ." Carter was just as much at a loss for words. "What exactly do you want?"

"What do you mean?"

"I mean, do you want us or not? Because I can't keep up the charade. I can't keep pretending like things are okay when they're not." He was holding her gaze now, his own eyes filling with sorrow.

Her voice had lowered to a whisper. "Why do you want me to take this so bad?"

She might as well have punched him the way his face collapsed with the question. His shoulders slumped and he glanced to the dance floor where his employees were immersed in pure joy and happiness. "No, I think the better question is, why are you so against it."

He left her there, drowning in her own sea of regret. It was torturous. She could only sit there, alone, while the festivities circulated around her. She knew she had to find him and apologize. Hell, even she knew the way she acted toward such a beautiful gesture was completely uncalled for.

April started to rise, but then paused when her eyes zeroed in on a woman in the crowd. A woman who looked suspiciously like Brynn. If it wasn't for the outfit, April may not have known that it was her. But she remembered that dress.

She remembered how they had gone shopping and Brynn had plucked it off the rack and made a joke about how it was wild with its iridescent sequins. And April had encouraged her to try it on because it was such a unique color, and the high split would accentuate her gorgeous legs. Brynn had laughed but she'd acquiesced and emerged from the fitting room to both of their amazement, looking absolutely stunning, like some kind of ethereal goddess. April had been right. It hugged her body like an extra layer of skin. And Brynn had wanted the dress, bad. Her longing had practically oozed from her pores. But she'd peeled it off with a leisurely reluctance that had saddened April. "I'm not like you," Brynn had teased. "I can't afford to buy clothes to put away just in case when just-in-case could never come." It hadn't even taken any convincing. April had handed over a credit card without so much as looking at the price. And Brynn had graciously accepted the gift, but she'd insisted the dress wouldn't see the outside of her closet because she had nowhere to wear it.

It couldn't be her. But that damn dress was causing April to do a double take, looking for the shimmery material among the rainbow of chiffon and silks and tulle.

Just as quickly, the mystery woman in the dress was gone, having blended back into the throng of inebriated party guests nearly obscured in the low-level lighting. April had to shake her head at the silly assumption. She must've been mistaken. Had to be. Sure, the woman had looked nearly identical to Brynn. But the dress wasn't custom. It could've been anyone from anywhere. It was improbable to think Brynn was even in the city (she rarely left Columbus, if ever). But it was even more of a reach to think she would be at this party for Carter. What were the odds?

April sat for a few moments longer when her cell phone buzzed with an incoming text. She grinned when she saw it was from Deuce, those two simple words like a melody to her ears: **Found him.**

Chapter Thirty-three

The rain pelted the windshield like rocks and April barely had time to dash it away with the windshield wipers before another sheet immediately took its place. The sky was pitch-black except for a dull glow from the moon, hidden behind the clouds. April's sigh came out shaky and fearful. No time to back out now.

She parked the car on another street and bundling her hair in a messy bun at the top of her head, she fit the baseball cap on top. She noticed the subtle shaking in her fingers as she fumbled with the plastic gloves. Get a grip, girl, she mumbled, the plastic cold and uncomfortable against her clammy skin. With one last look in the rearview mirror, she sighed, opened the door, and stepped out into the rain.

It was coming down in sheets now, nearly obscuring her vision. April squinted through the curtain of rain, the water chilling her cheeks numb. She stumbled blindly forward. The sidewalks were empty, the houses gloomy and ghostlike.

The pounding of her sneakers echoed off the empty streets as she ran toward Jameson's house. The metal from the gun was beginning to bite into her skin, and she almost wished she had somewhere else to hide it other than her waistband. Too late for wishes.

Jameson's house would appear to be the most sinister one, the sight seemingly reaching out and beckoning her like a crooked finger. The driveway was empty, the lights off in the house. With one last look around, April cut through the freshly manicured front yard and made her way to the back of the house. Her heart was hammering with every step, her breath coming out quick and desperate. She urged herself to keep moving forward as she rounded the house.

April knew from past experience that Jameson used to keep a spare key under the back doormat. Holding her breath, she stooped down to the soggy piece of carpet and peeled the corner back, nearly jumping for joy when the key winked up at her from the ground. Some things never change, she thought with a satisfied smirk as she shoved the key into the hole. She heard the locks click out of place and, licking her lips, she grabbed the doorknob and pushed the door open.

It opened easily without so much as a squeak. April pocketed the key and stepped into the kitchen, closing the door behind her. The house was quiet, the only noise coming from the creak-creaking of the ceiling fan in the living room someone had apparently forgotten to turn off. April crept on, waiting for her eyes to adjust to the dark. Her wet shoes made a squeak with every careful step she took on the hardwood floor. She listened to the rain plummeting outside, hitting the roof like bullets, splashing against the glass.

April went into the living room, her eyes scanning for pictures on the mantle or coffee table. But there were none. Only furniture dominated the room, yet not one shred of memorabilia was in sight. Boxes were scattered around the room, all closed and pushed out of the way.

A crackle of thunder rumbled outside and had April jumping; startled. She knew she had to hurry. The storm was getting worse, and it was only a matter of time before Jameson got home. She headed down the long hall, frowning when she was met with nothing but closed doors. She wiped a stray raindrop from her forehead. She swallowed and grabbed the doorknob to the master bedroom, then she swung the door open.

She winced when it creaked loudly, sending a ripple of uncomfortable fear through her spine. A king-sized bed was positioned in the center of the room, jeans and T-shirts cluttering the floor, and a female's makeup scattered over the dresser. Brynn's, perhaps? A mixture of cheap perfume wafted through the stiff room, making April turn up her nose in disgust.

April went to a drawer and pulled it open, frowning at the socks and underwear that rested inside. She pulled open the other drawers, remembering how Jameson used to keep important documents in one of them. She pulled open another one and sure enough, manila folders, envelopes, and loose-leaf papers were strewn through the drawer and she stooped to rest on her knees, snatched off the plastic gloves, and began her search. Her nimble fingers raced over the labels, her eyes quickly scanning the contents of each folder.

A picture caught her attention, affirming her suspicions about Jameson. She should've known. April took her time, folding the picture into quarters and stuffing it in her pocket.

April was rising to her feet, near the brink of giving up hope, when her head snapped back, her eyes ballooning in fear, her ears perked. Was that a door creaking open? April held her breath and listened to the sound of the rain, growing more persistent against the windows. Her grip tightened. No, she wasn't stupid. That was a door followed by heavy, determined footsteps muffled against carpet. April's breath caught in her throat. Someone was in the house.

Panic had April crawling to the side of the bed and stooping down, her mind racing through a desperate prayer she wouldn't get caught. The door opened and she watched a pair of black, clunky work boots stop in the doorway. The room seemed to be suddenly enveloped in the smell of blood and beer: both stenches she knew so well.

"I know you're in here." Jameson's voice was low and threatening and the terror brushed her spine like a finger of death. "I knew you'd come back," he was saying, his boots stepping into the room.

April's breath quickened as his steps came closer, slower, like he was trying to make her suffer. The scream erupted from her parted lips as he threw himself at her, tackling her backwards. He landed on top of her, his face shadowed from the dark room, his lips peeled back in a satisfied grin. "Hey you." He leaned down to kiss her. She closed her eyes as his mouth met hers, the moustache scratching her lips, his tongue dry and itchy as it made a desperate journey over her face. "I always did love you." He was mumbling. She pushed at his firm chest, wiggling desperately.

"Get off of me, you bastard." Lifting her knee, she smiled in triumph when it connected with its target between his legs, and he hissed in pain. He rolled over and she frantically scrambled to her feet and screamed again when she tripped over his foot and was again thrown to the floor. The pain was unbearable. Her body seemed to burn all over with previous bruises now awakened, as if in a reminder. Jameson grabbed her shoulder and whirled her around. She didn't have enough time to block the blow, but the punch landed on her eye with such power that it left her vision blurred.

"Stupid bitch." He was shouting now as his hand closed around her neck and he hauled her to her feet on rubbery legs. She was sputtering as she clawed at his arm, and she kicked her feet. Her lips began to swell and blood vessels felt like they were bursting in and around her eyes like tiny, red fireworks.

"Now I can finally do what I've been wanting to do, ever since I found out you killed my uncle. But now I can claim self-defense." He gestured widely with his other hand at the mess in the room. "Breaking and entering."

In that brief moment, Jameson looked like *him* and her flesh crawled with the visceral memory of the assault. The way his skin smelled like wet leather as he clamped his hand over her mouth so she could swallow her screams.

"Oh my God, Jameson stop!" The voice was familiar and April had just enough strength to roll her head toward the panicked voice. Brynn was standing in the doorway, soaked from head to toe.

Jameson seemed to find humor in the situation as he snatched April to his chest, easing up a little to allow her a greedy intake of breath.

"You brought this on yourself, you know," he snarled. "First, you tried that shit with my uncle, then you tried to steal from me. Where does it end?"

"I didn't—" she whispered and was immediately silenced by the abrupt jerk of Jameson's hand as it squeezed her throat.

They stood there, sizing each other up, as the rain pummeled the world outside. Jameson slung April toward the nightstand and weakly, she stumbled into the lamp, knocking it over, before collapsing to the floor. She got to her hands and knees. She was out of breath, but she could only think about Brynn. She couldn't have someone else get hurt because of her. Gasping, she stumbled to her feet.

Jameson was walking toward Brynn. Her lips were moving, but no sound came out. Before he had time to think or react, April rushed toward him, sending all three of them crashing through the window and tumbling outside.

April landed on her back in the wet grass, and she inhaled sharply at the pain. The glass had cut her in the face. She felt the blood trickling down her cheeks as she got to her feet. Her arm was killing her and her whole body seemed to vibrate with the abuse. Black and white circles peppered her vision as she searched frantically for Jameson. Her hat had gotten knocked off somewhere in the chaos and the rain was plastering her hair to her face. She spotted Jameson, stooping over Brynn. It looked like his hands were grasped firmly around her neck, struggling to choke the life out of her.

April reached in her jeans, her fingers numb against her cold skin before she pulled out the gun. It was heavy in her hands, and she clicked it open to make sure it was loaded. One bullet. Jameson's bullet. She sucked in a breath. Just enough to put the bastard out of his misery. She clutched the gun between trembling fingers as she stumbled toward them. Her finger itched on the trigger as she aimed right for the back of Jameson's head. April's lips curled up into a sneer as he turned to face her, his eyes at first growing large with surprise, then humorous as if doubting her. He rose, his large body facing her, and April kept her eyes steady, her finger on the trigger, the gun aimed at him.

"Oh, so what are you going to do?" he asked, his voice calm. "Shoot me?"

She was breathing hard, the fresh taste of blood in her mouth, the sound of her heartbeat roaring in her ears along with the rapid thunder that rumbled through the sky.

His grin was slow and devilish. She lifted her finger and clicked on the aim light, watching its red beat hit his forehead, signaling where the gun was pointed. She watched in satisfaction as his smile faded. The blinding rain nearly obstructed him from view, but she was able to see his eyes through the haze.

"Shoot me dammit. You want to see me dead? Shoot me!"

The words echoed through April's head, but she wasn't afraid. Not anymore. Her heart had settled to a calm beat and her hands were no longer trembling. Whether because she knew what she wasn't going to do, or with the realization of what she wanted to, she didn't know.

"You know what?" she whispered, glaring directly into his eyes. "I forgive you. And I'm sorry, Jameson. I'm sorry for you and for Warren."

But even as he came charging forward, a roar escaping from his lips, she didn't hesitate to pull back on the trigger, nor did she flinch when the bullet exploded, stopping him abruptly, and his eyes rolled back in his head. The gun felt hot and it vibrated in her hands as she lowered it slowly, watching him sway forward before collapsing backwards. His eyes were open wide and still, his mouth embedded in the frown he tended to keep planted on his lips.

She walked to him then, her throat burning, her left eye partially shut with the pain, and stared down at him. The rain pelted her in the back of the head, forming a curtain around her wet hair as she looked into the eyes reeking with death. He stared back up at her, blood oozing from the bullet wound in his forehead. Her chest heaved with the effort to gain air and she could feel the necklace of bruises circling her throat. She turned and knelt down beside Brynn.

Brynn's eyes were wide in disbelief, her breathing rampant as the rain slapped her face. April lifted Brynn's head into her lap as sirens approached from the distance. She looked up toward the street, as the first blue and red lights raced around the corner.

Chapter Thirty-four

April recognized the officer as soon as she was escorted to a waiting ambulance. She closed her eyes to ward off the familiar image, even as she struggled to calm her fearful shudders. Detective Hill. Memories of their last encounter flooded back to haunt her. She wasn't a "person of interest" in Warren's death anymore. But for the longest time, she had lived in fear thinking he would eventually come for her; discover a piece of incriminating evidence he had overlooked. Then, as the days grew to months and months into years, she had finally convinced herself that she was indeed free from her past.

He was perched against that same dusty, gold Ford Taurus she remembered from years ago. Hell, he was even dressed the same. Light gray Polo and navy slacks, like he was some cartoon character with a closet full of the same clothes. The years had aged him a bit, with more defined wrinkles in the pale skin around his eyes. His eyes, one feature she would always remember because his always carried suspicion, even as his mouth formed to deliver bad news she didn't want to hear. She would recognize him in a lineup, though she was sure he wouldn't recognize her. Because if he did, there was no way she would be walking from this scene except in handcuffs.

As if he had been watching her the whole time, Detective Hill was already looking in her direction as she passed by. His brow furrowed as if he was attempting to place her, but the confusion etched on his face let her know she was as inconspicuous as she had been before. It was funny, because she knew she physically looked different. But even she had to do a double take in the mirror at times because she surely was not the same woman.

The officer motioned for her to have a seat on the bench in the back of the ambulance and she did as she was told. An EMT began picking and prodding and swathing her arm in bandages, all the while asking her questions about her pain level and the various bruises decorating her ashen skin. April answered as best and as vaguely as she could, blaming her lethargy on the traumatic events that had just taken place. Meanwhile, she could feel Detective Hill watching her.

"Ma'am." A short, stocky police officer with *Officer Miller* emblazoned on his name tag, approached with a grim smile. "You mind if I have a word?" Years of cigarettes and bourbon had stripped his voice of all-natural appeal and its raspy tenor made it seem as if he constantly needed to clear his throat.

April nodded and quickly averted her eyes. Suddenly being in the officer's presence brought on this imminent feeling of horror that made her fearful.

Officer Miller pulled a notepad and pen from his breast pocket. "Can you please begin by giving me an account of what happened here tonight?"

April did. She relayed what she and Brynn had practiced. Brynn was currently living with her boyfriend and April had come over to visit. Brynn had let her know she could let herself in to wait as she was near the house. Jameson had arrived home and came on to her, and things got aggressive when April refused his advances. That's when Brynn came home and Jameson had attacked her and April, in self-defense, had to shoot him. Both women agreed, knowing what they knew, it was best to embellish the truth.

"Well, we are certainly glad you're okay," Officer Miller said with a nod after April was done. "Most women don't make it out of that kind of situation alive. I'm glad you and your friend were here to protect each other."

April nodded, her gaze unwavering. "Yeah, me, too."

"Do you have somewhere to go? Someone to take you?"

April glanced over to Brynn being treated in a separate ambulance. A small smile crossed her face. "Yes, I'm good. I have a place."

By the time Officer Miller nodded and trudged off, April glanced over to assess Detective Hill. But the man was gone.

———⋙◦⋘———

It felt weird being back in the old neighborhood.

April leaned against the window and watched Brynn's car crawl through the old streets that she remembered driving to visit Ramsey. There was something about being back that felt wrong and forbidden. Like she was no longer welcome here given the history and like a tornado, the destruction she'd left behind. But you couldn't tell now.

The neighborhood looked completely serene while it slept. Until they pulled past the residue left behind from the fire. April's breath caught in her throat. She hadn't seen the house in the aftermath of the wreckage. Hadn't wanted to. Besides, Brynn had given her a good idea of the damage and she'd left the rest to April's imagination. Still, not even what she visualized could compare to the fire-damaged shambles where her house used to stand. There was nothing left but soot and ash like a gaping black hole. It was hard to believe that was where she'd lived with her husband and his mother, now the home, the lives, and everything in it had been destroyed.

"Don't look," Brynn murmured as she eased the car by.

Too late. April shut her eyes against the harsh imagery, but she could still see it. She could still smell the smoke and hear the flames as if it were tattooed on the subconscious. For a brief moment, she wished for death, because being haunted by the mistakes of her past was much worse.

April didn't open her eyes until she felt the car stop and the engine cut off, enveloping them in a thick stillness. She peered through the windshield to stare at the two-story, split-level house tucked away from the street and slightly obscured by a dense cluster of trees. As long as she had known Brynn, she had never been in her house. Which was weird, considering Brynn had always been at hers.

Brynn broke the silence, stifling a yawn. "You going to be okay crashing here for a few days?"

April nodded. She was actually looking forward to it.

Brynn walked around the hood and helped April from the car. She leaned all of her weight on Brynn, only wincing once when she put too much pressure on her leg. It took a minute, both grumbling through their injuries, but together they were able to make it to the door.

Inside, Brynn immediately began flipping switches to flood the house with light. "Home sweet home," she announced. April followed Brynn into the living room where she collapsed on the couch, grateful to be off of her feet. It had been a long evening.

April noticed that Brynn's house was just as vibrant as she was, decorated with eclectic patterns and foolish accessories that didn't match. The juxtaposition between the sleek, modern furniture and the laid-back floor tiles, eclectic throw pillows, and settee created a fun air of irreverence that April could appreciate. The familiar smell made the home that much more nostalgic.

"Can I get you anything? Water? Juice?" Brynn went into host mode, hurrying to the kitchen.

"I'm good."

"You need to drink something, girlie. And when was the last time you ate?"

Without waiting for a response, Brynn returned with a glass of water in hand. She held it out to April, who shook her head with a weak smile. "I'm going to need something stronger," she teased.

"You and me both." Understanding, Brynn sat the glass on the coffee table and plopped down beside her.

"I'm so sorry about everything, Brynn," April started. She had been going over and over how to broach the subject and an apology seemed the best place to start. After all, everything that had happened was all her fault.

Brynn rested her head on the back of the couch and shut her eyes. She blew a staggered breath. "You don't have to apologize, Erin."

"No, I do. The whole thing with Jameson had nothing to do with you but I put you in harm's way."

Brynn nodded with a small smile. "Can I ask you one favor?"

"Sure."

"Can you tell me the truth?"

April looked away, her eyes resting on the mantle. "About what?"

"Everything. Why did we have to make up that story to the police about Jameson? Why were you even over there? None of it makes sense." Brynn paused, waiting for April to look over at her. "Look, it's okay if you don't want to. I understand. We all have secrets, right? I just thought that maybe with everything you could trust me enough with yours."

April sighed. It was time to get it all out in the open. Her mouth felt ashy, and she wished she could drink the water. But she knew it was best to get this over with. "I'm not who you think I am," she admitted.

Brynn's eyebrows furrowed in confusion. "What do you mean?"

April rose and began to pace. If there was a time for one of Erika's cigarettes, it would certainly be now. Her eyes swept the living room with its luxurious finishings and gorgeous interior. She then turned to face Brynn and spread her arms apart. "Okay. I'll give you the truth," she said. "I know who you are, Brynn. And I know you're the one trying to kill me."

Chapter Thirty-five

Brynn's eyes widened in shock. "W—what are you talking about?"

April stood by the glass scale paperweight on the mantle, the one she'd seen in Warren's office enough times to identify every angle, every crack and crevice off the sculptural piece. Her voice softened as she spoke. "Warren," she said. "I know you think I killed him. That's why you've been after me, right?"

Brynn remained silent, obviously too stunned to confirm nor deny the allegation. April took the opportunity to keep going. "I have to admit, you had me fooled, Brynn. You really did. Acting like my friend. Getting close to me. Hell, even coming on to Ramsey every chance you got and whispering in his ear about me to get him to do some digging. You were really trying to destroy me. Then, I saw you at Carter's party and I realized you were following me. Everything else started to come together. I went to Jameson's house for answers, and wouldn't you know it, I found exactly what I was looking for . . ."

A picture caught her attention, affirming her suspicions about

Jameson. She should've known. April took her time, folding the picture into quarters and stuffing it in her pocket.

April pulled the picture out of her wallet. She unfolded it and held it up for Brynn to see, though she was sure the woman knew exactly what the evidence showed. It was the rest of the pictures from what April had found in Warren's things. A wedding photo. Warren was standing with his entire wedding party this time, including his nephew, Jameson. And right by his side, grinning from ear to ear like she'd just won the lottery, was his blushing bride, Brynn.

April let the picture go and both of them watched it feather to the ground. Silence. "I gave you the truth," April said after a tense moment of silence. "Now, it's your turn."

Brynn inclined her chin. "What do you want to know?"

"Were you and Jameson in on this together? To track me down and destroy me for what happened to Warren?"

A pause. "Yeah."

"And you killed Ramsey?"

"That was an accident," Brynn croaked. "He came to Jameson's place because he thought you two were having an affair. He wouldn't listen to reason. There was a fight and . . ." she trailed off.

April grimaced. She hadn't meant to sound so callous, but she pushed herself to keep going. She had to get it all out. She had suspected, but now that Brynn was confessing, she wasn't going to stop. Even if it pained her. "Whose idea was it to put him in the storage unit?"

"Mine. That way we could frame you. But you found him before we could send the police."

"And the fire? Was it really an accident what happened with Mama Edith?"

Brynn lowered her eyes. She had the nerve to be sympathetic as she sniffled. "I didn't mean for that to happen. You were supposed to be in there . . ."

"Hey, girlie," Brynn chirped. *"I came by the house looking for you. I'm headed to work a little later, but I thought we could grab something to eat. You close by?"*

Brynn was talking fast as she explained, as if it would help. As if it would absolve her guilt. "I left and came back, and a light was on in the kitchen. I thought it was you . . ."

"I'm sorry, girlie. I didn't mean to hold you up. Is Mama Edith with you or is she with Tabitha at the house?"

"And because you had said Mama Edith was away with Tabitha for a while, I assumed the light in the kitchen—" Brynn's breath caught and her breathing quickened as if she were suffocating.

April could only stare at her in disbelief. "You killed Mama Edith." It was said as a statement, rather than a question.

"I—it was an accident!" She was sobbing uncontrollably now. "All of this is your fault, April! I knew Warren was cheating on me, but I loved him."

"It was you." April was still trying to wrap her mind around the facts as the realization sank to her bones like an anchor. Her enemy had kept her close and she hadn't even realized it. "All of this time. The necklace. The flowers. The flattened tire . . ." The memory from the storage unit throbbed in her mind. "The assault with the knife. And what was Jameson in all of this? An accomplice?"

"We had something in common. You took someone from both of us. You needed to suffer."

April gestured toward the door. "He wasn't really attacking you when I shot him, huh?"

Brynn's jaw clenched as she stood. "No, I needed him out of the way. He didn't want to get with the plan."

April looked at this woman, this shell of herself, fractured by rage and grief. She wanted to be mad at her, but all she felt was sorrow. "You're wrong about me, you know," she murmured.

"No, I'm not. You killed Warren!" Her tone had taken on something dark and sinister. Something not of this world.

"I didn't—"

"Yes, the fuck you did!" Brynn pulled herself to her feet and that's when April saw it. The gun. *Her* gun that Brynn had obviously taken from Jameson's house. The purple tint was piercing in the lamplight. Her voice was quivering as she spoke. "You took my entire life. My family. Everything! So how dare you get to have your happily ever after? How dare you get to erase your deeds and change your name and hair color to do it over and over again."

April lifted her arms in the air in surrender. "Brynn, please—"

"No! It stops here. You're not going to get away with this."

April's vision wavered once more but through the haze, she saw Brynn's brooding smirk. As she watched her finger stroke the trigger, April let her heavy lids flutter.

When she opened them again, she saw Brynn's face but slowly, as if she were watching some sick and twisted supernatural metamorphosis, the face transposed until it was her own. Staring back with that malicious grin and pointed gun. April gasped as she watched the lips move, *her* lips now, even though it was Brynn's voice that came out. "I deserve my happily ever after, dammit!" she yelled, pain coating her voice.

The words slapped April in the face, and she wobbled under the weight of the final piece of the puzzle. That made what she had to do even clearer.

Chapter Thirty-six

April didn't bother thinking anymore. Only reacting. With a burst of renewed energy, she grabbed the glass scale paperweight and hurled it at Brynn. She ducked to dodge the makeshift weapon, but she wasn't quick enough to keep it from shattering across her arm. Her finger slipped on the trigger. A gunshot popped like a firecracker, the hollow explosion echoing off the walls, penetrating the plaster just a little too close to April's head.

Mustering through her own pain and injuries, April lunged for the gun. She gripped Brynn's wrist and forced the firearm in the air as Brynn snarled like a rabid dog, cursing and spewing a decade's worth of hatred. April turned slightly, just enough to pit her back toward the flailing woman and rammed her elbow in Brynn's chest with enough force to send a rippling sensation through her arm.

Brynn took a choking breath, struggling for oxygen, and stumbled backwards. April gripped the gun with both hands and whirled to face the fractured woman. She didn't want it to end this way. But she knew. Even as she raised the gun, this was the consequence she had been running from.

April swung the pistol, bringing the butt of the gun to Brynn's head with exponential force. Brynn grunted and shifted, and all of her unleashed fear propelled April's arm to repeat the ramming, five, six, seven times until Brynn's body went limp and tumbled to the ground with a sickening thud. April felt the warm blood splatter on her hands, saw the speckles grazing the front of her sweatshirt from the crimson puddle seeping from the gash in Brynn's head. The woman lay unconscious, but April couldn't tell if she was still breathing.

April held her breath and chanced leaning down to feel against Brynn's parted lips, then the pulse at her neck.

"Oh God," she whispered, watching now as more blood poured from her head like a faucet and stained the ivory carpet. She held her own hands up to her face. Her vision was hazy, but sure enough, she could tell her blood-soaked fingers were trembling. *Shit. Shit, shit, shit.* She had to remain calm. She had to think. She had to finish this.

April picked up Brynn's cell phone and punched in Erika's number. She picked up on the second ring and April didn't even bother to let her speak before she conjured sobs. "Erika, please help me." She gripped the phone with both hands, tossing quick looks over at Brynn's body. She didn't know which was more troubling: The thought of Brynn being dead or her *not* being dead.

"What's wrong?"

"I did something bad. I—she's—dead . . . I—I—"

"What are you talking about?"

"She figured out the whole thing. She fought me and, oh my God. What do I do?"

"Get out of there. Now!" Erika was already giving instructions. Her voice was laced with urgency. "Go to a hotel. Do you understand?"

April's mind was racing as she struggled to clear her head. "Yeah, I got it."

"Go now." *Click.*

Her clothes were a mess so, thinking quickly, April used her pocket as a makeshift glove in order to open the closet door without her fingerprints marking the doorknob. There was a long trench coat hanging among the feminine jackets, and she knew instantly that it belonged to Warren. With a labored sigh, April snatched it from the hanger and put it on. Fueled by pain and adrenaline, she gathered Brynn's things, panic quickening her pace as she swept the rooms for everything she would need.

The cool night air tickled her skin as April stepped outside. It was dark and too damn quiet. She could hear her own breath loud and raspy in her ears and her heart was drilling double-time against her rib cage. But damn, it felt good to be outside.

Brynn's blood was beginning to itch as it dried to a crust on her skin. The smell was growing stronger, ripe and metallic and she swallowed bouts of nausea. Her body felt like jagged shards of glass were grinding against her flesh and down to the bone. She gritted her teeth against the searing pain.

April made it safely to Brynn's car and slid into the driver's seat, stretching against the crisp leather. She started the car and the engine hummed to life with the gentle blow of the AC chilling the interior. She didn't breathe until she had wound down the circular driveway and she saw the black aluminum fence ease by the back seat windows.

For the first time, the silence felt peaceful. She had no regrets and she damn sure wouldn't speak about this. The less people knew, the better. The air on the other side of that fence even tasted different. Less stifled. Less restraining. It tasted like freedom.

PART VI: ACCEPTANCE

The final stage of grief where you're finally able to accept the reality of what's happened and begin to look for avenues to move on.

Chapter Thirty-seven

April struggled to restrain her rising panic as she approached the hotel desk. Usually there was a rush of adrenaline. But not tonight. Not this time. That had been superseded with a fear so chilling it left her breathless and trembling. Would it work? Would they recognize something was off? But she kept those thoughts to herself. As far as everyone else was concerned, she was just another guest, weaving through the maze of elite patrons peppering the hotel lobby. Blending in was the easy part. Not getting caught—well, that was the challenge.

Muffled laughter and music wafted to greet her, evidence of a party in full swing in the ballroom. The merriment was almost mocking and April quickened her pace. She had to get away. She had to think. She knew if she acted on impulse, she would make another mistake. And she couldn't afford any more of those.

April scissored her legs across the floor with a panicked urgency. A laptop bag was slung over her shoulder and knocked against her hip, throwing off her stride. She wheeled a Montblanc suitcase along, with a grip so tight it felt like the handle would crack the bones in her hand.

She was nearly nauseous. It was his musky vanilla scent that clung to the trench coat she wore. She hadn't wanted to take his, but it was the only one she could find in her haste. Anything to hide the blood coagulating in the fleece of her sweatshirt.

The hotel attendant—Wendy, by the gold name tag pinned to her breast pocket—looked up with a warm smile. "May I help you?"

April forced a smile, hoping her face relayed the casualness she didn't feel. "Checking in," she greeted.

Wendy nodded and began pecking away on her keyboard. "Of course. Name?"

April's voice quivered over the name, and she licked her lips. Breathe, just breathe, she coaxed herself. "Brynn Sunderland."

Her head was pounding.

April opened her eyes and groaned with the weight of the throbbing pain. For a moment, it sounded like fireworks. The memories flooded back with a crippling intensity. One could easily assume the entire night's events had all been a dream if it wasn't for the bandages wrapped around her arm. She lifted a hand to her forehead and cringed when she felt a knot forming underneath the hair matted to her sweat-dampened skin. Movement drew her eyes to the window. Tiny pellets of rain beat against the glass and added a soundtrack to the overcast clouds darkening the sky.

April summoned as much strength as she could to drag her weakened body from the bathroom floor. The pounding continued. Not her head—well, not so much *in* her head. The door. Hadn't she requested not to be disturbed? Which could only mean . . .

Relief eclipsed annoyance when she pulled open the door to greet the visitor. "Hey, Erika."

Erika Garrett marched into the room in a haze of chiffon, vanilla, and alcohol. The acute click of her stilettos echoed with resolve, and she was already shrugging out of a wool dress coat, no doubt a head-to-toe profit from their recent exploits. She looked amazing—how could her mother look amazing, when April looked like she'd been dragged from the edges of death?

Noticing her daughter, Erika hesitated for the briefest of moments. April caught it. Then, it was gone as swiftly as it had arrived.

"Did anyone follow you?" Erika asked as soon as they were closed and locked back in the room.

Did anyone? Everything from the last few hours was a blur so though April couldn't be 100 percent sure, she shook her head anyway.

"Good." Erika's tone was laced with irritation as she lowered her voice. "We already have to clean up your mess. Can't have you broadcasting a murder up and down Peachtree Street."

"I don't need you—"

"Don't tell me what you don't need." Erika narrowed her eyes at her daughter's visceral vulnerability. "You fucked up and now you have to deal with the consequences. I'm trying to help you as best I can, but I'm not going to let you unravel everything we've built. Put your emotions in your pocket."

Typical Erika. Even though April was desensitized to her abrasiveness, it didn't make the words sting any less. She shouldn't have been surprised. Love wasn't something in Erika's genetic makeup, unless of course it was for herself. Oh, and money. She loved that, probably more than herself.

Erika pulled a trash bag from her purse and took a peek in the bathroom. She frowned at the disarray. Soiled clothes lay in a pile on the floor. Remnants of dried blood speckled the shower pan. "Lord, girl, do you *want* to get caught? Get the envelope out of my purse."

April reached in the purse and her fingers closed around a thick manilla envelope, nearly bulging from its seams. She didn't have to open it to recognize the protruding shape of money stacks.

"IDs and passports are in there too," Erika affirmed. She was squatting on the floor—expertly in high heels, no less—shoveling April's clothes in the trash bag. Her mood had noticeably shifted, her movements subdued, her voice now sounding cold and distant. Well, more than usual. Like this was a premeditated business arrangement between them.

April swallowed, her saliva tasting putrid in her throat. It was taking all of her energy to fight off dizziness. How had she not seen any of this earlier? "How . . ." Her voice cracked. She took a breath and tried again. "How did you get these?"

"I know a guy."

"Is the body—"

"No questions about what happened. The less you know, the better."

April nodded her understanding. The envelope of money felt like bricks in her grasp. Somewhere far in the distance, a police siren wailed, and her eyes darted to the door. "Do I have to worry about cops?"

Erika didn't seem fazed. "They won't come looking for you, April. We took care of that."

That was what she needed to know. The realization began to settle like a heavy smog around her. A terrifying, suffocating smog. The silence around them had a heaviness about it, like a breathing entity with a life of its own. April wasn't sure what her mother was thinking, but her mind was reeling with the events that had taken place. And the new life she was about to assume. She had never felt more alone and some part of her had to question: Was she making the right decision?

April chanced peeling back the flap and peeking into the envelope. Sure enough, there was money. Plenty of it. And, just like

Erika had said, a stack of driver's licenses and passport books were nestled in a Ziploc bag.

"See?" Erika was grinning now as she rose and tossed the trash bag over her shoulder. "It's easy to have more than one life, you just have to know how to balance them."

April eyed the driver's licenses, the names, all with her face on each plastic card. Erika's words were more unnerving than reassuring. But at this point, what other choice did she have? She had started it. Now she had to finish it.

Her mother continued to clean the bathroom while April moved about the suite, stepping into her shoes and gathering her belongings. She didn't stop when Erika looked her way in apparent confusion.

"What are you doing? You not staying here for the night?"

April shoved the envelope in her—well, *Brynn's* purse—and cast a dejected look in Erika's direction. "You know, it took me a minute to put all of the pieces together," she started, her eyes reflective. "I have to admit, I never thought myself as smart as you, Erika. Never did I think the truth would be hiding from me in plain sight."

Erika smacked her lips. "Girl, what the hell are you talking about?"

"Jameson was Warren's nephew. Brynn was Warren's wife. They worked together to *bring me out of hiding*, so to speak, to avenge his death." She paused. "But it wasn't until tonight that I began to question, How in the hell did they find me? Who sent Brynn to me? And then I realized, it was you."

Erika stood, unmoving in the threshold, her lips pursed so tight they had paled through the lipstick.

"I saw the way you hesitated when you came in the door," April said, her voice calm. "It's because you thought I was Brynn." She had to shake her head at the absurdity of it all, even as the words fell from her lips. "I called you on her phone intentionally, to see your reaction. I told you I killed her and you assumed I meant that she had killed me. This was all part of your plan."

Erika was shaking her head, fiercely. "You're wrong," she snapped. "Yes, I thought that you were Brynn. Yes, I assumed she had killed you. But that's not what I wanted. I sent Brynn your way for you to kill *her*."

April could only stare at this woman, this *stranger*.

Erika rushed on at April's continued silence. "Okay, okay. Yes, it was fucked up. But I was fucked up when I realized that Warren had another wife. I had no idea about Brynn. After he died, I thought we could cash in big on his life insurance. I never in a million years thought all of his money would go to his wife. His *real* wife. I tracked her down and told her about you. All the while, I knew if she died, she couldn't have Warren's money."

"Why didn't you just kill her yourself?" April bit off the words with malice. "Why bring me into your twisted mind games?"

"Because I could tell you were pulling away from me," Erika shot back, her words sharp like poison. "All of your life, I had been there for you and you were trying to rid your hands of me. I knew if you thought you were in danger, you would come back to me. Come back to Mommy. Where you belonged. You needed me, dammit!"

"I can't say I expected any less of you, honestly," April mumbled. "All my life, you have always been consistent. You've always shown me who you really were. I just allowed myself to be manipulated by my *love* for my mother. But it's done now, Erika. Just like you told me, and then you told Brynn, I deserve my fucking happily ever after too."

April started for the door with Brynn's belongings and now, Erika's money. Erika was shouting desperately. "April, wait—"

"No!" April whirled around. "My name is Brynn. April died last night. And according to this letter, *you* killed her, Erika."

That startled a gasp from Erika's lips. To prove her point, April pulled her journal from her purse and flipped to the back where she'd written one last entry. She ripped the page from the spiral binding.

"*It's taking a lot for me to verbalize this,*" April read. "*But April Garrett is dead. I killed her. As I'm writing this, I don't even know how to feel. Numb, maybe? Relief? Part of me feels her death was almost merciful. Or maybe fate if you believe in that sort of thing. Sure, it was an accident, but I would be lying if I didn't say how much I think she deserved it. I can only hope that she forgives me. And God forgives me as well. Maybe now I'll finally have some peace within myself.* Signed, Erika Garrett."

"How could you write that?" Erika's voice was nothing more than a staggered whisper.

"Because it's true. You killed your daughter. You killed her every day, all of her life. And if you don't want this to make its way to Detective Hill, I suggest you leave me the fuck alone. For good."

Stronger than she had ever been, April pulled open the door and walked out. This time, she didn't even look back.

Chapter Thirty-eight

She should've gone straight home, but she felt compelled to make a detour.

April slowed her car in front of a crossing guard and waited until she was waved into the elementary school parking lot. It was crowded as it usually was around this time. Cars flanked the curb in the carpool lane and April wheeled past them to park in a far corner in the parking lot under a tree. The position gave her an excellent vantage point of the front door while keeping her removed from the congestion.

She was early, so April pulled out her phone and dialed a number. Thanks to Deuce's excellent tracking skills, she had finally located the bastard. The phone rang once, twice, before he picked up.

"Hello?"

She hesitated for just a moment, not sure if she should say something.

"Hello?" His voice heightened with agitation, so she finally felt compelled to speak.

"Hi, Warren." She heard his sharp intake of breath at the name, and probably the fact she was calling. She had promised never to do it. "Listen, you don't have to respond," she went on, her eyes trained on the building as she spoke. "But I wanted to let you know I have transferred the last bit of your money to you. So, you don't have to bother me ever again. I've held up my end of the deal. It's over."

"It's not over until I say it's over," he barked. "All of this shit is your fault. You and your thieving-ass mama."

April took a calming breath. "I know," she admitted. "And I've had to live with it all my life. But in all fairness, you didn't tell me and Erika you already had a wife before you married me. You got a lot more than you bargained for. We both did."

"Listen, bitch," he growled. "You still owe me. Do you hear me, April?"

A ghost of a smile touched April's lips as she heard the school bell and the doors swung open. "You'll have to find me first, Warren." And with that, she hung up just as the first few children spilled free in a frenzy of innocence and laughter.

April climbed from the car and stood quietly by her door, her eyes searching through the sea of colorful book bags. She was looking for one in particular. A black one embellished with glitter and snowflakes and Disney *Frozen* characters embossed across the huge front pocket. She'd had the same one year after year, her small stature continuing to grow until it fit the oversized bag.

Sure enough, April caught the little girl in the crowd. Her hair was braided this time, long cords with colorful beads on the ends that bounced with her steps. She was dressed like a big girl instead of the young age of eight, with mustard yellow leggings and a cream sweater dress with matching snow boots with fur. She wore a pink headband with rhinestones that sparkled in the sun, and April knew, even without reading the words affixed to the top of the headpiece, what it said. *Birthday Girl.*

And then just as quickly, she disappeared into the backseat of a red Ford Explorer and April's spirit deflated, as it always did, when the truck pulled off. She wouldn't be there for this birthday, like she wasn't for any of the birthdays, but part of her felt some sort of contentment having seen her daughter. Also, thanks to Deuce for locating her. And that would have to be enough. For now.

Epilogue

April Garrett's Journal

FIRST ENTRY

I know this is a weird first entry, but I have to write this down somewhere. Because if anything ever happens to me, I want there to be a record of it.

My mom had this "brilliant" idea to have me marry her boyfriend so we could steal from him. Well, I did it and it backfired. Because Warren caught me red-handed. I was so scared. He's never hit me before, but he certainly looked like he wanted to. The way his fist was clenched and his whole body was trembling with rage I knew for sure he was going to kill me and bury my body in the backyard. I started crying as he walked toward me, and I had no choice but to cower in a corner. I was begging and sobbing and apologizing for my life. He lifted his hand to punch me, and I yelled out the secret I had been keeping hidden from everyone. "I'm pregnant!"

It worked. He didn't do anything. Not yet anyway. He told me to leave the money and get the hell out of his office. Which I did. I threw the money on the floor, I think it was like $1500 and when I ran by him, he grabbed my arm and told me to go straight to the room and don't say a word to Erika. As scared as I was, I would've agreed to anything.

I sat in that room for what felt like hours. I didn't dare go to sleep because I didn't know if I would've woken up with a pillow over my face. Or the cops at my bedside. I didn't sleep, blink; hell, I didn't even breathe. And when he came in the room a few hours later, I was ready to pee on myself.

His expression was unreadable, which scared me even more. Because what was he thinking? What was he going to do? He sat down on the bed while I tried my best to make myself disappear.

"How long have you been stealing from me?" he asked.

And I told him the truth. Ever since we got married, so almost two years. He asked me how much had I taken and again I told the truth. That I didn't know but it was a lot. He asked me if Erika knew and I nodded yes, that it was her idea. Then he said something that I would never forget.

"You didn't steal just from me," he said. "You stole from my clients. And when I didn't have their money, it got me in a lot of trouble. I could kill you right now," he said. "But I won't because you are indebted to me. And you're going to do two things. Pay back every fucking penny. And help me fake my death."

I was shocked as hell to hear that last part. Granted, I didn't know how I would pay him back either, but at least that wasn't an unrealistic request. But help him fake his death?

He told me that at any moment if I ever breathed a word that he was alive or didn't uphold my end of the bargain, that he would kill me. He told me there was nowhere I could run, no place I could hide to get away from him because he had people who could track me down.

But sitting right there with my life literally hanging in the balance, I nodded yes. As far as I was concerned, I had already signed my death certificate. I was dead anyway. Had always been.

He asked me was I serious about being pregnant and I told him that I was. He said he would take me to have an abortion and I cried because I couldn't do that. Instead, I asked him one small thing. My only saving grace. I wanted to hide the pregnancy and afterwards give my baby girl up for adoption. I couldn't bear the thought of Erika getting ahold of her. Or worse. Be a part of the same vicious circle that had killed me in every way possible. He agreed. And I knew why. Because he knew having this baby somewhere in the world, alive and well, would hurt me every day, for the rest of my life. And that amount of anguish was incomparable to an abortion. He didn't want kids and we both knew this child was better off without me. As much as it hurt.

We were in agreement. I would help him fake his death, I would lie, cheat, steal, and do whatever I had to in order to pay him back. In exchange, I could walk away with my life and the life of my baby girl. I couldn't tell a soul. Not even Erika.

I think I still got a fair end of the deal given what I had done. I just have the rest of my life to live with the consequences. And in a way, that judgement is worse than death.